Greetings from the Vodka Sea

Glenda
886-3365

greetings from the
VODKA SEA

Chris Gudgeon

GOOSE LANE

Edited by Laurel Boone.
Cover illustration: Veer.
Cover design by Paul Vienneau.
Book design by Julie Scriver.
Printed in Canada by Transcontinental.
10 9 8 7 6 5 4 3 2 1

Library and Archives Canada Cataloguing in Publication

Gudgeon, Chris, 1959-
Greetings from the Vodka Sea / Chris Gudgeon.

Short stories.
ISBN 0-86492-383-X

I. Title.

PS8613.U44G74 2004   C813'.6   C2004-904085-5

Published with the financial support of the Canada Council for the Arts, the
Government of Canada through the Book Publishing Industry Development
Program, and the New Brunswick Culture and Sports Secretariat.

Goose Lane Editions
469 King Street
Fredericton, New Brunswick
CANADA E3B 1E5
www.gooselane.com

To H.B.

Contents

Liberation

At approximately eight-fifteen on a mild Montreal morning, a black LaSalle taxi pulled up to to 1279 Redpath Crescent, a large, three-story house in a quiet neighbourhood that claimed, by right of affluence, a view of the city from half-way up Mount Royal. Three men got out of the taxi, one of them carrying a wrapped present, and asked the driver to wait. There was a long flight of stairs to the front door, so the taxi driver could not see the men as they approached the door and rang the bell. He could not see the Greek maid answer the door and could not hear the young man say, in broken English, that he had a birthday present for Mr. James Cross, the British Trade Commissioner to Canada. A receipt was required.

The driver could not see the woman hesitate — why would anyone need a receipt for a birthday gift? — and missed the part where the three unmasked gunmen pushed past the clucking housekeeper and forced their way in toward the bathroom. The radio was on, and the driver could hear, but paid no attention to, Janis Joplin, who'd died that very morning of a drug overdose. *Freedom's just another word for nothing left to lose. . . .* The driver was engrossed in his paper. He liked to keep up on the news.

The detail "unmasked" is not superfluous, since the gunmen were supposed to be masked — the plan clearly called for the men to wear hoods to cover their faces — but in their excitement the kidnappers forgot to put their hoods on. It was a serious mistake in an episode in which one serious mistake followed another. They'd encountered Cross just as he stepped out of the bathroom, wiping the excess shaving cream off his face with a dry towel. "Get down on the floor," one of the men caw-cawed to him, displaying his gun like proud plumage, "or you will be fucking dead." Cross complied.

The gunmen handcuffed Cross, then pushed him — comfortably dressed in a checked sports jacket and slacks — toward the front door. It was a mild Montreal morning, a Monday, and the three young men took it as a sign that fate was on their side. Not God. He had been exorcised from their province ten years ago and now clung only to old women and curates, *tapettes* mostly: fairies. They stopped at the door and told the commissioner's wife that they were members of the Front de Liberation du Québec and that they were taking her husband hostage. It was the twelfth terrorist kidnapping in the West since September 1969 and the first outside Latin America. It was October, 1970. Revolution was in the air.

Two details stuck in Sondra's mind. The first was the checked jacket. Every single reporter went out of his way to mention that Cross was wearing a checked sports jacket at the time of his abduction. One guy on the TV even gave great detail about the jacket, describing the size (42 short), the fabric, its texture, the brand name; he went to a men's clothing store and found another jacket of similar colour and style and tried it on for the benefit of any viewers at home who could not at that moment go to their own clothing stores and try on similar jackets for themselves. Considering that it was off the rack, Sondra thought, it fit the reporter well, accentuating the breadth of his shoulders while masking somewhat his slight hunch and little potbelly.

The second detail was the birthday present. Was there actually something in the gift-wrapped box, Sondra wanted to know, or was it empty? And if there was something in the box, what was it? These were the sorts of questions a man would never ask. They were more interested in times and dates and jacket sizes, the measurable data. Objective reality.

She was studying the Polaroid picture of James Cross in the paper and thinking of the difference between photographs and statues. He was seated on a wooden crate, looking up at the camera. He wore a dark work shirt, obviously a gift from his captors, and played a game of solitaire. Sondra would have liked him to move the jack of hearts onto the queen of clubs. Statues, she concluded, are an imposition of history, an attempt to lock the past into the present, the past imperfect, so to speak. Photographs, specifically snapshots like the Cross photo, freeze the present and pull it outside of history. (There are, of course, historic photos, that is, photos of historic significance — the Cross photo is only one example — which exist almost wholly outside history.) Photographs are a kind of literature, in which attention must be paid to character and setting and voice and tense and the powers of light and darkness. Cross was looking up, neither smiling nor frightened, appearing, in fact, a little peeved for having had to stop his game and pose.

James Cross had laid his cards on a battered storage trunk used as a makeshift table and sat on a wooden crate turned on its end. On closer inspection, Sondra saw the word "dynamite" stencilled on the side of the box. She wondered if the photographer had asked Cross to smile or say cheese, or did he just call his captive's name and catch his subject, as lovers sometimes do, off guard. She wondered if James Cross was comfortable, seated on the box, and thought that perhaps he might like a cushion.

. . .

People assumed, when they heard Sondra was a feminist and unmarried, that she was a man-hater. Of course men reacted this way, particularly the older ones who'd grown up when notions of paternalism went unquestioned, but women too, and not just some women but most women. That she had been married was irrelevant (indeed, it only offered further proof of her hatred, or better yet, it clarified her bitterness — not that she was bitter, but she'd heard the talk and mapped the logic on her own). The fact was that Sondra was not a man-hater. The fact was that she loved men. Her own father, for example, she'd loved dearly, although he'd died when she was barely a teenager. And others, many others. The only difference between her and other women was that she'd made a conscious decision to free herself from the archaic thinking that allowed a man to behave as he pleased while a woman had to suffer by another standard. Her decision to take a married man for a lover, for example. She was not Étienne's mistress, as no doubt others (and no doubt he) thought. She chose him exactly because he was intelligent and elegant and *married*, and in that way could offer her everything she wanted from a relationship without bringing into it expectations greater than she was prepared to manage. And the others. Her position at the university, not to mention her private practice, afforded her plenty of opportunity. No. She wasn't a man-hater. She loved men, and she respected them. If they saw something they wanted — a job, a car, a lover — they didn't pussyfoot. They took it.

She was discreet and as honourable as she needed to be. Patients — clients, as she preferred to call them — were generally off limits, as were students. Generally. Avram was an exception, and there had been other exceptions who typically fell into one of two categories: men who were particularly together, who entered the relationship, like her, with their eyes wide open, expecting pleasure and novelty and temporary companionship and nothing more; and those who were apart, who seemed in need of the sexual attention of a woman who was particularly sexually attentive. These were not, to use the vernacular, mercy fucks, but carefully crafted therapeutic interventions. Then there was a third, much smaller category, which in actuality consisted entirely of Avram, a category reserved for men (and, up to this point, a man) who, unlike men in general, whom Sondra loved, not despite the fact they were men but because of it, she found herself loving in the particular. To be clear, these three categories applied only to men with whom Sondra had relationships, as opposed to men (like Étienne) with whom she had *a* relationship. So while she was in love with Étienne, a respectable heart surgeon with a quiet, sturdy wife, a man with whom she was having a relationship in a very specific sense (and within the very clear, in her mind, criteria she had set up) and was comfortable with that, she had found herself falling in love with Avram, with whom, by her own definition, she was not having a relationship, and with whom she would never, for a variety of reasons (his age, her intellectual needs, their long-term sexual incompatibility), have a relationship. This was unprecedented, and it concerned her. More than anything, she disapproved of the indiscretion. The photograph. That was a mistake. A tactical error that captured Sondra in a moment of weakness and froze it in time. She had resolved to get the photograph back. Not ask for it back, as a woman might. She had resolved to go to his apartment herself. She would go to Avram's apartment and take it back, like a man.

She hadn't noticed him at first. He was one of those boys who sat at the back of the class with his head down and his mouth shut. He had never once raised his hand to ask a question, and Sondra had quickly learned not to bother asking him one. He would stare at his notebook without answering. Not that he wasn't attractive. When you finally noticed him you realized that he was beautiful, with fine features and smooth skin, still wrapped in the androgynous petals of adolescence. But he was shy to the point that Sondra suspected he was suffering from some manner of neurosis, perhaps stemming from a deep-rooted sexual conflict. He was, no doubt, a virgin. And she was content to let him remain one, deciding almost consciously to pay no attention to this student who clearly did not want attention to be paid. There were plenty of other young people in the psych survey course, many of them quite eager and a few of those, she suspected, rather brilliant.

One morning, though, on her way from her car to her office, she noticed him — Avram — sitting at the edge of the fountain. He had his head lowered, as if he were reading a book in his lap, and remained almost motionless. His long hair fell before his eyes, and Sondra had the feeling that he was peering through this brown veil, watching her.

He was there again at the end of the day when she walked from her office to her car, and again the next morning, and so on and so on for days, his head down, the invisible book open. She began to notice him in class too, not that was he taking a more active role, but that he seemed to concentrate his energy on not looking at her. But, and this is critical, she did not sense any aggression on his part. There was this tremendous, pervasive passivity in his body language, which reminded her of clients who were victims of physical or sexual assault. He shared the impassive affect, the lack of eye contact, the centripetal gravity that drew all the extremities inward, sucking him into a fetal ball. There was one significant difference between this boy and her clients, though. What they lacked was the aura of innocence that encircled Avram. They had been corrupted, spiritually speaking, by their experience with the world; he had yet to open up to that experience; he had yet to be corrupted.

In the beginning, Sondra overlooked the boy's attentive non-attention. She was almost flattered in her way; one never knew how to react when a student had a crush on oneself, and surely that lay at the root of his behaviour: an adolescent, biochemically charged infatuation, perhaps inflaming his ambiguous sense of sexual self. In time — and not a long time, frankly — she found herself growing more irritated with Avram. She'd catch him in the middle of class with his head lowered and turned away from her. If she was on the right side of the room nearest to the door, he turned his head left, toward the window. If she strolled to the back of the class, as she now sometimes did almost to observe to what absurd lengths Avram would go to avoid looking at her, he would avert his eyes to the front of the room, concentrating on a square of tile near the blackboard or the metal wastebasket by her desk. And then she found herself angry at him. It was Étienne who first pointed out the significance of this. They were having lunch at the hospital commissary — they were very open about their relationship, or as open as one could be when one was having an extramarital affair in Toronto's airtight atmosphere — and she was going on about Avram. She was saying that she might report him to the department head or even ask to have him removed from her class when the elegant doctor, beads of potato soup condensing on the tips of his old-fashioned moustache, remarked that she had now been talking about Avram for, by his watch, a full thirty-eight minutes.

"There must be something very special about this young man that he should arouse," Étienne spread the word like warm butter, "your passion so."

That stopped Sondra cold.

"I'd suggest," he said goodnaturedly, "and bearing in mind that I've seen inside more hearts than any man I know, that you're harbouring some feelings for this student, and I'd suggest further that your anger stems, as anger usually does, not from the boy's behaviour per se but from your inability to control his behaviour. No — I see that look and I agree. Control is not the right word, or rather, it is the right word but the wrong connotation. Let me put it this way. You are frustrated because he is just a child, yet he has out-manoeuvred you through the deliberate manipulation of his inattention. By not wanting to look at you, he has made you want him to look at you. Of course, he has carried it to a ridiculous extreme because, I think, as you do, that when you get right down to it, he is rather disturbed."

It was Étienne who encouraged her to take Avram as her lover. He looked on it as a challenge and maintained that, without engaging in such adversity, the human spirit, to use his perfect term, calcified. Of course, she immediately became suspicious. When a woman encouraged her partner to take a lover, it was because she was utterly tired of having him in her bed. But when a man suggested it, it usually meant he was about to sleep (or had slept recently enough that he still felt remorse) with someone else. Étienne sensed her concerns and protested that, with her and his wife, he already had more women that any man could reasonably handle. He assured and almost convinced her that he had only her best interests at heart. In fact, he said, he found the whole idea of her taking a young lover rather erotic.

Now, it's one thing to decide to take on a lover and another thing entirely to actually take that lover on, although in Sondra's experience, the woman always had the upper hand. It was a matter again of subjectivity versus objectivity. Approached by a woman who offers to take him to bed, a man never looks beneath the surface. *Of course she wants to take me to bed,* the man tells himself, regardless of how unappealing he considered himself moments before. A woman in the same circumstance will always ask herself why. Why me? Why now? By the same token, a man has much less capacity for turning a woman down because objectively, based purely on the observable data, it doesn't look good. Does he find her unattractive? Well, surely, after a point, that doesn't matter. Is he afraid he doesn't measure up? Is he a homosexual? Rarely does a man want to explore this subterranean universe, so he almost always takes the easy way out. If a woman asks him to bed he says yes. Society demands it, the fraternity of men demands it, the cock demands it.

But Avram was not so simple. Being an introvert, he was less inclined to be swayed by the forces of society and fraternity, and being grotesquely shy and (as Sondra surmised) ambivalent about his own sexuality, he was disinclined to follow the capering of his sex organ.

"Why don't you take him to one of your little orgies?" Étienne suggested. He was teasing, of course. It was something she noticed that older men often did to younger women, tease them, a subtle way, she supposed, to reiterate their dominance.

"They're not orgies, they're encounter groups. And I'm afraid this boy's ego isn't ready for such an intense experience as that."

Sondra favoured the direct route. One morning, on the way from her car to her office, she stopped at the fountain and invited Avram to join her for coffee. That's when he did it: he looked directly at her for the first time. That's also when she realized how beautiful he was: brown-black hair which fell into his eyes and nearly reached his shoulders, black eyes, unblemished skin the colour of weak tea, lips as thick and tender as a young woman's, and recognized too that his discomfort (he was visibly embarrassed; his face and ears flushed, his hands shook, his voice quavered as he almost whispered,

"No") enhanced his beauty for her. His vulnerability excited her, and her own aggressiveness in the face of this vulnerability increased. She noticed how her body language changed in response to Avram's passivity. She stood more erect, her shoulders fully back, and her eyes were as unwavering as his were unfocused. And suddenly she understood why men didn't need foreplay: the chase was stimulation enough.

The next morning, he wasn't waiting at the fountain and did not come to class. Sondra began to worry that she'd been too aggressive, too direct. She found herself passing the fountain five or six times that day and the next and had almost given up on seeing him again, perhaps ever, when, later that evening, as she was returning to her car to go home, there he was. Sitting at the fountain, desperately not looking at her. He was in his shirtsleeves and seemed even from a distance to be shivering in the descending cold. He coughed, and, picking up the cue, Sondra went to speak to him again. This time she was more tactful. She'd missed him in class, she said, and had worried that something had happened to him. She told him the class valued his input and managed to make a lot out of a trifling thing he'd once said during a discussion on manic-depressive illness. He coughed again, and Sondra offered him a ride home. Avram sat for a very long time, measuring his frozen breath, before he wordlessly assented. The car ride was predictably quiet. Sondra made an effort to start a conversation, then lapsed into a monologue, then simply turned up Stravinsky on the eight-track. He almost seemed relieved when she shut up. He relaxed in his seat.

"Do you think they'll kill him?" he asked, after a long, long silence.

Sondra was taken aback. She had no idea what Avram was talking about, and she found the question and the way he framed it with silence almost a threat in itself.

"Kill who?"

"James Cross. Do you think the FLQ will kill him?"

Illuminated, Sondra relaxed, but before she could respond (the simple answer was no, but Sondra was prepared to give a much more detailed analysis), Avram stopped her. "I like your car," he said. "I want to get a car like this someday. I want to get a car exactly like this."

And that was it. She dropped him off a few minutes later by a rack of student apartments near the bus station. He thanked her very politely, exactly the way, Sondra thought, his mother had taught him. And he looked at her again as he shut the door and kept his eyes on her as she drove off. He stood on the corner and watched as she drove away and did not move until the car was out of sight.

In a note left in a garbage can for the reporters at radio station CKLM (the unfolding crisis was the last great radio news event in the country, perhaps the world), the FLQ took credit for the kidnapping of Cross, a "representative of the old, racist and colonialist British system." In retrospect, the separatists' demands were realistic: there was no call for the overthrow of a repressive political system, and while they did refer to the goal of "total independence" for Quebec, they clearly held no illusions that this kidnapping would further that end. What they wanted was the release of twenty-three "political prisoners" — men who'd been arrested for a variety of terrorist acts perpetrated by the FLQ over the previous ten years. Men like François Schrim, a Hungarian-born career terrorist and former French Legionnaire, who shot and killed the manager of the International Firearms Company during an attempted robbery, and Robert Levesque, a twenty-nine-year-old plumber who faced a string of convictions including armed robbery and bombings. Along with freedom for their comrades, the kidnappers wanted safe passage to Cuba or Algiers for themselves, the political prisoners and any family members who wanted to join them. They also wanted half a million dollars worth of gold bullion to help finance their new life, calling it a "voluntary tax."

The Cross ransom note was unsigned, but police already had a very good idea of who was involved in the plot. Central was Jacques Lanctôt, who had been picked up eight months earlier in a rented delivery truck carrying a sawed-off shotgun, a man-sized storage trunk and a press release announcing the never-perpetrated kidnapping of Israeli trade consul Moshe Golan. Lanctôt and his accomplice, charged at the time with possession of a restricted firearm and conspiracy to kidnap, disappeared into Quebec's underworld shortly after they were granted bail. Along with Lanctôt, the police also had their eye on his sister Louise (who did not go to the Cross house) and her husband Jacques Cossette-Trudel (whose father had been named five days before to the National Energy Board by Prime Minister Pierre Trudeau), Marc Carbonneau and Pierre Seguin. Collectively, they called themselves the Liberation Cell.

In Sondra's estimation, two discoveries had advanced the cause of women's independence above all else: the pill and the Polaroid camera. The pill granted women power over their own reproductive cycle and in an instant turned the traditional patriarchy on its head. Women were now free to enjoy sex without having to worry about its consequences. While Sondra was certain that motherhood was one of the greatest joys a woman could experience, she was equally certain that the demands of motherhood — the burden of taking responsibility for a child — forced women into subservience. Meanwhile, the Polaroid camera was helping women move to the next stage of evolution: for the first time, women could not only create and distribute images of sexuality that appealed to them directly (and specifically, these instant pictures gave every woman the power to be her own pornographer), but they now had the power to objectify men as men had historically objectified women. And that was not necessarily a bad thing, for the key to the liberation of female sexual expression, and therefore the key to the political and socio-economic emancipation of women in general, lay in their ability objectify men, to see them as sex objects.

It was this political inclination toward Polaroids that led Sondra to pose for Avram. Even at the time she had her reservations but convinced herself that they were hypocritical. In the encounter sessions she led, Sondra often encouraged participants to strip down and photograph one another, literally tearing away their boundaries and baring themselves before the unwavering eye of the camera. It was Sondra's belief that people had to become comfortable with their bodies and with the image of their bodies they carried inside their heads, before they could become comfortable with minds and egos and souls.

So Sondra agreed to pose, although "pose" is an extreme exaggeration. They had only just finished making love for the first time (Avram coming, almost the instant he'd entered her, under the stern watch of Che Guevara) when he caught her unawares. He'd gotten up on the pretext of going to the washroom, and Sondra saw the flash a moment later. Avram stood like a guilty child as Sondra's eyes adjusted to the light.

"I want . . . I want to have a picture to remember you."

And that was Sondra's opportunity. On the one hand, she felt violated; on the other, there was a certain charm to his passivity, to his fear. So Sondra did not object and did not, as she easily could have done given the circumstances, grab the photograph from his hand. Instead, she let him keep it but insisted that he must now pose for her. She made him lie on the bed with his head on the pillow. At first he tried to cover himself with the blanket, but she kicked it aside roughly.

"Put one arm behind your head," she told him, adding, when he did not immediately respond, "quickly now. And now lift your leg a little. The other leg, please. Just let your foot lie on the bed."

He seemed willing to comply with her every instruction, and with each order and response she found herself growing more forceful.

"Now touch yourself, with your free hand. Not there!" She leaned down and positioned his hand over his tired cock. "I want you to play with yourself. Close your eyes and play with yourself. And keep it up until I finish taking the picture."

How she'd finally got him into bed was another story. It took weeks of gentle manipulation to get in a position where she could make her move. Eventually, he allowed her to come up to his apartment. They stood by the doorway for a very long time, but each time she leaned forward to kiss him, he would recoil and turn his head. She would retreat, and he would turn to look at her again with his soft eyes. Advance, recoil, retreat. Advance, recoil, retreat. Finally she'd had enough. She pushed him back against the door and kissed him hard on the lips. When he tried to turn his head, she held his chin firmly with one hand. Soon she pushed her tongue into his mouth, and she could feel his body responding. That's when, and this is the funny part, she picked him up (surprised at her own strength, her own force) and carried him into the apartment. She looked around the barren room and saw, under a huge black-light poster of Che, a thin mattress lying directly on the floor. She dropped him on the mattress, which served as his bed and, no doubt, his couch and kitchen table and work desk, and ordered him to undress. And when he didn't, she started to do it herself.

Sondra did not keep the photograph. It neither aroused nor disturbed her but only de-eroticized the experience. This skinny boy caught in the unflattering shadows was not the beautiful young man she'd taken to bed. She tore up the picture to give the moment entirely back to memory.

Étienne had laughed when she told him about the picture Avram had taken (laughed, that is, not in a condescending way, but with empathy, from the perspective of one who understood completely the pitfalls of taking a lover). He laughed again when she told him he she was going to get it back.

"To the victor go the spoils," he said, perhaps to tease her, or perhaps because he knew that, at that moment, he needed something elegant to say. And he laughed one more time, almost to himself, and again, not to put Sondra down but in simple appreciation of her adventure.

It was a season for adventure. The Cross kidnapping, the FLQ, the declaration of martial law, not to mention the waves of political, social and sexual liberation sweeping the country, made this Anglo-Saxon enclave where she lived seem almost cosmopolitan, almost dangerous. Everyone knew anything could happen (although certainly nothing would); Toronto — Canada — was growing up. Sondra found herself rather sympathetic to the FLQ. She saw in the kidnappers kindred spirits, not just in the larger political sense, striking a blow against oppression and the parochial status quo and its corporate-military sponsors, who espoused democracy while dictating a rigid social order, but also in the smaller, personal sense. They had come to reclaim what was theirs: their identity, their nationhood, their sense of self. That was her goal too. Both were victims of a conquest of sorts, the only difference was scale. They wanted liberation, the right of self-determination over their own land; she, on a political level, wanted equality and self-determination for womankind, which meant, in large part, the destruction of the artificial borders that define ideas of gender. And on a more personal level, she wanted self-determination over her own image; she wanted her damn picture back.

Avram lived on the top floor of a three-story building with garbage piled up in front. The squalor was typical of not just the student slums but much of the ethnic quarter of inner-city Toronto. She could smell the food cooking on a dozen hot-plates: some chicken soup here, a curry there, something heavy, bacon perhaps. Radios and record players sang from every corner, rock music and arias and even a fiddle, as static-coated announcers talked excitedly about the kidnappers and the crisis they'd precipitated.

Sondra knocked and waited. Avram had called her several times since the night they'd had sex; she could tell it was him because when she answered the phone there was no one on the other end. He hadn't been to class either, but there was not much different about this. Sometimes he came, sometimes he did not.

Sondra knocked again, then, finding the door unlocked, she let herself in. The light was on in the tiny bathroom, and Sondra could hear the shower running. Better for her; she could finish her work without causing a scene. She quickly searched the room. The dresser drawers were empty except for a few clothes. She found the Polaroid camera on top of a makeshift bookshelf, but the photograph was not with it. She looked in the bed and under the mattress and on top of the miniature fridge and in the coffin-sized Ardmore that served as his clothes cupboard and pantry. Nothing anywhere.

That's when she thought of the poster. She peeled back the yellowed tape and turned up the corner and then, in her shock, tore the poster down.

She stepped back. The water was still running. She could hear him moving in the little stall: maybe he was thinking of her right now? Pleasuring himself, perhaps?

Sondra counted. One, two, three . . .

She stopped at thirty-six. Not because there were too many to count, but because she realized that the exact number was meaningless. Woman and girl and boy and man — all of them captured unawares, some covered, some half-draped, some fully naked. Some seemed surprised by the sudden flash, others angered; most smiled, the way we are conditioned to do whenever a camera is pushed in our face. Here and there — the younger ones mostly — had thrust their legs apart or moved their hands onto themselves. Already they were looking to the future, anticipating the pleasure this photograph would bring to the photographer. Individually, the pictures seemed poorly composed and constructed, with far too much shadow and black space, but collectively they held a certain unmistakable power. They were dark and sexual and cold, and every person (again, thanks to a quality of the light) blended into one.

Her own snapshot was near the bottom, wedged between a much older woman, probably in her fifties, heavyset, who managed to smile just in time to have her picture taken, and a teenaged boy, still with his baby fat, the camera flash making a ghost of his white skin, apparently sleeping.

Sondra looked toward the tiny bathroom. She thought of confronting Avram, of pulling him out of the shower by his ear, like a cartoon schoolmarm, and force him to explain himself.

She felt now as if she were captured in a larger photograph, a moment glazed and mounted in time. She looked again at the collection. She wanted to reach for hers, in the bottom right corner, flanked by the old housewife and the ghost boy, but her hand would not go there. She felt a soft anxiety — guilt, perhaps, or a momentary wish for atonement — then began plucking the other photos from the wall. Avram could keep the one of her, it meant nothing now, just another image in a series of disconnected moments. The rest of them she'd take. She piled them neatly in her hand, careful not to crease the edges. This had been Avram's secret. It belonged to her now.

A Collection of Suicide Notes

The coroner has one of the best collections of suicide notes I have ever seen. Of course, he has an in. That's often what separates the true collector from the gifted hobbyist. My own assemblage is eclectic, with a few documents of historical interest and a couple pieces that I would call real gems from an artistic point of view. But all in all my collection is wanting. I don't have the access.

You shift your legs, uncrossing them, crossing them the other way, and I can see that my revelation is making you uncomfortable. Maybe I'm kidding, or maybe the darkroom fumes have gone to my head and left me dizzy. That's happened before. Like the Sunday when I'd been developing photographs all afternoon and I came out finally and poured milk on your sister's head because I thought her hair was on fire. That, I'll admit, was a legitimate hallucination. This time I'm telling the truth.

The coroner says that it's not always easy to get his hands on the suicide notes. They are, after all, evidence, although perhaps not evidence in the strictest legal sense; no real law has been broken. The notes are the unofficial certification that the deceased did in fact kill themselves and were not, as the coroner is always careful to establish, victims of foul play. So as you can see there is nothing truly illegal about our little avocation. It's a bit voyeuristic, morbid even, but essentially harmless. No need to look alarmed; I assure you there is nothing of a sexually deviant nature to this hobby, speaking for myself in any case. I can't honestly say what goes on in coroner's mind.

While my collection pales beside the coroner's, I have over two hundred and fifty original suicide notes, and another five hundred-odd if you count certified photocopies. The very youngest writer was a boy of eleven. I bought his from a serious collector from Seattle, who'd found it pressed between the pages in an antique bible. The note is very old and simply reads: "I'm sorry I am not a better son. I only want you to be proud of me." It is addressed to no one, so we can only speculate, and signed simply "Owen." (A suicidal eleven-year-old is not as unusual as you might think; the coroner says he often sees children as young as three and four who have taken their own lives, although, out of compassion, he lists these deaths as accidental.) The oldest writer in my collection is a man named Dolby, who, at the age of one hundred, shot himself in the head. This letter is definitely authentic, I bought it off the man's grandson, although rather rambling and disoriented.

What would your sister say? It's not as if she's without her own little peculiarities, is it? Everybody has secrets and collections. You yourself have your preferences, which I have been very tolerant of, and I don't think I need to remind you of the way you used to collect baby things until you gave it up. And your sister — your sister used to boast, "I collected lovers like holiday spoons." We've both seen her in action at the supermarket. Pretending there's something wrong with her cart, or that she can't reach the oyster sauce on the top shelf ("Could I just ask you to reach that down for me thanks I don't know why they make these shelves so high a woman's got to be some kind of amazon or basketball player to get things down it's so hard to go shopping when you're just cooking for one"), or, when all else failed, as it usually did, offering the delivery boy a little something extra for carrying her bags. It's in our blood; we evolved from hunters and gatherers, and hunters and gatherers we continue to be. So don't give me that what-would-my-sister-say look, please.

Your sister once said something along the lines of, "I'm the type of person who remembers the lovers I almost had better than the lovers I did have." Maybe you weren't there, but I remember it like yesterday. We were in Niagara Falls, the time before we were married that we went to the Falls, before I really knew you, in the days when I contemplated your sister. You remember. Your sister had just left the Spanish man, Carlos, in Montreal. Your sister had black hair then; this was several months before she became a natural blond. My cousin had the red Trans Am with the sun roof. He drove for a day and a half straight through by eating those little caffeine pills you'd taken from your father's shaving kit. The four of us went to Niagara Falls to forget. You had gone to the wax museum with my cousin, and your sister and I were left on a beach together with nothing but our best moves. We did try to grope and grapple for a while, but then she told me about you. She said you were like the air inside a tennis ball. I laughed, of course, assuming that your sister, who was never one to wax philosophical, was somehow being sarcastic. But she wasn't. "She has such secrets," your sister said on your behalf. "No one knows what's inside or how she keeps it there." Of course, by the time you and my cousin returned from the wax museum I'd forgotten about your sister; I was over you like a plastic raincoat. You seemed surprised that someone would prefer you to your sister. And to her credit, your sister easily switched to my cousin. I'd like to know what she thinks now. Maybe I am one of those best remembered almost-hads; I've often wondered that.

It's an erroneous belief that every suicide victim leaves a note. Most do not. In fact, most people go out of their way to make their suicide look like an accident. A car drives over an embankment. A woman out for an evening stroll stumbles into the sea. A lonely young man in a rooming house falls asleep with a cigarette in his hand. Psychologists, the coroner tells me, believe most "accidental" deaths are suicides of one sort or another: contrived, conscious, deliberate, premeditated and otherwise. Who wants to be remembered for taking their own life? (Worse, who wants to jeopardize their life insurance policy?) Not in our society anyway. Maybe in Japan, where I think hara-kiri is still acceptable if not honourable; maybe in ancient Rome or Greece. But in our culture, only a very few — the bravest or the most foolish — leave evidence. A survey of my collection suggests that most people feel a need to apologize; exactly sixty-two per cent of the letters in my possession start with the words "I'm sorry" or some variant. The coroner concurs. Of the letters in his collection, easily ten times mine, most are a kind of justification, although he also sees another force at work, what he calls "the last gasp of the creative impulse." I know what he means. Many of the suicide notes in my collection are, for example, written as poems. Sometimes they rhyme — I have a least eleven sonnets or poems that take a rough sonnet-like structure, and dozens with less elaborate rhyme schemes — but free verse is more popular, in particular the haiku. This reflects, I think, a general belief that free verse is easier to write than rhyming poetry. Granted, it is easier to sound important with free verse, no one wanting, I think it's fair to say, an insignificant sounding suicide note. It's another interesting statistic that most suicide notes are written by men, despite the fact that the overwhelming number of suicide attempts and a significantly higher proportion of successful suicides — there's an oxymoron for you — are carried out by women. This supports the coroner's "last gasp" theory, I think. Men are much more drawn to the notion of their place in history than women are — I'm not being sexist here, it's just what I think. Men are much more inclined to need a last burst of literary achievement, a demonstration of their creative prowess in the face of what they see as the ultimate act of sacrifice and destruction. Don't roll your eyes, that's how men think. For many women, I suspect, suicide is a creative act in itself, which needs no justification.

I have not been a collector as long as the coroner. In fact, I did not start my collection until after I met you. It was on the drive home from Niagara Falls — the second time, our honeymoon — that I realized two things: I loved you, and I needed a hobby, something to collect. You made a remark. Remember, we'd stopped off at your mother's house, and just as you stepped out of the car, your teal pumps sinking halfway into the mud, your sister opened the screen door with her new hair and a new man on her arm. What did you say? You always say the right thing at the right moment, and that was the perfect thing to say. Your sister came and took your arm and helped you through the mud, and her friend took the suitcase from my hand gallantly and carried it to the house. He was an investment banker from Mexico, the wetback with the greenbacks, your sister said; she always had a thing for Latin men. Your mother met us in the hallway, and she hugged me tightly and kissed me like we'd known each other all our lives, like she was my mother, not yours, or our mother, even though I'd never met her before. Your stepfather forced himself out of his chair and shook my hand and said, "I guess you're part of this crazy circus now." You sat on the red settee, rubbing your swollen feet, with your hair piled high and your sunglasses on like a movie star; that's the moment. That's when I knew I loved you. Your sister talked about a springtime many years earlier when you tried to hatch a robin's egg that had fallen out of the nest. You kept it on the hot water pipe in your bedroom in a cereal bowl full of torn-up yellow toilet paper. And finally a beak appeared and a tiny head, and your sister said she wanted to crack the egg open to let the chick out. But you wouldn't let her. You said it would have to get out on its own or it was as good as dead. (Where did you bury the chick, I forget, by the birch tree in the back yard?) And all the time your mother sat there on the edge of the sofa, both hands supporting her cane, correcting your sister and shushing your stepfather whenever he opened his mouth.

And when she could contain herself no longer, your mother burst out, "So you're married, honey, I can't believe it! I'm so happy for you." (Although the family politics, the sharp look to your sister and her rolling her eyes, did not escape me.) Then your stepfather saying out of the blue, before your mother could hush him, "I've married off five and buried two myself. That's not bad batting." The Mexican laughed majestically, then suddenly stopped, embarrassed. And in the silence that followed, that's when it struck me: I had a family now; I had a crazy circus. An urge overcame me, the urge to hunt and gather. The urge to collect.

The most celebrated piece in the coroner's collection is a suicide note by none other than Sir Winston Churchill. The great statesman never in fact killed himself, but that does not diminish the value of the piece in the eyes of a collector. Churchill was hounded most of his adult life by the Black Dog of Depression and drafted at least seven suicide notes. The coroner's is considered to be Churchill's finest. It is written on ivory vellum and still has, if you hold it close to your nose, the raw scent of leather, like a magnificent leather-backed chair from, one imagines, Churchill's study. While most of his other notes are pathetic, he simpers in a most unChurchillian manner, the coroner's note is beautiful. I've copied a passage, which I keep in my wallet. *I have wallowed in the trenches; I have whined in the streets and mewed on the hilltops and in the lowest valley; I have suffered You to make this bleak wind kiss my lips and comfort me with the cold; I do not ask much, my Lord, just the comfort of the cold.* You can almost hear the great man's voice as you read. The coroner picked up the Churchill note while he and his wife were on holiday in Zurich. (She, by the way, is completely aware of his hobby and finds no malice in it; she is happy he has an interest outside his work, which can be very consuming, and has on several occasions presented him with suicide notes for his birthday or at Christmas.)

The coroner had the good fortune to come across an antique dealer who specialized in suicide notes — the Europeans, as always, being much more tolerant. The owner, a Pole, first tried to sell the coroner Adolph Hitler's authentic suicide note, which, to a collector, is suspect, in the same league as a sliver from the true cross or a deed to the Statue of Liberty. Once the Pole figured out that he wasn't dealing with a rube, he got out the real goods. The coroner picked up the Churchill note, along with a certificate of authenticity from Sotheby's, for just under twenty-five thousand Swiss francs, which is, I can assure you, a bargain. While I haven't anything as exciting as the Churchill note in my collection (the coroner has given me a certified copy, under the stipulation that I neither sell nor reproduce it), I have a couple of pieces of which I am justifiably proud. Of some historical significance is a note from Edwin Miles, the only survivor of the Charge of the Light Brigade (in truth, the validity of this piece is in some doubt). My favourite piece is a note by one Günter Polphner, Herman Goering's personal chef. Written on the back of a recipe for stuffed green peppers, it says simply, "Dear Lord, turn me over when I'm done."

I think it's true what you said, that every man must spend time in the company of strangers. It was years ago, I know, but every time I look at you I hear you saying it again. We were on the sand by the lake, and the moon's light fell across your face; I could see your cheeks and lips; your eyes were shadows. You had just revealed to me the first of your secrets — how you concealed it from me I'll never know. It seemed at first only a small bump on your chest, but when I looked more closely I could see that it was in fact a third nipple, just as you said. "It's not so uncommon, really . . ." But you didn't need to apologize. I kissed this and all your nipples, and, enjoying the compression of you above me and the warm sand below, I fell into a kind of sleep. In the distance I could hear your sister talking as always. What colour was her hair then? Black or white? In my near-sleep I remember the sound of the paddles as they stirred the water, and I think by then the Mexican ambassador was singing to her in Spanish, something vaguely familiar, like a lullaby, although the words and melody didn't register. Yes. That's it. "London Bridge." In Spanish. I've always wondered if you heard it too. I did not hear the splash as your sister dove into the water, and I don't recall anything before the ambassador called her name. By then, you were calling too. I followed the trail of clothes to the water's edge and saw you waist deep in the water, calling, calling, calling your sister's name. The ambassador, who once worked as a pearl diver and had tremendous breath control, scoured the bottom of the lake, while we did the best we could from the cumbersome rowboat. It was almost dawn when the police divers arrived with their scuba tanks and sonar equipment. You stayed on the water in the rowboat the rest of the day and into the following night. It's not so strange that we never recovered her; the police captain, the one with the twitch and the stammer, said that the lake was cluttered with sunken stumps; a four-foot layer of mud and silt covered its bed. Finding her would have taken a miracle. The search continued for a week, but all we came up with was her waterlogged hairpiece, which had drifted to shore on its own. I've always wanted to ask you, how come you never cried? Not when she went missing, that's understandable, there was work to do. But not even later, when the police called off the search, or when we found your mother in a heap on the floor of her living room with her dress wet with tears and a photograph of your sister in her hands, which she held so tightly that it tore when we tried to take it away from her. I'd thought you'd cry then. But you seemed indifferent, cynical at best. You laughed at the funeral and ridiculed us for spending two thousand dollars to bury a thirty-dollar hairpiece. Afterwards, you laughed when your stepfather tried to put things into perspective. "At least this tragedy has brought us all closer together," he said. And later as I drove you home from the cemetery I confessed to you that I had never felt more alive than I had during the search, working shoulder-to-shoulder with the police, all of us focused, and that I had never felt closer to anyone than I felt to you right then in that car. That's when you said it. "Men need the company of strangers. Men only come to life when they're surrounded and involved with people they don't know."

The coroner says most people wait until the spring to kill themselves. Death in general is more abundant in the spring; hospitals and old folks' homes routinely report the highest number of deaths in March and April. The coroner sees this in a positive light, and I agree: people hold on to life for as long as they can. Surviving one more winter is, if not a small victory over death, at least a slap in death's face. I've come to think of you as this kind of person, the kind who plans to make it through one more winter. I think you'd like the coroner. In a lot of ways, he's similar to you. Stoic, that's the word. Stoic, but in the good sense. Not like an institution, but stoic like a well-fed farm animal.

I wanted to tell how I came to collect suicide notes, but it's not a very interesting story. A fluke, more or less. I chanced upon a note. I must confess that I was very apprehensive about telling you anything at all, especially at this time. But in a relationship like ours, we should be able to tell each other our deepest secrets as easily as we say "I love you."

I wanted very much for this to be about someone else, but it's about you.

I've read your note. I was going to put it in my collection, but the coroner's offered me a handsome sum for it, and, at this point in our relationship, I think I should accept his generous offer.

Greetings from the Vodka Sea

They'd heard rumours of marauders sweeping down from the hills to rob tourists and worse, but the sun, the salt air and the stillness of the Vodka Sea immediately put their minds at ease. The hotel, the Crown, was even better than the brochure promised, with the recent addition of two huge kidney-shaped pools linked by a swim-up bar nestled in the plaster grotto. The bar was called the Queen of Hearts, and the heart motif was echoed in everything from the heart-shaped stools rising out of the warm salty pool water and the heart-shaped waterproof doilies (what was the point of those?) down to the cupid cherry skewers and the complimentary heart-shaped chocolate mints, wrapped in red or silver foil, that accompanied the bill. The romance of the place was breathtaking, and the two of them, Dr. and Mrs. Hammond, let themselves be drawn into it. On the first night the normally shy and reticent Monica unselfconsciously gratified her new husband manually in the shadowed hot tub (oddly spleen-shaped) that bordered the grotto, even though they ran the risk of being caught (slight, given the lateness of the hour and Bruce's unmoving, impeccable silence that gave nothing away) or at least discreetly witnessed from a distance. In fact, the thought that they might be being watched (discreetly, that is, from a distance) heightened the experience for both of them. They relaxed and snuggled in the aftermath of Monica's handiwork and tried not to think of the bubbling unhygienic residue of the hundreds or thousands of similarly indiscreet couples who'd honeymooned before them. As they watched the stars vying for attention in the incalculable distance, they could hear the Vodka Sea caressing the shore. It was, they would agree later, the happiest moment in their lives.

That first morning they walked to the sea. It wasn't far, just past the mango grove (Bruce was quite certain that mangos were not native to this part of the world) at the far end of the grounds beyond the pools and tennis courts. One could cut through the grove (although they had been warned to watch for a small green snake, a kind of viper that could deliver a nasty and mildly toxic bite), or one could take the asphalt laneway that wound along the outside of the grove. That first morning they took the laneway; however, as time and their sense of London slipped past, they favoured the shortcut more and more.

The beach itself was splendid. Perfect round beads of pinkish-white sand, the colour of Monica's skin, tickled and massaged their bare feet. No sharp stones or rubbish or aluminum flip tops or bits of broken glass, so unlike Bristol's shaggy shores or those impossibly filthy beaches on the continent. Just warm, gentle beads. Monica said she'd love to lie in those beads fully naked, allowing the sand to surround her and warm her every cranny. Bruce squeezed her shoulder, and she understood that he would take her right then and there on the warm soft sand, if it weren't for that couple with two small children, on holiday from America, enjoying their morning coffee. Monica walked to the shore and put her pink toe in the water. It was colder that she imagined, not that it was cold, in fact it was probably just a few degrees below body temperature, it's just that she'd imagined it would be warmer. She breathed deeply. The smell of salty air (with a slight tinge, a wisp, of vodka) filled her lungs and invigorated her.

"Do you think it's safe to swim?"

Bruce was way ahead of her.

"Bathing is permitted and encouraged," he read from the full-colour brochure. *"The salt density is five times greater than that of the Atlantic Ocean. No one has ever drowned in the Vodka Sea."*

Monica nudged out another couple of inches.

"I wonder, are there fish in it, then?"

Bruce plunged into the brochure. "I'd suspect not. The alcohol combined with the salinity — well, bugger me. *The Vodka Sea supports several unique species of aquatic plants and a high concentration of free-floating crustaceans, close relatives of the brine shrimp. These are the single food source of the Bolen's dwarf whale. No bigger than a carp, this Lilliputian leviathan is the largest inhabitant of the Vodka Sea."*

There was a picture of the whale in the bottom left corner of the brochure, a cartoonish drawing of a miniature blue whale breaching, curls of water rolling from its blowhole. At the top of the spout tumbled smiling shrimp sporting top hats. Bruce scanned the horizon.

"What are you looking for, love?"

"Whales, Peachtree," he said.

She hugged herself, almost blushing. "Miniature whales! Isn't this absolutely the most romantic place on earth?" She turned back and smiled at Bruce and he reciprocated. And at that very moment a tiny whale surfaced not ten feet from them and fired a handful of mist into the air before surrendering to the sea again.

.   .   .

McGuffan told them all about the Vodka Sea over dinner that night.

"The whole thing sits on a kind of peat bog," McGuffan explained. "Layer upon layer of castings and roots that have decayed and built up since time began."

Monica and Bruce carefully forked their pâté and sweet-breads — they hadn't the courage to try the whale brochettes — and hung on McGuffan's every word.

"At one point, it all lay underground in a subterranean cavern, isn't that what the tour guide said, Alice?" Mrs. McGuffan, who was midway through a long sip of claret, snuffed her agreement. "The whole thing acted like a natural still — the minerals in the rocks, the vegetative bog, the salt water, all compressed and contained for millennia — until one day the earth above collapsed, and the Vodka Sea was left exposed to the world. It's a geological wonder but not as uncommon as one might think, what with the Argentine Gin Flats and what-not." It was McGuffan's turn to test the claret. A rather portly Aussie who'd made his fortune in industrial plastics and, more recently, lost half his nose to skin cancer, McGuffan and his wife had been coming to the Vodka Sea for a decade.

"The first time we came it was a collection of rustic cabins, and that's being generous," Alice was saying as the waiter served their entrées.

"The room had snakes and these giant blue spiders. Remember those, love?"

McGuffan nodded. "You don't see the spiders anymore. I wonder what happened to them."

"Yes."

"They were attractive in their way. A most wonderful blue hue, right, love?"

"Yes. Deadly."

"Deadly's overstating it, love. Paralyzing. Coma-inducing. But you'd be hard-pressed to find anyone who'd actually died . . ." McGuffan's voice faded into another glass of claret. He smacked his lips and dove into his whale fillet. Monica and Bruce looked meekly at their mutton and new potatoes in a light grape-shrimp coulis.

"Fancy a bite?" McGuffan offered a forkful of whale to Bruce. "It tastes just like chicken, only saltier, with a hint of — what's that flavour, love?"

"Vodka, dear. I believe it has a hint of vodka."

.   .   .

The Vodka Sea hadn't been their first choice. Spain. Spain is what Monica's parents decided, and her sister and Anthony, Bruce's best man, concurred. But Spain seemed so . . . *Spanish*, so *done before*. And besides, the spicy food didn't sit at all well with either of them. France, of course, and Italy were options, but didn't everybody who didn't go to Spain go to France or Italy? Mrs. Perkins, across the hall, had been to Berlin on her honeymoon, but that was eons ago and her husband was, after all, a survivor of Dresden. Who goes to Germany for their honeymoon? You might as well go to Iceland. They asked Barbara to find them something different, something completely off the map. It would be their only holiday for quite some time; they wanted to make it memorable. Barbara looked at them for a whole minute before speaking. She was a handsome woman, middle-aged, in a crisp grey dress boldly bordered by a pearl choker. She looked more like a head-mistress than a travel agent. "I've got something perfect, I think."

Bruce and Monica had to lean forward to hear her. Barbara got up and closed her office door, then chose the yellow key from a small coffee cup, souvenir of Barbados, at the side of her desk. She unlocked the bottom drawer and pulled out a single file folder. She removed a brochure and held it out for Bruce and Monica, without actually letting go.

"Have a look at this," she near-whispered. "But I must ask you to keep it to yourselves." Bruce and Monica looked at each other, and on her signal, he took the brochure. "The Vodka Sea isn't for everyone, and we want to keep it that way."

Louise was not impressed. Monica told her about the Vodka Sea (she hadn't meant to, it just sort of slipped out, it's hard to keep secrets from your sister) and showed her the brochure. But Louise could not understand. "Why go someplace no one's ever heard of? Why take the chance?" Then her eyes narrowed. "Is this one of his money things?" It was a common theme in her family, Bruce's thriftiness. "It must be the Scot in him," her father would say, glad, for once, to see another familial male taking the heat.

"This isn't about money, Wheeze. It's the perfect place for us. It's so unknown."

"Everything's unknown until you get to know it." She wore an earnest smile with her blue and green pantsuit. She looked more like a travel agent than a sister.

"That's deep. Have you been listening to Tracy Chapman, then?"

Louise rolled her eyes and laughed. "Am I being a bitch?"

"You most certainly are, sister. I mean, it's *our* honeymoon . . ."

And that's when the waterworks started. The whole pressure of the wedding hit Monica like a monsoon, and large pituitary-gland-shaped tears tumbled down her cheeks. Louise reached out and hugged her and rocked her back and forth and understood completely, like no man, no husband, ever could, the emotional maelstrom swirling inside her little sister's heart. "There, there, Monkey. It'll be all right. Everything will be fine. He's a fine man. A fine, good man."

Things were no easier on Bruce. Dr. Welsh, head of OB-GYN, offered his villa (in Spain, no less) free of charge and rather angrily rebuked his young protégé for turning it down.

"You shan't want to go portside in Chocko with no bullets in your backpack," he said, or words to that effect; in moments of high emotion, Dr. Welsh often reverted to an incomprehensible public school patois. Bruce calmly held his ground (the cool head went a long way toward explaining his meteoric rise through the hospital hierarchy: thirty-two and already Senior Fellow) and said both Monica and he were quite comfortable with their choice of venue. Dr. Welsh, who was one for the parry but not the thrust, spent the week lunching on his own and didn't entirely return to form until after Bruce had made him a present of Wagner's complete Ring cycle on CD.

It was only through such machinations and breakdowns that Bruce and Monica were able to go to the Vodka Sea with more or less everyone's approval (his mother was a problem, but that went without saying). Dr. Welsh even called up and made sure there were roses and champagne waiting in the room for them when they arrived.

. . .

McGuffan had cautioned against drinking the water. Not that there was anything wrong with it, per se. It was just the thirst it caused. The salt, he supposed, combined with the vodka. You could drink and drink and drink, he said, and never be quite satisfied. But Monica wanted to taste it just the same. Their second day on the beach, and already they were feeling more daring. They'd woken up at sunrise with the vipers and birds and invisible blue spiders and made love on the bed (and loveseat and floor) without bothering to shut the blinds. It was early, she said, setting her tongue on the skyline of his belly. No one was up to see, and damn them if they did. She took him in her mouth (which silenced the last of Bruce's half-hearted concerns) and led him from bed to loveseat to floor to the kitchenette (Bruce resisted the passing urge to put the clean cutlery away in the drawer) and back to bed again before bringing him to what just might have been the loudest single orgasm in English history. He looked at her afterwards rather sheepishly, which is when Monica suggested they go down to the sea, in part so he could escape his ear-shattering embarrassment but mostly because *she wanted to*.

The sea, smoother than a freshly shaved patient, beckoned to Monica. They'd already been through the question of the tides. Monica believed that the sea had its moods, its highs and lows, its empathy with the moon. Bruce did not. He wasn't forceful or even particularly rude, just dismissive in that matter-of-fact way he had. No. The Vodka Sea was not tidal. Entirely landlocked, no bigger than a dozen of your smaller football stadiums, Stamford Bridge, say, or Upton, pushed together — it didn't seem practical that the moon would have a discernable effect. They'd asked around, but no one had a definitive answer. McGuffan wasn't sure, and Ricki, the treacly hotel manager, had never been asked before. Even the brochure was silent on the matter, which rendered it, to Bruce's mind, a non-issue. But before entering the morning sea, Monica mentioned the idea of tides again, perhaps because she believed in them, or perhaps, and she was surprised to find herself even thinking this, because she wanted to get a rise out of her newly minted spouse. He could be so flat, so constant, so damned reassuring (and again, she only became aware of these feelings at that moment, as she stepped into the Vodka Sea, the taste of him still in her mouth, the unwashed morning smell of him on her hands and face).

"It's definitely tidal. You can see the line where it came up to."

Bruce looked. In truth, there was nothing there.

"It is rather unlikely, Peachtree. But maybe you're right."

Monica took another step. The water did not cover her ankle.

"I wonder how deep it gets."

Bruce shrugged. "The manager said it doesn't go much deeper than ten feet."

"That was McGuffan."

"I think it was the manager, dear."

"I'm sure it was McGuffan. He said so only last night."

"Perhaps it was both, then. It's hardly worth arguing over."

"I'm not arguing."

Bruce thought to say something, then shut his mouth, which annoyed Monica more than just about anything he could have said. She wanted to be mad, but those eyes, those eyes of his, caught her and lifted her up. It was the eyes, the eyes that had first attracted her. Bruce was really not her type. Far too angular, too milky, too British. Monica liked men with a dash of pigment in their skin, a hint of something other than public schools and holiday motor trips south and skin that burnt and peeled at the mere memory of sun. When he'd first asked her out (she was Anthony's sister's boyfriend's neighbour; it was a much-brokered deal) her inclination was to say no, doctor, as she told her sister, or not. But then she caught a flash of those eyes. Very dark, a black, black chestnut, almost evil, somehow rather American. She liked that. She liked those eyes. And when he fixed them on her with a sexual confidence that surprised her, she said yes. Their first date was antiseptic: luncheon (that's the word he used) in the hospital cafeteria (an emergency compromise), Bruce on his cell the entire time, shards of perfunctory conversation. She'd figured that was that. But at the end he apologized and asked for a chance to make things right. Part of her wanted to take a pass, she was definitely the kind of girl who could turn a man down, but those eyes, those eyes engulfed her, and she granted him his second chance. Was he conscious of the power of those eyes? Did he (an only child, whose mother was, in the most charitable term, difficult) understand English women so completely, understand their need to find a sliver of darkness beneath the facade? Or was he simply a sexual savant, a self-absorbed, hypercritical, handsome head in a jar? He'd shown his passion: on their second date, an Irish concert and then the pub, he'd kissed her at just the right moment in just the right way with just the right amount of force and just the right amount of discretion. It was not the chaste kiss of a woman's romance (she was far from virginal, after all, but not too far), and she and he allowed their hips to slide together, and he pushed with little force on the small of her back, drawing her in even closer, and she allowed herself to press into him and felt how big he'd already become and looked again into his dark, dark eyes, into nothing but more darkness. And that's how love was born.

Monica waded out several feet, until the water snuggled her hips. She wanted to wash her face, get the smell of him off her; she wanted to take a drink, get the taste of him out of her mouth. She bent down and cupped her hand, but as she raised the water to her face, a dwarf whale surfaced and spouted inches from her head. Monica jumped back, bringing her hand across her chest. And then she laughed. She threw her head back and brayed in delight.

"It startled me!" she cried, when she'd caught her breath. "Aren't they just the cutest . . ." And she dove in head first, quickly bobbing to the surface and rolling to her back. "It's like flying! You float, you float without the slightest effort."

"It's the salinity," Bruce said, but what he meant to say was that Monica had never looked more beautiful to him than she did at that moment; he had never been more in love. That's when she did it. She turned her head and drew a mouthful of water, then put her head back and spouted a mist of vodka water into the air.

"Thar she blows!" he called, as playfully as possible, resisting the urge to caution her against drinking the water. Monica turned her head again and took another draw, not as long as the first. She seemed to be swallowing this one, closing her eyes as she did. She scrunched her face.

"Yuck. That's awful."

"Remember McGuffan's caution, love."

"It tastes like . . ."

She turned her head and took another drink. "Cor. That certainly doesn't hit the spot."

Bruce was watching his floating bride and inching out himself when Ricki, the manager, appeared, holding two yellow towels.

"It's a beautiful morning for a swim, sir. Of course, sir, it always is." Ricki smiled and handed the towels to Bruce. They were still warm from the laundry.

"The water, is it safe to drink?" Bruce asked.

Ricki looked almost insulted. He stumped his pinkie finger into his hairy ear and corked it around, evidently composing himself. He had a large oblong head, like those mystery men of Easter Island, and rounded, bulky arms and legs, simian. Rumour was that Ricki had fought on both sides of the civil war that had ravaged the countryside in the decades before. (Alice said she'd heard the International Tribunal at The Hague had a standing warrant for his arrest, although McGuffan, in the most comical manner imaginable, pooh-poohed her. They really were quite a couple.)

"I can assure you, sir, no one has every come to harm . . ."

"McGuffan said . . ."

"I understand, sir. Mr. McGuffan has shared his concerns with me. But they're folk tales, really, to amuse the peasants and their children." Ricki's voice faded, politely. His gaze fell on Monica, who was standing again. The sea had pasted her t-shirt to her bra, and in the cool sunlight, Bruce could track the gravy-coloured outline of her aureoles and the harsh stubs of her nipples (hard, Bruce assumed, hoped, from the cool morning breeze). He glanced at Ricki, and had he been a jealous man he might have thought that the manager was giving his bride the once-over. It's funny. Bruce had never thought of Monica as particularly beautiful. Not plain, no. Louise was plain, in that flat-chested, horsy-faced, hospital-cornered British-matron way. Monica had a certain virginal sexiness, an attractive middle-aged nunnishness (Sister Grace, for example, Nursing Head of the chemo ward, who turned a resident's head or two). But this morning, in the cool sun, with stubbing tits all glisty wet, her fleshy cheeks peeking out from her bikini bottom, that orgasmic smile, that don't-give-a-damn glaze to her eyes — this morning she was a bit of something. Ricki held up his arms.

"Towel, ma'am?"

Monica took a towel and rubbed her hair, messing it up in such a way that she only looked sexier. Ricki extended his hand and helped her out of the water.

"I'll think you'll enjoy the breakfast today, Miss. Strawberries, fresh from the fields, and local blood oranges — better than the Italian. And Monsieur Langour was up very early preparing his apple-almond croissants. I'd suggest you try them with yellow pepper marmalade: spicy, sweet, a house specialty."

"That sounds wonderful," she said, as Bruce drew the other towel around her shoulders (trying discreetly to cover her visible nipples) and led her by the arm toward the mango grove.

"He's an interesting man," Monica said.

"Yes. Hairy, too."

"Yes, indeed. Hairy."

.   .   .

That afternoon they took the boat tour across the Vodka Sea. McGuffan and Alice joined them, although they'd taken the tour a dozen times before. McGuffan was the sort who'd interrupt the tour guide to offer his own by now much-practiced insights; the Australian was quickly losing his lustre. Likewise Alice's calculated hee-hawing and endless slogging had worn thin. (Bruce had quickly come to hate the sight of her lips as they snarled over yet another bottled vodka spritzer.) They were like two tireless party guests who refuse to leave even as you stand there, hats and coats in hand, yawning and blearily eyeing your bedroom door.

"Is it true that, at its deepest point, the Vodka Sea is barely ten feet deep?"

(*Objection, your honour! Counsel is leading the tour guide.*)

"Yes, sir. Even at its deepest point, the Vodka Sea rarely exceeds ten feet." The tour guide, they called him John, for convenience, smiled at McGuffan, calculating, Bruce supposed, his tip.

"Remarkable," McGuffan declared, although there was nothing remarkable about it. He turned to Monica, beaming, and raised his eyebrows like an excited ten-year-old auditor who'd just found a KitKat amongst the debits and credits. Monica smiled back and tilted her head in a motherly fashion, then she shifted in her seat slightly, adjusting her dress. She wanted to give Bruce, sitting directly across from her, a better view. She wanted him to see that, under the crepe sundress, white, translucent, she wasn't wearing any panties. She'd done that for him, she supposed; she'd thought about it for a long time as she readied herself after lunch. She stood in front of the mirror with panties on and panties off and panties on and panties off just to get the hang of it. She felt so free without out them, but did she dare? It's not the kind of thing a nice woman, a decent woman such as herself, did, walk around in a crepe sundress (it hardly hid anything, and in any case, concealed only as a roundabout way of revealing) with no panties and no bra (her nipples were clearly visible, if she looked hard enough) in broad daylight. But every time she made up her mind to go with them, she slipped them off again, the soft fabric brushing her soft skin, bikini-waxed at Mercury Spa not four days before, just to see if she could dare go without them. It wasn't a matter of comfort, because she felt more comfortable with her panties on. It just seemed different, like something she would never do and may never do again.

"And the tides? Our friend here," McGuffan nodded toward Bruce, "was wondering about the tides. What about the tides?"

John shrugged. "The tides are still a matter of some debate." The tour guide had a vaguely Oxfordian accent. Perhaps he'd studied there. Perhaps he was the son of a local potentate and had been afforded the advantage of a British education.

Monica continued twisting one ankle and raised her knee and looked expectantly at Bruce. She could feel the fabric of her crepe dress drop below her (just as she knew it would, as if the fabric was now part of her), although the top of it still lay respectably on her knee. She felt the breeze move up her skirt and across her trimmed pubis, and with one more minor adjustment — there! — she awaited Bruce's reaction.

He caught her gaze and was smiling back at her now. She rather dramatically ran the back of her hand across her brow, then slowly lowered it to rest on her knee. She drew her sun-dress up another inch and watched her husband's eyes widen. He seemed at first to panic, to signal her with urgent nods that something was amiss. But she only drew her hem up, dis-creetly, another notch, and slowly let her hand fall onto the pocket of fabric that tented her crotch. A finger lazy brushed the skin along the inner thigh, and Bruce's signals became more frantic. The other passengers were engrossed in the tour and paid no attention as she casually let her hand drop to her thigh, and slipped two fingers along her smoothed skin until they lightly brushed the ruffled, raised flesh. Bruce crossed his legs and tried to look away. Was he angry? She couldn't tell.

"The Bolen's whale, then, is it related to the humpback?"

"Exactly right, sir. This whale is a close relative of the hump-back. Scientists believe that the Vodka Sea was once part of a vast oceanic corridor that stretched from pole to pole. Way back, as the oceans receded, a pod of humpbacks may have become landlocked. They practiced the elementary rule of evolution: adapt or die."

"What about the marauders?" It was Bruce's turn to ask the question. John hesitated. This was not the kind of question he normally faced. Bruce watched the guide scan his memory bank for a moment. John had one of those ageless foreign faces; he could have been anywhere from fourteen to forty. (Bruce thought of a story Anthony had told him about how his sister-in-law, ex-sister-in-law now, had once befriended an orphan during some South American getaway and decided to take him home and adopt him. They'd done all the paperwork, at least they thought they'd done the paperwork, but as they were entering the airport the chief of police stopped them. Turned out their orphan was a twenty-six-year-old midget with a wife and children of his own. The kicker to the story, as Anthony told it, was when his now-ex-sister-in-law lamented, "What's the world coming to, when you can't even trust a midget?")

John cleared his throat, suitably recovered.

"Everyone has heard such stories," he said, beading in on Bruce. "But it's important to remember that our government has never supported the — what's the word — notion? Yes, notion of a resort on the Vodka Sea. First of all, they mistrust foreigners in general, even Australians," John turned to the McGuffans and smiled; Alice hee-hawed appreciatively, "and wish to do anything to avoid encouraging them to come here. And second, the government is given to a certain," he paused again, grasping for the right word, "fundamentalism. The notion of a sea of alcohol, well, they don't quite know what to make of that. First they tried to ban it, but as you can imagine, it's hard to ban a sea."

The small crowd tittered.

"Then they tried to regulate it: no swimming on Sundays or after eight o'clock, that sort of thing. Now, they simply tax us to death. There's a twenty-six per cent room tax, a fourteen per cent food service tax . . ." He waved to indicate that he could go on forever. "It's the perfect antidote for a pious, avaricious, ambivalent government. Condemn with one hand, profit with the other."

"But the marauders? What of them?"

"The marauders?" John grunted. "That's just an old wives' tale, sir. Spread by the government to scare off tourists. The old women believe it, and the children. But I can assure you, you're perfectly safe on the Vodka Sea."

On cue, a whale punched the surface and rolled its back through the air, and then another and another until the sea around the cruise boat boiled with these bobbing self-contained fists. John pulled a bucket from under his seat and spilled its shrimpy brine into the water; in their rush to get at the food, the little whales smashed into one another quite comically.

"Look, the whales have come to say hello." John uncovered another bucket, and with a professional conjurer's flourish, poured it over the side. "A most intelligent animal indeed, ladies and gentlemen. Stories are told of I don't know how many drunken fishermen, who, after falling overboard in a stupor, have been safely buffeted to shore by the vigilant whale."

Bruce looked into the water. The sun was already beginning to set, and the broken water sparkled sharply in the whales' small wakes. Two or three of the creatures begun ramming the side of the tour boat, hungry for more, It was all quite comical, like a small child play-fighting a giant dog. *Ping. Ping.* Their little heads echoed off the aluminum hull. Bruce looked in the water and watched the curious whales, immersed in his own tiny sea as surely as Monica (leg slightly raised, fingers discreetly but vigorously working) was immersed in hers.

. . .

There were ups and downs. At times they seemed to be moving in different directions. If Monica wanted to go to the bazaar, Bruce wanted to go to the ruins; if Bruce fancied the ancient burial grounds, Monica insisted on the sixteenth century frescos. She called her mother.

"It's a give and take, sweetheart. Your father and I never really agree on anything. That's why we have two tellies."

"Three tellies, Mum."

"What's that?"

"Three tellies. You and Dad have three tellies."

"Yes, three tellies. One for the children, of course." Monica envied the way her mother could reduce any problem to fit into her dollhouse world of social teas, the ladies' squash ladder and Third World charity boards.

"It's just that I sometimes wonder if — not that I think I've made a mistake, mind you, but — I wonder if maybe we didn't rush into this a little too fast."

"Surely you're not having second thoughts? The man's a doctor."

"That's not what I'm saying, Mummy. I just don't know him. I should have eased into him a little more, I think."

"Monkey, sweetie, you're on holiday. You're a thousand miles away from nowhere. You shouldn't have a care in the world. I know what it's like. I get to Provence or Gibraltar, I'm weeks before I can settle in. It takes time to shake the city out of your head, to let yourself go and just relax. Go have a nice mineral mud bath — have you tried the mineral mud bath? Treat yourself to something nice and stop worrying so much. You're just like your father."

And Monica took her mother's advice. She treated herself to a mineral mud bath (it was as good as she'd heard; she emerged, hours later, thoroughly rested, her skin tingling), then wandered down to the sea. She took a sip of the salty water, and then another and another. She spent the rest of the afternoon on the shore, drinking from the Vodka Sea and watching the tiny waves rise and fall.

The week was almost over, and they'd planned a coach trip to the coast. At the last minute Bruce got an urgent call. They needed his advice on a complicated case (Bruce had pioneered the use of non-invasive procedures, almost single-handedly pulling London out of the Dark Ages of reproductive surgery); they wouldn't have called but it was, quite literally, a matter of life or death. Bruce kissed Monica's forehead.

"I'm afraid you'll have to get used to it, Peachtree. A doctor's life is never his own." He urged her to take the motor trip without him. The McGuffans would be there, and that new couple from Bingly (married, it turned out, the same day as Bruce and Monica), and besides, he would likely be in and out of consultation all afternoon. She reluctantly agreed.

The coach was cramped and hot (air conditioning was yet to be discovered by the locals, it seemed). Monica had a seat mostly to herself, although John sat with her whenever he was taking a break from his guide duties. They drove due west, past the government checkpoint a few kilometres from the resort compound, up into the rolling hills (several rows of barbed wire separated the road from the untended orange groves), and through the gentle grasslands. They drove right past the Hanging Gardens, heralded in several languages as the Tenth Wonder of the World. It looked broken down and unattended, and judging by John's smirk, it must of been something of a local embarrassment. The coast was . . . well, a coast: rocky shoreline and sandy beaches, although the water looked cold and muddy and violent; it had nothing of the Vodka Sea's soothing charm. And so they trudged through the half dozen grim tourist shops, each selling the same cheap t-shirts and shell animals, and the dirty bistro (where a mercifully Spartan lunch of fish soup and herbed bread was provided) and out along the same breakwater where pirates and crusaders, centuries before, had stopped to ask directions. Their last stop was an icebox-sized bar, named simply 1234. A glass of local wine was included with the tour (somewhere between a Merlot and a Cabernet, with a peaty, almost mouldy, aftertaste). Monica had one drink, and then John, who'd latched onto her, the Single Englishwoman, bought her another and another.

"It's a long ride back." He smiled. He skin smelled of coconut and motor oil.

And a long ride back it was. Dusk had come, and the coach fairly crawled along the unlit gravel highway. John gave up his patter ten minutes into the trip, and settled into the spot beside Monica.

"It seems so curious to me," she said, after enduring a few moments of silence.

"What's that, miss?"

"You seem to be somewhat above this." The wine had made her unusually brave. "I mean, you're obviously educated. A man of some character and breeding. Surely you aspire to being more than a tour guide."

John shrugged.

"We do what we can, miss. And when we can't do what we can, we do what we must."

"Come now, John, there's no need to play the inscrutable foreigner on me. You and I both know that you are cut out for bigger things than pampering fat Americans and buying squeaky English women drinks. I could see you doing quite well back in London."

John smiled. "Two things, miss. First, never look at a postcard and think you're getting all the picture. And second, this isn't London."

A few minutes later, he seemed to drift off to sleep, his head tilting onto her shoulder. It was not uncomfortable, it just wasn't comfortable. Some minutes later, John let his hand slip casually against Monica's knee. Slowly, glacially, it marked its way up until it rested on her thigh. A slight grunt as the pretending-to-sleep tour guide pretended to turn in a dreamy fit, and the hand was on her lap. He pressed lightly, his hand vibrating and jumping as the coach slithered along the ancient road. She let it stay there, pretending now to be asleep too. Casually, she let her legs unfold a few inches, so that the tour guide's hand pressed firmly against her. And there it stayed for the duration of the trip.

·   ·   ·

At supper that night, Monica ordered the whale, grilled on an open flame and served with a peppercorn-garlic mash. There were potatoes too, the brownish red kind, apparently a staple around these parts, roasted with a variety of sweet local squash. Bruce watched his wife as she ate. He expected her to approach the whale with caution; she attacked.

"Mmmm." Her eyes were shut, the sound stretched into a barely muffled moan. Bruce felt embarrassed. Surely nothing could taste that good.

"You must try the whale, Bruce. It's . . ."

"I'd rather not, thank you."

"But it's . . ."

"No thank you, Monica." Bruce pulled on the wing of his game hen, which tasted rather more game than hen, and looked around the dining room. McGuffan was there, chewing on his whale steak and kidney pie as his wife neatly filleted her whole poached whale in a vodka Béarnaise (spécial du jour in the Imperial Room). The Americans were there too, he sucking the marrow out of a whale's spine, she helping the young children slice their battered whale and chips into manageable pieces. There were others, couples mostly (new couples, honey-mooners, seemed to arrive every day) who collectively, and silently save for the gnawing and sucking and appreciative smacks, were devouring an entire generation of Bolen's dwarf whale. Monica took another slug of her Blue Whale (fresh-drawn vodka, blue curaçao and grenadine), downed the last drop, and signed to Ricki, pulling double duty behind the bar, for yet another glass.

"Haven't you had enough to drink, Peachtree?"

"We're on bloody holiday."

"But angel, that's six . . ."

"Give it a rest, granny." She offered Bruce one more bite, just, she didn't doubt it now, to rub it in. His priggishness was suited to back home; the hospital and great city demanded no less, but that was a thousand miles away. The more kempt and parcelled he became, the more Monica unstitched herself. It was stupid, really; Monica knew it. She'd set Bruce up as some sort of authority figure (not unlike, as distressing as this was to admit, her father), and now she tilted and tumbled at him like a temperamental teenager. He'd challenged her when she headed off to supper in shorts and her bikini top (although that's how the other women were dressed, for godsake, what with the nights so stifling and the atmosphere of the restaurant so informal), and sternly swatted her hidden hand away during appetizers as she quietly tried to breech the fortress of his trousers. The reactions were expected. Anticipated.

Dessert was served, mango ice in hollowed coconut shells (definitely imported, he was certain of this) as Bruce diligently avoided eye contact with McGuffan. It had become ritual for the Australians to come to their table for coffee and dessert, and Bruce couldn't bear the thought of entertaining them again. He strategically selected a minuscule table at the far end of the dining room, beyond the pampas divider and prostate-shaped dance floor. They ate their ice in a pleasant silence. The sound of a folk guitar washed over from the Queen of Hearts (and here and there, an odd cracking sound from across the water, fireworks, no doubt, for some local saint's eve), riding the rhythms of the distant waves. The fingers of their free hands interlocked, and they looked deep into each other's eyes the way lovers should.

He was talking to his wife about London, about how the city had changed.

"I don't see the difference," she was saying. "It's the same old city it's always been, only there's more of it, I suppose."

"Nonsense!" Bruce was surprised how aggressive his tone had become. Already a Senior Fellow and department head, he'd learned not to have a lot of patience. "I mean, it's not really English any more, is it? You won't find any real English people in London. You've got to go far out of the city to find real English people."

"We're real English people, aren't we?"

"You're twisting my meaning . . ."

"And my family. And your friends. Even your mother — Christ, her father was assistant to the Home Secretary."

"Let's leave Mother out of this."

"Her uncle was a Churchill by marriage. How could anyone possibly be more English than your mother?"

"I mean the city as a whole. It's become . . . cosmopolitan." Bruce emphasized each syllable, as if each one represented a particular shade of decadence. "Just try getting a decent meal. It's all McDonald's and halal meats. Just try getting some decent fish and chips . . ."

"You hate fish and chips."

"Or a decent glass of beer. You know what the pub across

from the hospital sells? Molson's Canadian. And Coors Lite. Coors Lite? What the hell is that?"

"I hardly think fried potatoes and beer are reasonable grounds for dismissing an entire city."

"That's not the point." Bruce was shouting at Monica now. "It's the people. The people have changed. When I was a boy, the people were still English. Now, everyone in London is an immigrant or a tourist or a businessman. Christ, even the prostitutes are Russian. And when I go to work, I need an interpreter — and that's just for my staff. In the wards, it's like a UN refugee camp, its all coloureds and Asians and Indians . . ."

Bruce's voice trailed off. Monica sat in silence. This was a side of her husband she had never seen or even suspected. Underneath the starched shirt and school tie was a starched shirt and school tie, an Englishman dying to get out. Bruce tried to smile.

"I'm only saying the truth. You know it as well as I." He reached for her hand, but she pulled it away. She was thinking of the years ahead, the chubby, pasty children, the women's club, a mistress perhaps, a lover for her, a friend of his no doubt, a protégé.

"Honey, please don't be that way." He reached for her hands again. She let him hold them but turned her head toward the sea.

"Fancy a bit of company?" McGuffan had rooted them out.

"Actually, we're just going to our room." Bruce pushed his chair back.

"Splendid! But we've only just ordered fancy coffees. Imperial Room specialty. You must try one."

"Caffeine doesn't agree with me."

"Caffeine doesn't agree with you. Did you hear, that Alice? We'll make it decaf, then. You really must try this drink. It has — what's the stuff, Alice?"

"Anisette, dear."

"Anisette, yes . . ."

"And a splash . . ."

". . . of vodka?"

"That's right, love. Vodka."

Bruce looked at Monica pleadingly. She tilted her head and ran her bare foot up his leg.

Bruce collapsed just a little. "One drink, then. Only one."

"Splendid." McGuffan rubbed his hands together, excited at the opportunity to play the congenial host. "Ricki! Café spécial, for four."

"Make mine a —"

"And make one a decaf, for the good doctor here."

"One drink, and that's it."

But one drink became two, and two become four, following the physics of alcohol consumption, and soon even Bruce had become dizzy. He remembered singing with Alice (in French? Something from *Cats*?) and parading, almost obscenely close, to Ricki and one of the serving boys in some strange folk dance involving tea towels, bare chests and a kind of frog-hopping two-step.

And at some point the whole crew, the McGuffans and Monica and Ricki and a regiment of servers, made their way to the hot pool, as Bruce took a walk to the beach to clear his swimming head. It was a strategic move; as soon as he hit the sand, Bruce shoved two fingers down his throat and forced himself to vomit. Once. Twice. Three times. He gasped for several moments, his knuckles and knees planted in the still-warm sand. He pushed off his shoes. That was better. His stomach was not so sour, his head clearer. He pulled his shirt off (vomit had drooled across the pocket) and rinsed it in the water. Then he dipped onto his haunches and, sitting like a dog, looked out to sea. There was something out there. It took a moment for his eyes to adjust, but there — there it was. Not twenty feet from shore, a small whale, poking its head into the air, watching. And there, nearby, another whale, and another and — there were almost too many for a drunk to count. They simply bobbed and stared at Bruce impassively (of course, as Bruce quickly realized, they were whales; they could only be impassive). It was the noise. Yes, that was it. The retching song — that had confused them, attracted them. Bruce reached for a stone. He felt a wide flat one. Perfect. He pushed himself to his feet and flung the stone onto the water. It skipped half a dozen times, jewelling the water with moonlight each time it scratched the surface, stopping finally in the space between two buoyed whales. From across the sea, firecrackers clacked again. Quietly, together, the whales withdrew.

Bruce took the main path back to the hotel. He expected, hoped, to find Monica there waiting for him, perhaps a little worried (where had he been?). But the room was still dark, the bed empty. Bruce went to the window. He looked down into the courtyard. There, near the shadows of the grotto, in the hot tub, Monica, Ricki and John, close but not too close. Alice and McGuffan sat at the other end. She may or may not have been singing. In any case, he was nuzzling (or at least, from Bruce's vantage point, appeared to be nuzzling) her throat. Monica was leaning forward, relaxed (almost overly so); Ricki and John sat motionless, their faces blank, revealing nothing. Ricki tilted his head back and seemed (from where Bruce stood, it was hard to tell) to close his eyes. Aimlessly, Monica turned her gaze toward the window. Bruce stepped back, half hiding behind the curtain. Nevertheless, she seemed to find his eyes. She seemed (though the distance and darkness could have been playing tricks) to be staring right into his eyes. Her arms moved vigorously now under the bubbled surface — Monica made no attempt to conceal what she was doing. The realization that her husband must have been watching (discreetly, that is, from a distance) heightened her excitement. Ricki arched forward as John thrashed in the water (Bruce found himself growing excited despite himself, knowing she must have been watching him watching her), and the tour guide moaned so loudly that Bruce could clearly hear him, three floors up and through the glass. A moment later, the hotel employees had sunk back into their spots, but Monica still looked up to him and, in fact, had never averted her gaze. These eyes, his eyes, she was trying to reach inside them, to dive inside them, find herself in his eyes, look through his eyes and see herself as he saw her. Bruce drew the blind. He went to the kitchenette and opened the drawer beneath the microwave. There were several knives in the drawer, and he selected the long one with the serrated edge. He shut the drawer, then slipped into bed to wait for his wife.

.   .   .

Monica stood up. She didn't need to towel, the night air was that warm. The breeze, hot as it was, cooled her wet skin. There was that sound again. The firecrackers. McGuffan stopped himself mid-nuzzle to listen.

"Marauders, eh, Ricki?"

The manager grunted and shrugged.

"Marauders?" Monica looked toward the sea.

McGuffan nodded. He'd been through it a couple of times, he said. "Hadn't wanted to mention anything earlier, what with the honeymoon and all."

"What do we do?" Monica strained to still her voice.

McGuffan ran a hand through his thinning hair. "Remain calm, that's always best. And wait. The government usually re-establishes a safe corridor within twenty-four hours. Isn't that right, Ricki?"

"A day, maybe two. There's an election coming up, so who knows?"

John broke in. "They're like the tide. They ebb, they flow."

"Who? Who is like the tide, John? The government?"

"The government . . . the marauders . . ." His voice drifted off lazily; they were one and the same for him.

Monica looked to the hills across the water. Several fires were spreading at an alarming rate (almost comical, from this distance). A wave of panic washed through her. She must find Bruce. Where could he be? He'd gone to the beach hours ago. And a different kind of panic overtook her. Perhaps he'd seen? Perhaps he'd been coming up through the path and caught sight of her — the lot of them — in the Jacuzzi. Of course, the idea had struck her before, and, in fact, at the time, it was this idea that appealed to her most. It wasn't so much the foreign men, naked, leading her on (Alice bleating, "Go for it, love, you're on bloody holiday," but the thought that Bruce might see, would see, and approach in anger (slightly aroused but angry, righteous without being self-righteous) and grab her roughly (but not ungallantly) and, with a few threatening, understated words to the foreigners, whisk her off to the room — this is what excited her. She'd been stupid. A stupid girl. She couldn't blame the men. They were attractive and aroused (not a big deal, really, for her, but it did tip the scales slightly) and so adolescent in the obvious-ness of their intentions, their earnest, almost pathetic actions (they must have thought English girls were such sluts), tugging her hands towards them (not forcefully, but with such vague and, again, pathetic deference it was almost sad; she pitied them, as people tend to pity foreigners). No. She'd never been so stupid. Not even in school. She was a married woman now, for godsake; and even if she weren't —

Monica hurried off toward the beach to find John, all the way reproaching herself. But you can say only so much, and by the time she reached the sand (there were his shoes, and there, his shirt) she was already repeating herself. It was agreed: she'd been stupid. But now they'd have to live with it and move on. The waves washed almost to her feet. It was the sea, she thought. The damned sea. They'd put it in everything: the sauces, the cocktails, the dessert, the aperitifs. The sea was everywhere. The waves licked her toes. Monica squatted. She dipped her hand into the sea and, almost without thinking, took a sip. It was awful stuff, horrible. How could anyone . . .

She took another drink. From across the water, she heard the shouts of men, some angry, some, it seemed, frightened. Women too were screaming, and children, she thought she could make out the sound of children crying for their mothers. It didn't matter that she couldn't speak the language; the sound of children crying for their mothers was something you just instinctively understood. Now she sat and wondered, where was Bruce? Perhaps he'd gone for swim. Or a long walk along the beach? He liked to do that when he'd had a bit to drink.

There was another *crack*. The gunshots were getting closer. The marauders were sweeping down from the hills, and where was John? She wanted him there with her. She wanted to hold him. She wanted him to be angry at her, to reproach her. She wanted to be hated and forgiven. She rolled onto her hands and knees and reached into the water for another drink, then she bent forward and began to lap the water like a dog. Nearby, a stone's throw, really, a whale surfaced. It was close enough for Monica to look into its eyes, to read the blankness, and she realized for the very first time that these friendly whales weren't friendly at all.

"I know your game," she said, then lapped another mouthful of water. She felt around for a rock and found one almost the size of her fist. She pulled it towards her, nestled it in her lap, held it tighter. Bruce would come for her soon, she was sure of that. She wanted to be ready.

The Klingon Opera

Murph found the kit at the back of the basement walk-in, in a plastic storage box stuffed to the gills with memories and other shit. Why he hadn't disposed of the kit years ago, simply thrown it away, he couldn't say. He was a pack rat. You never knew when you'd need something. He'd asked Rudy to help him, but the kid was on his computer and refused to get off. Murph got pissed and started into one of those lectures about allowances and certain teenagers who never lifted a finger to help around the house, but he kept his cool in light of the fact — the irony, hypocrisy even, that he was asking his son to participate — indirectly, in a major felony punishable by up to twenty years in the federal penitentiary.

Leave the kid to his conversational Klingon, Murph decided as he started to reorganize history, one box at a time. "Wedding Stuff" . . . "Misc. Photo" . . . "Xmas '96" . . . "Income Tax" . . . "Marg's Office." In "Rudy" he found *Baby's Memory Book*. It listed the stats of the boy's birth: weight, 6 pounds 8 ounces; length, 20 inches; hair colour, none; eyes, yes; and on and on. Murph's wife had even updated the book: first tooth, first steps, first haircut, first words. Sometime before First Day of School, Marg had petered out. She was good at that.

Twenty-five minutes into it, Murph reached "PM: Personal." He peeled back the plastic lid and swept aside the packing of old *Penthouse* and raunchy letters from ex-girlfriends and found the kit still wrapped in a striped tea towel, the way he remembered it, the way it had always been. And once he had reinterred his past, all but the kit, a holographic shard revealing more of Murph than seemed possible, he returned to his study to finish the job. Muffled synthesized music trembled from Rudy's room. He was working still on that damned opera. But such was adolescence, Murph supposed, all about obsession and the creation of tinkly epics never to be heard outside inner space. Besides, it kept Rudy off the streets, away from their wantonness and dangers. The kid, thank God, wouldn't know Colt 45 from a Colt .45.

The product was spread out on the table. While it hadn't exactly cost Murph his live savings — those were somewhat below zero, an ex-wife and a teenaged son would do that to you — it had substantially increased his debt load, the VU meter of his underamplified life. When he got together with his buddies for a drink or some herb, it always came back to that. What's your debt load? How much of a burden are you? How big is your nut? It was the cost of living, in monthly instalments. Everybody had a plan. Moonie sold his truck but blew most of that in a Vegas chicken ranch. He came home, used the leftover money for a deposit on a new truck, and settled back into the faithful, forgiving arms of his debt load. Lloyd lucked out when his mother died. He got the family home, which he unwisely converted into a four-bedroom rancher in the valley, a nice little setup up for his girlfriend and her two brats. Now he's amortized into oblivion. Dicky D did the best of all. He took out a second mortgage, then a third and was working on his banker to spring for the fourth. His plan was always the same: consolidate debt. But every time, the debt wound up consolidating him. Now Dicky hoped to die before he turned sixty-five, having no desire to endure sunset years of cat food suppers in a fixed-income flat.

Murph had already cut the coke into six smaller sections. He'd thought to weigh it, to make sure he'd got a whole kilo, although what would he do if it was light? It's not like there was a complaints department he could go to. Things had changed, but not that much. Murph dabbed a bit of the product with his baby finger and stuck it into his mouth, swishing it around to test the bouquet, just like they did on cop shows. Real life cops never did that. Real life cops never knew if they were getting a finger full of up or down or potassium bromide or Draino. But Murph already knew that this was the real deal. He'd done a line with that kid with the limp, the wholesaler. *Double U.* Not that he'd really wanted to do a line, but he felt he should, to put the kid's mind at ease. Murph was a fresh face in a business that didn't like fresh faces, and an old fresh face at that. His brother had vouched for him — that helped — but it was possible he could have been a narc, a stupid, shitty narc, in the worst look-at-me-I'm-a-narc disguise any narc ever concocted, so he took a line for the cause. It was like he'd never left home. The taste (not sweet, not tart, nothing you could describe because there was nothing else you could accurately compare it to: almondy, barely, that's the best he could do), the sugary burn in his sinuses, the up that came and went with a bang. Kaboom. He'd swore he'd never do it again, back when he'd given everything up and swore he'd never do anything again. But never is a long time, and defeat is often easier to swallow (or in this case inhale) than complete humiliation.

He hadn't quite figured out what to do. His first thought was to process it, make crack. The wholesaler said that that would net him the biggest return; his brother concurred. He could move a point of crack for ten bucks, net five or six times his investment. The downside was that Murph had never made crack before, and he didn't feel he had the wiggle room to fuck around with the product. Plus, he didn't understand the market. Crack was after his time. Up he understood. He understood who used it and why. There was still a measure of respectability to it. Doctors did coke. Professional athletes.

Bankers. Crack was something else, and crackheads moved in different (and, as far as Murph could make out, ever-diminishing) circles. It was the Kmart of the drug world, the bad name brand, the unwashed slut who went down on anyone and brought everyone down with her. He'd just cut it with soda and package it in Baggies. Simple. Understated. Hard to trace. A classic.

An electric rhythm kicked from Rudy's room. *Boom-cha, boom-boom ba-cha.* The Klingon Opera was going to be the first ever acid-rap musical. *Boom-cha, boom-boom ba-cha.* It told the story of Kahless the Unforgettable, patriarch of the Klingon Kingdom, who, through a set of complicated and contrived circumstances, is forced to choose between the two Essential Truths: Honour and Duty. The libretto was complete. Rudy had read it to Murph over the Christmas holidays. Upside: mercifully short. Downside: Murph woefully untutored in conversational Klingon. Now there was just the music. *Boom-cha, boom-boom ba-cha.* Murph liked that rhythm. It was animal. Angry, in a sexy way, like a good fight, or the way a good fight used to be, years ago, the kind of fight that just happened, where someone'd just look at you wrong and you'd fall together and kick the shit out each other for five minutes, then both collapse at the same time and walk away without even saying a word, like some anonymous perfect macho fuck, and the buzz stayed with you for days; sexy in a fantastic way, a more-gorgeous-than-life sexy, like a beer commercial or *Penthouse* spread. Sometimes Murph would crawl into his bed as the rhythm thumped from Rudy's room, just crawl into bed with a couple of good mags and pull himself off and take himself home listening to that rhythm — it was that kind of sexy. Murph wondered what kind of effect the music had on Rudy. Did it awake the animal in him? Was there an animal in him?

Murph measured out fifty Baggies in ten-, fifteen- and fifty-dollar sizes only. It was more cumbersome that way, but he'd have a level of protection. If the cops caught him — not that they would, but if they did — he'd only ever be carrying enough for himself, they couldn't ding him for dealing. In high school, when he'd really been a dealer and not just some guy trying to make ends meet, he found it hurtfully hypocritical that a society which so worshipped capitalism, and the entrepreneurial spirit so deeply abhorred the dealer. True, dealers didn't pay taxes (neither did IBM) and contributed, in the most theoretical terms, to general human suffering (so did Dupont and Ford and just about every corporation you could name), but dealers also brought pleasure and gratification to many willing, wilful people. Back then, he'd managed to convince himself that he was on a crusade to turn on the world. Now, he didn't give a shite about the big picture. All he wanted to do was get out of the hole and not, repeat not, go to jail. Murph had an itch to try another line, bolster his nerve. But he just kept weighing and cutting, weighing and cutting, weighing and cutting. This was strictly business and would remain so. He had work to do.

.   .   .

Wilson turned the corner at full trot and crashed into the cans, just like on TV, and it hurt like shit, like it never did on TV, and it wasn't funny in the least, like it always was on TV. He dropped his Glock. Wilson got up right away because the adrenaline was rushing and because he was spiritually, emotionally, intellectually and physically shitting his pants and mainly — mainly — because he didn't, under any circumstances, want to die. Wilson was his real name, but nobody used it. They called him by his street tag, which right now seemed so stupid and pointless, and worse, so utterly unproductive, that he thought of himself only in terms of Wilson. In TV shows — and don't get Wilson wrong, he liked TV shows, he's not blaming TV shows for anything — but in TV shows, no one ever got scared shitless. They were shot at, shot back, chased and were chased, they swore, they threatened, they fought, but no one ever got scared shitless. Afterwards, they might say they were scared, but in a really emotional way that real scared people, people like Wilson, never used. Wilson was scared shitless, and his entire body, his soul, was scared shitless, and he shook and could barely breathe, and if he'd had to talk, say something colourful for the cameras, he wouldn't have been able to say a word. The problem? The problem was simple. There might not be any afterwards. You're always guaranteed an afterwards in a TV show when the drug deal goes bad, if you're the right guy, the good guy. Wilson didn't necessarily have an afterwards, and he knew it.

He ran down the alley, his knees shaking with every step, his bad leg holding him back, and came, just like in the TV shows, to a wire mesh fence, maybe nine feet tall. When this happened on TV, Wilson always thought, how *fucking* convenient. Right in the middle of nowhere, for no fucking point, someone had stuck a fence. That's not contrived, he'd say to Cherry sarcastically. Now here he was, unpleasantly contrived. He jumped and grabbed the top of the fence (whether the sharp unshielded points of metal at the top of the fence dug into his fingers, like they sometimes did on TV, he couldn't tell) and pulled himself up almost whimpering, almost ready to cry like a baby. People never cried like that in the TV shows. Maybe the bad guys or the wimpy guys, the comic relief. But guys like Wilson, the good guys, the anti-heroes, they never cried like that. Maybe if you killed a guy's partner or raped and murdered his wife he'd cry. But then it was such a deep, rooted, tearless, gushing, snot-effusing cry — wrathful almost, foreboding. Not like this. Not whimpering. But Wilson couldn't help it. It went with that feeling he had, growing in half-lives inside him. He wanted his mother. Wilson wanted to be with her right now. He wanted to be four years old and wrapped in her big arms and warm and protected and fucking loved so absolutely that nothing else mattered. He'd felt that way sometimes with Cherry, in a little way, tucked up beside her, his whats pressed up against her big ass, the two of them in tight as one. Now he wanted to feel the comfort again, in a big way. And so he cried, not just because he was scared — he was, shitless — but also because it was comforting, made him feel that if he kept it up, maybe those big arms would reach down from above and pick him up and hold him until it was all over.

Wilson slipped. *What do you think of that, Cherry?* The toe on his bad foot didn't catch in the mesh and he slid two feet back to the ground. *Pretty convenient, huh?* He could have kept going, and he wanted to, he really did — he really didn't want to die. But the gun was in the back of his head. It was so close he could smell it, he could taste it on his teeth, a steel popsicle. Colt Pocket Nine. ("How d'ya like my little dildo, motherfucker? How 'bout I stick it right up your ass?") Usually it wasn't like this. It wasn't this intimate. Usually it was anonymous. A shot in a bar. A drive-by. It happened like that because they were scared too, the shooters. Scared in a different way, but scared all the same. Wilson tried to look him in the eye — not move his head, mind you, but roll his eyes far enough to catch a piece in his peripherals. *Homey's got red hair.* He didn't know the kid's name. Maybe he had once, but that was lost in the fog of fear and time. He knew his street tag, but what good was that? That was kid stuff, teenage bravado. This was something different. This was intimate. Man to man. He should at least know the fucking name. *Homey's got red hair.* It was a stupid thing to think. Quite possibly the last stupid thing he would ever think.

Out of the filthy, starless sky, two enormous hands, beautiful hands, reached down to Wilson. At first the hands caressed him — he could still smell the soap on those hands, lavender soap, and a wisp of Pinesol — and then they lifted him, comforted him. And from deep inside his reptilian brain, the place, perhaps, where fear itself was born, a cry bored out like a tapeworm almost covering the sound of the gunshot.

"*SoS!*"

His accent was flawless. Perfect Klingon.

.   .   .

Murph called Starky to confirm the deal. They talked in code. *Our friend has arrived from out of town,* etc. It was stupid but had to be done. Starky was the perfect start. A doctor, discreet as all hell, who just liked some blow every now and again. His old score had gone up the river, literally, having retired inland to his private ranch. Business had been that good. Starky shot hoops with Murph, recreationally. They called him Doctor No, because he was always trying to nullify a good play with an after-the-fact penalty call: "Sorry, no, that was travelling"; "Sorry, no, that was goaltending." No one really liked him, which made it even better. It was hard to sell to someone you really liked.

Starky was Murph's anchor tenant. He wanted a lot of product to squirrel away. Starky hated dealing with dealers (Murph hated to think of himself in such reductionist terms, but there it was) and wanted one big score to minimize contact. The plan was that Murph would make several small deliveries over the course of two days, to reduce the risk to everyone concerned. That was Russell's idea too. He'd been in the game since forever and never been dinged. That's not so remarkable when you think about it. Like anything — traffic violations, shoplifting, murder — the cops only caught the tip of iceberg, and in fact, when it came to the product, they really only seemed to care about nailing the crackheads, black kids, mostly, who hung out downtown. It wasn't just racism at work, but, as

Russell explained, it was a matter of self-preservation. First of all, the crackheads (Murph loved the term, it sounded so dumb, like something middle-aged women would say to make themselves sound cool) all carried guns. Every one of them. That made the cops nervous. Second, crackheads don't give a shit about anybody but themselves or about anything but their next hit. They'd kill their best friend to help them fuel up again, so cops — cops were nothing. It was the nature of the beast, Russell said. That was something Murph understood. The focus. The single-minded purpose. The beast. The addiction.

Boom-cha, boom-boom ba-cha.

.   .   .

What precipitated the downfall Kahless the Unforgettable?

Some say it was hubris, an excessive reaching. Not content with unifying the Klingon peoples, he strove to lead them. Not content with leading them, he strove to rule them. Not content with rule, he strove to conquer. It was his discontent, his lack of respect for Order, that brought him down.

Others believe that agents of Morath were at work, sowing the seeds of revolt. The Empire was still in its infancy, and many local warlords and chieftains were ripe for rebellion. In this context, Kahless's death could be viewed as a sacrifice, and ultimately, as the singular event that consolidated and confirmed the Klingon Empire. He needed to be dead, because only in death could he attain mythical stature. And that's what the Klingon Empire needed more than anything, a mythology upon which it could hang its politics. The living could subjugate and contrive: only the dead could unify.

Still others take a more romantic perspective. Kahless abdicated for love. While there is no direct reference to this in the formal canon, there are hints throughout the literature. Among historians, it is one of the most vigorous areas of research, hypothesis and speculation.

Regardless, Kahless the Unforgettable found himself by the Cleft of HurghtaHghach, faced with a simple but impossible choice: on the one side Honour, on the other Duty. He had to jump, but which way, and why, he could not say.

Moonie was at the door. He came in without being asked and sat at the kitchen table, silently waiting for some coffee. He had a great idea, he said. A money-maker.

"This one's a sure thing — hear me out."

Then there was a big long build-up about how everybody, the lucky ones at least, got old someday, and what with the baby boom and all, more and more people would grow old each and every year. "The trick is, the question is, how can we profit from this demographic phenomenon?"

"If the answer has anything to do with sponge baths or enemas, count me out."

"Let me put it to you another way, Murph. There's four things everybody's got to do, no matter how old they are, right? They got to breathe, they got to pay taxes, they got to shit, and they got to eat. Well, I can't help 'em with the first three, but I got a great idea about the fourth." Moonie paused for full dramatic effect. "Home cooked meals. Delivered right to the door."

"Don't they already do that?"

"Don't who already do what?"

"Meals on Wheels. They cook dinner for old people, deliver it right to their doors. Dirt cheap, too."

"I'm not talking soup and a sandwich here. I'm talking a real meal, meat and potatoes, gourmet stuff. But reasonably priced. You got to keep the price reasonable. That's the whole key."

Murph shut up and let his friend talk. He must have been getting restless again. Every four or five months Moonie'd lift himself out of his funk by getting excited about some new scheme or another. Last year it had been real estate, he'd even taken the test for his license; before that, it had been home cleaning products.

"The biggest problem, as far as I can see, is start-up money. We'd need a couple trucks, of course, and a professional kitchen. We could run a store front operation too, you know, retail the food to take-out customers up front, and move out the deliveries from the —"

Moonie was dead in the water. Murph had never noticed before, but now he saw it clearly. Moonie had given up, completely surrendered. Somewhere between high school and death he'd taken the wrong turn, and defeat had piled up like an eternal snow. The snow was up against the door, and Moonie couldn't get out. That made Murph even more anxious to get to work. Addiction — addiction, he could understand. It was two notches up from defeat, so at least it was somewhere. Moonie was snowed under, he was frozen solid. His little schemes were just phantom limbs, invisibly twitching and jerking, the remnants of Moonie's amputated ambition. He got stuck looking at the hole, the bad decisions and hard luck that had left him ever on the edge of financial ruin. That was the last thing you wanted to do. You could itemize the mistakes you made — the bad marriage, career choices — but that wouldn't change a thing. You couldn't look at the hole. You had to look for a way out. Murph, he had a plan. It had its risks, in fact risk was at the heart of it, but risk also gave it a tremendous upside. He'd maxed everything, every credit card, every overdraft, his mortgage — everything — to get himself as liquid as possible. It wasn't much, $35 k and change, but with the right investment, the right product, he knew it could roll into something better. He wasn't greedy. He needed $90 k to clear his debts and cover interest, and what with the product he had — it was good shit, real good shit — that was totally doable. And then? He'd be back at square one. It wasn't great, but it was a hell of a lot better than where he was right now, too rich to walk away, too poor to file for protection.

He wasn't complaining. Murph knew he had no one to blame but himself. First, there'd been the marriage. It started poorly, with Marg knocked up and all that, and ended badly, with Marg hiding in a woman's shelter and the house breathing a sigh of relief. Another good love gone bad. Second — second he could sum up in two words: business machines. Faxes. Copiers. Computers. For a while there, you could say he was addicted to them, not in the key-lock way he'd been addicted to blow after high school, but addicted emotionally, like, say, the difference between lust and infatuation. Business machines weren't really the objects of his addiction, but the subjects, the representation of promises never quite fulfilled. See, he'd dropped out of college, then hung around for a while before cleaning himself up (he did it for the baby, he did it for himself). And then business machines just sort of fell into his lap. They gave him prestige and a territory, but Murph quickly maxed out on both of those and slid into the Great Recession, where his returns diminished even further. By the time all the smart money was moving out of the corporal (hardware) and into the cerebral (software, dot-coms, IPOs), Murph had gone from being a player — a young guy going places in Eastern Standard Business Machines — to a blocker, an old guy who'd reached his limited potential and was now just standing in everyone's way. And so he pushed harder, tying to move more product, and even started carrying other things, small stuff (staplers, postage meters, calculators) to push his margin, and in the process, found himself in hock up to his asshole. Which is precisely the moment Marg decided to walk, with neither a bang nor a whimper, just a handful of unsubstantiated accusations (even the counsellor at the sheltered conceded that) and an overriding need to hate her ex-husband for the rest of her natural life. Murph went liquid, bought her out of everything, and that was that.

Murph made his way back up the stairs. Moonie hadn't gone anywhere fast, and now time was getting tight. Murph'd promised to meet Starky at four-thirty. That left him less than an hour to finish scaling and packaging and get his ass to the mall uptown. *Boom-cha, boom-boom ba-cha*. The damned opera. Murphy knocked but got no reply, then knocked again, then just walked in. Rudy grunted some abuse and tried to cover the computer screen with one hand as the other scrambled for the delete. Murph had seen enough to get the gist. A Klingon woman, naked save for her helmet, sprawled on a rock as a Klingon warrior, hung and hard, prepared to ravish her.

"Are you just going to sit in your room all day?"

"I'm working on my opera."

"Well, I could use a little help around the house. It's a pigsty. Maybe you could mow the lawn or —"

"Don't I get any privacy?"

"We're not talking about privacy —"

"You didn't even knock."

Murph shut up. He could see where this was going. Nowhere.

"Look. I just need a little help around here, that's all. I'm not going to bark orders at you all day long. I'd just appreciate a little help."

Murph backed out of the room, shutting the door as he left.

Rudy uttered some words in Klingon (*Vav qatlh ghaj SoH lonta' jIH*) and went back to work.

.   .   .

Cherry had just put Baby down. Baby was a good sleeper, a sound sleeper. You could put her to bed at seven, sing her a little song or two, stroke her head, and she'd go down like a garage door. She'd stay down too. Twelve hours, no problem. The other mothers talked. Their kids would be up four or five times a night, crying and nursing and needing their little nappies done. But not Baby. Shut her eyes and that was it. She was down. Just like her father.

Cherry made herself a sandwich from the steak that was left over in the fridge. There was a little wine left too, so she finished that off. She tried not to think of the pipe in the bedroom. It was right there in the dresser, bottom left-hand drawer. She'd always thought of finding a better hiding spot, but when she got right down to it, she couldn't be bothered. If they were going to get you, they were going to get you. It was easier to keep it in the same spot. That way she wouldn't forget where she'd put it, which could be tricky. She watched a show or two on TV, then phoned her mother. They talked about Baby. "Are you sure she's getting enough to eat?" her mother asked. She always asked the same question. After that, she went back into Baby's room and just looked at her, just watched her sleep for five or six minutes. Baby was so precious when she slept. Cherry went to the crib. She stroked Baby's cheek. *If only they stayed babies forever*. If she could give her daughter one thing, it would be that: babyhood, forever. Cherry went into the bedroom and got her pipe. She only had a couple of rocks left and smoked them both. Then she was up for hours. It was two or three in the morning when she finally fell asleep. She had the strangest dream. She was some kind of princess, standing on the crest of a hill. A sea of warriors approached from behind, screaming and waving their swords. Princess Cherry pitched herself into the darkness but woke before she hit the ground. It was morning already, and Baby was crying. Baby was crying and Wilson wasn't home.

．　．　．

Russell had one piece of advice: don't think you're better than it. The *it* he'd left open. He could have been talking about the product, which made sense. You had to respect the product — Murph learned that the hard way, years ago — because the product was the undisputed heavyweight champion. Lots of guys figured that the product could never beat them, that they were on top of it. They were the first to go down.

Russell might also have been talking about the game itself, and again, while it wasn't earth-shattering advice, it was a welcome reminder. Don't ever underestimate the cops; don't trust anyone, not your supplier, not your client, not your best friend, not your kid, not your dog; and, most important, keep your big mouth shut. Chances are you wouldn't go down, but if you didn't respect the game — if you thought you were too smart or too fast or too lucky or too much above it all — you were inviting trouble. Then again, Russell might have been talking about the customers, which was bang on too. Whether it was cocaine or copiers, you had to have a healthy respect for the enemy. It was a buyers' market (outside of love and sex, Murph figured everything was a buyers' market), and you had to work for every sale. Of course, there was one more possibility Murph barely considered. Maybe *it* was everything. The house, the kid, the failures, the small success, the debt, life — everything. Don't think you're better than it. That was the kind of thing Russell would say.

Murph brushed the soft powder from his chest. He'd been in such a hurry to leave the house, he'd spilled half a kilo down the front of his shirt and pants and onto the black tile floor. He didn't have time to change. He grabbed his coat. It was an expensive mess, but he'd have to deal with it when he got back. The irony was that Starky was late. And not just late, Murph was sitting on his thumbs in the mall for an hour and a half. He had a coffee, then a latte, then a bowl of soup, then another coffee. He finished with pie. Lemon meringue pie, just like Mom used to make.

Starky rushed in with an air of urgency and sat down without apology. They chatted for a few minutes, small talk about people they knew. Basketball. Then Murph took the book out of his briefcase — *Gray's Anatomy*, a nice touch. He'd burrowed a hole in the pages, making a safe little nest for the coke. Starky looked it over once, than quickly handed it back.

"Look, Sticks"— Stark always called Murph Sticks, he had his own nickname for everyone — "Look, Sticks, I don't want it."

"What?"

"I changed my mind. There's just too much heat right now. My wife"— here the doctor lowered his voice — "my wife's not acting herself these days. I think she's fucking around. Can you believe that? Fifteen years of . . ." Starky searched for but could not find the right words to describe his marriage.

"It's going like mad, Starks. I can't guarantee I'll have anything left by the end of the week."

"I can't take the chance. You know, I caught her going through my office yesterday. She's looking for something she can hold over my head —"

"Cost, Starker. I'll give it to you at cost, because you're a friend. I want to move it, that's all. I'm trying to make room for new inventory."

Starky stood up. No. Sorry.

"Tuesday night, Sticks. Shoot some hoops, okay? You gonna be there, Sticks? You gonna shoot some hoops?"

.   .   .

Rudy liked Duke. They'd gone to a Duke game once, maybe five years ago, back when Murph was still clinging to the diminishing dream of his son one day playing pro hoops. Rudy had the time of his life. Murph took the kid to the locker room afterwards (he was friends with a friend of the trainer), and all the guys had come over and said hello and signed a hat for him. Rudy wore that Duke hat every day for two years, until it was finally nothing but a band of tattered cloth and plastic, stapled together.

Maybe he'd get Rudy a Duke hat. Notre Dame was on sale. He asked for the sale price on the Duke hat. The store owner said no. He'd got a deal on the Notre Dame hats. The Duke hats were cost plus as it was. He couldn't give Murph a break. He'd like to, but he couldn't.

Murph cut through the park on the way back to his car. He'd still wanted to get something for Rudy, something for Rudy to remember. They hadn't had many memories lately. He thought of *Baby's First Book* and all the things it missed and all the things he'd never know about his son. His first kiss. His first orgasm. His first screw. His first disappointment. His first betrayal. His first bad trip. His first crime. His first good love gone bad. Everything. It.

Murph passed a couple of teenagers, lurking in the shadows by the monkey bars. He could tell one was holding, he knew the look, he'd worn the look himself; maybe he was wearing it now.

"OH vam QaQ shit?" the one kid asked.

The young dealer closed his eyes and nodded emphatically. "HIja', ioD, vam shit 'oH QaQ . . ."

.   .   .

The Klingon concept of Honour is tremendously complex. Unlike contemporary Western culture, which renders every complicated idea into an abstraction (honour, love, valour, truth, peace), Klingons leave nothing up to interpretation. Their Code of

Honour, the paq vo' quv, runs some twenty-five thousand pages and is constantly being expanded and reinterpreted by the Klingon High Council. In fact, like Earth's Eskimos, who have some fifty words to cover every nuance and grade of the concept snow, Klingons have some eight hundred and sixty degrees (counting changes in inflection and dialect quirks) of honour. There is the honour of a warrior in his first battle ("quv lak"), which varies greatly from the honour *of a warrior in his last battle ("quV LuZ"). There is the honour a Klingon woman shows her living mate (for example, "qUUv lOn," although this can vary depending on the mate's standing within in the community), which should not be confused with the honour she shows her deceased mate (which, again, varies greatly depending on the manner in which her mate died). Surprisingly too, for such a essentially conservative culture, there is the honour of a divorced woman, which ranges from the lowest order, "quvV tU," for the woman who quietly acquiesces as her mate takes another lover, to "quv tulG," reserved only for those great women who kill their mates in a highly choreographed and physically demanding divorce ritual. This honour code is a highly fluid system, with built-in safeguards that allow it to adapt to changing cultural demands. Only one kind of honour has remained consistent throughout the ages: "QuV SoS," the honour of a child for its mother.*

The concept of duty is less entrenched in the Klingon system, having been introduced only at the end of the second millennium. Still, the pac vo' kA includes more than four hundred entries, delineating what amounts to a state-sanctioned caste system. A careful reading of the pac vo'qua (High Counsellors specializing in this branch of Code must be logicians of the highest order) clearly delineates the duty any one individual within the Klingon Empire bears to any other individual. In fact, over time, as the Klingon culture has become more entrenched and therefore, by necessity, more hierarchical and more political, Duty, in practical, pragmatic terms, has risen to the level of, and in some senses supersedes, Honour. Honour still holds the greatest symbolic power for Klingons, but it is Duty that, as the counsellors like to say, gets the job done.

This is the subtext of Kahless's dilemma. It is a question less of choosing between two abstract and equal concepts (and all abstractions, like all men, are created equal) than of selecting the course for one's life, or rather, the course for one's legacy. To the left, Kahless faces quv, the sacred tradition of his peoples that gives meaning to ka. To the right lies ka, the profane system through which quv is sustained. One is eternal and decadent, the other perverse and sustaining. But Kahless, as the legends tell us, chose neither left nor right. He dove into the middle of the abyss. He is falling still and shall continue to fall without end. That is his legacy. In the shadow of his greatness, that is his tragedy.

.　　.　　.

Moonie was still talking about food. At first Murph had thought the talking was cathartic. But now it seemed the opposite, whatever that was.

"The drivers themselves should be chefs, that's part of the key, I think. Who wants to see some pimple-face snot delivering a wet bag of food? That's what most of those other fast places do, have pimple-faced snots deliver the food. It's always cold. The bag is always wet."

"Uh huh."

"But our drivers will be professionals. They'll be professional drivers and professional chefs. We'll even get those chefs' costumes and little white hats. In fact, maybe we can save ourselves a bundle and just buy the outfits. That way, we don't have to pay real chefs. We can just hire drivers who look like chefs. But professional drivers. And no snotty-faced kids. I hate that, when they come to the door with cold food."

"And the bag all wet?"

"Exactly. I hate that."

Murph had picked up Moonie on the way back from the mall. Quite frankly, Moonie had been getting on his nerves lately. But also, quite frankly, Murph didn't want to be alone. In the back of his mind he half thought that he could unload some of the product on Moonie. But who was he kidding? Even if Moonie took it he'd have to take it on credit, and in that case, he might as well just give it away.

"Maybe we could hire girls. Seventeen, eighteen. That'd be even cheaper. And instead of chef suits, they could wear those little French maid outfits."

"French maids?"

"Yeah."

"And not chefs?"

"Yeah."

"Isn't that somewhat incongruous?"

"Yeah. Exactly. It's funny."

A moment of silence. Murph figured Moonie was mentally undressing one of his French maids.

"You ever made a stupid decision, Moonie, fucked up real bad? You know, gotten yourself into something that looked simple enough on the outside, but once you're inside, you found yourself . . ."

Moonie waited for him to finish.

"Found myself?"

"Stuck."

"Stuck?"

"Stuck."

Moonie tuned the radio on. Coltrane checked in from 1956.

"Do you want to talk about it?"

Murph shook his head.

"Jesus, man. You need a holiday. You and Rudy, go some-place nice. Get yourselves a plane ticket, and go someplace nice."

.   .   .

Baseball. Crackers. Pearl. Lady. Bush. Candy. Da Bomba knew every word. Hotcakes. Raw. Scotty. Scramble. He even had his own words, he'd teach them to his bitches. Glo. Like "glow" but no "w." Glo was candy. Or jizz. That was rock. Glamour Pussy, that was a girl who'd go down on you for some jizz, not to be confused with a smoker, a chick who'd suck you off for some jizz. He called a pipe a bracket, no one knew why, that's just the word he used and he liked it. He called customers gooks, he called suppliers fairies, he called his posse his bitches. They didn't like it, but what could they do? Da Bomba had a word for everything. He told his bitches how he'd fixed that gook with his dildo, the gook what owed him the grass (which is what Da Bomba called money), and how the gook had shit himself and cried like a baby, and his bitches laughed until they almost shit themselves. Da Bomba, he was one crazy mother-fucker. He was all fucked up. He was only sixteen, and already the police were afraid of him. Shit, his own momma was scared of that crazy red-haired motherfucker Da Bomba. And that night when Da Bomba got home, he cried. He cried and he cried and he cried. His momma came into his room and held him in her big warm arms. She just held while he cried and cried and cried. He didn't want to die. He didn't want to die and go to hell. She was the only one who knew how scared he was. Da Bomba, that crazy motherfucker, he was scared shitless.

.   .   .

Murph knew the drill. He'd seen the cherries flashing a quarter mile back. He almost crapped himself. He nudged the wrinkled Barnes and Noble bag closer to Moonie, not entirely sure that, if push came to shove, he wouldn't let Moonie take the fall. He checked his speed, but he was in the limit. It crossed his mind that maybe Dr. No had ratted him out. Maybe the whole thing had been a setup. Maybe Starky was wearing a wire and recorded their conversation. It's possible he was already in deep with the cops and rolled over to protect his own ass. He was just that kind of self-centred son-of-a-bitch.

"What's the matter, officer? Was I going too fast?" Murph unconsciously wiped his shirt as he spoke. The officer didn't respond. He asked Murph for his driver's license and registration. The cop took the papers back to the hog and called them in. Murph slid the bag forward and tried to kick it under the seat. He was careful. Cops were always on the lookout for suspicious movement. For a moment, Murph thought of flooring it. He could easily put a quarter mile between the cop and himself, then ditch the book out the window. It was a question of the lesser of two evils.

The cop returned to the car. Murph thought he looked funny in his little costume, his puffy motorcycle pants and high boots, the white plastic ovum that covered his head, the empty shades meant to convey dispassion, to strike fear into the heart. This was make believe for children. It was not how police should dress in this day and age.

The cop handed Murph his papers.

"Thank you, Mr. Murphy. You have a nice day, y'hear."

.   .   .

Peter Murphy returned home. Peter Murphy parked the car. Peter Murphy did not know what to do next. Dr. Starky had knocked the wind out of Peter Murphy's sails. The cop had taken the wind out of Peter Murphy's sails. Rudolph Murphy stood on the steps waiting for Peter Murphy to come up to the house.

"Hello, Father," Rudolph Murphy said. His tone was unusually expressive.

"Finished your opera, then?" Peter Murphy asked, shifting the Barnes and Noble bag from one hand to the other.

"No, Father. In fact, I scrapped the opera altogether. The libretto was forced, the overture likewise. Parts of the first movement are salvageable, I think. But the rest is gack."

"Perhaps you're being too hard on yourself, son," Peter Murphy said. He thought that maybe he could have been more supportive. Peter Murphy patted his son on the head, then entered his house. Peter Murphy was tired. Frank Montgomery had said as much when Peter Murphy dropped him off minutes earlier.

Rudolph Murphy smiled. It wasn't enough to write about Klingons, he thought. The highest good, the greatest glory lay in becoming Klingon. Right now his father would be passing through the kitchen. He'd notice the counters were cleaned and uncluttered. Jars and boxes had been put away in the pantry like his father had asked he didn't know how many times. Those crumbs that seemed to breed like Tribbles by the toaster. Eradicated. Swept into the sink abyss. Rudolph Murphy was enlightened. He felt, for the first time, that he understood the nature of the Kahless dilemma.

Now, his father, Peter Murphy, would be ascending the stairs. Towels and clean shirts were removed carefully, properly folded and hung. Next he'd come to the bedroom. Rudolph Murphy had deliberately left the door open. It was a sign of welcome, a sign of submission, not the dispirited surrender of the broken, but the humble submission of the strong. An exercise in Duty. Rudolph's bed was neatly made, his father would see that now, and the sea of dirty clothes was packed away in the proper receptacle. Books and CDs neatly stacked, arranged alphabetically by genre; carpet, precisely vacuumed. One could eat off that floor. He wondered if his father would understand. All this time, Rudolph had tried to *approach things from the outside. A dispassionate observer, shielding his weakness through the pretence of art. But now he understood.*

It had come to him as he laboured over the ending. He wanted to understand Kahless the Unforgettable, he wanted to uncover the wisdom where others found only folly. And that's when it struck like a blow from Gowran's 'etlh: Duty and Honour were not exclusive. Kahless had chosen to merge the two, had chosen to accept the uncertainty of the void over the certainty, and servitude, of Essential Truth. At that point, Rudolph Murphy understood: he must jump too. He must pitch himself into the darkness, openly, happily, joyously. That was the essence of Klingon — quv'ka, united as one.

Quv lIj vav — honour thy father, that was it. Honour and Duty, perfectly expressed.

By now his father would have moved through his own bedroom and found it respectfully cleaned, bed made, shoes lined up neatly, clothes hung neatly, respectfully. The floor vacuumed spotless. It was funny; Rudolph Murphy had discovered an unexpected joy in carrying out these menial duties, slipping seamlessly from life as object (someone who is done for) to life as subject (someone who does) — quv'ka instantly internalized. He felt strong.

And now his father would be moving into the den, plants watered, magazines unscattered and alphabetically arranged, videos likewise, tile floor carefully swept and scrubbed (his father, Peter Murphy, seemed to be growing more careless these days). It was spotless now, one could eat off that floor.

Rudolph Murphy wasn't sure what he'd expected, but Peter Murphy's reaction was a complete and unanticipated delight. It started low, so low that Rudolph Murphy wasn't sure it was a sound at all. It could have been the earth shifting or the sound of the sun as it inched across the sky. But then it grew louder, a bass, constricted howl that rose now like a powerful wind. It was his father calling to him in the language of a warrior, an unspoken and unspeakable recognition. The sound wrapped around Rudolph Murphy, it lifted him up and held him, comforting him. The sound was so beautiful it was almost harrowing. Rudolph Murphy could imagine the tears of joy raining down his father's, Peter Murphy's, face, standing in his room, cleansed, as it were, the floor, swept clean, even the walls scrubbed. Rudolph Murphy thought of the tears, the powerful tears, and imagined that if those tears could speak they'd say: Today my son is a man. No, better than a man. Today, my son is Klingon.

Secret Friends

Talk to him, the doctor had said. Act like nothing is wrong. She kissed her son on the forehead. Dougie did not stir. She thought of his green, green eyes, the most beautiful shade of green, almost emerald, like no other child, no other person.

"Tomorrow I'll take you shopping, grocery shopping, we need some things, and how about some shoes? I think it's high time you got a new pair, your old ones look like they're ready to walk away on their own."

Diane could fit both of Dougie's hands in her fist, but she was positive that the night before, when she had put her son to bed, his hands were as big as or bigger than hers. Diane decided to keep a journal, to record the length of particular limbs, his height and body weight.

Diane tugged on Little Doug's shoulder. "Wake up," she said. "Wake up, Dougie. Wake up, please." Her voice stern. "Dougie, wake up now, it's time to wake up." What were the magic words? When they first brought Dougie into the hospital six months ago, the doctor believed the boy suffered a delayed concussion or perhaps a stroke. The EEG revealed nothing. His brain patterns were as regular and erratic as those of any twelve-year-old. Dr. Sidhu handed Diane a scroll of computer paper marked with rows of jagged lines, like nervous handwriting. "These are alpha lines." Dr. Sidhu pointed with his pencil. Diane noticed that the doctor always held a pencil in his hand. He left a small grey shadow on everything he touched. "When the lines are very concentrated in this way, they show your boy is in a profound sleep. He sleeps deeply, in what we call the REM sleep." The doctor stroked his thin moustache with the pencil. "Have faith, we'll get to the bottom of this, although it is a very unusual thing to see a boy sleeping so."

The yellow house where Diane and her husband lived was an hour's drive from St. Joseph's hospital, along roads which grew progressively rougher: the highway to the lake turnoff, the twisting country road through the Indian reserve, the dirt logging trail that circled the lip of the reservoir, then finally down the steep gravel driveway to the yellow house.

Her days were the same: off to the hospital in the morning, then four hours at Barkley's Pharma-Centre, and back to the hospital until visiting hours ended at nine o'clock. Usually the nurses let her stay with Dougie an extra half hour or so. Then the long drive home. She couldn't wait for her moment of peace at the end of the day. She'd put on her flowered house-coat, careful not to wake her husband — it was easier if she let him be — then stand at the kitchen sink rinsing her face with cold water. Diane sipped a cup of tea as she stared out the kitchen window to the saltwater inlet below. Seagulls circled outside her window, always lots of seagulls, bumping into one another as they flew, Diane could almost see the surprise on their faces. They scuttled across her balcony, fat, armless businessmen hurrying to catch a bus. Most evenings she could not sleep. She never liked the TV. She would sit at the kitchen window and watch the world of seagulls and silence.

Thursday night, Diane's mother-in-law called just as the kettle boiled. Mrs. Flannigan had to tell Diane her dream.

"Jesus appeared before me in a yellow robe, his arms outstretched, light radiating from his eyes and from all about his body. He spoke not, but smiled, and I remember in my dream feeling calmed and at peace. When I awoke I turned immediately to the scriptures, reading verses at random. The Holy Spirit directed me to Psalm 121, A Song of Degrees. 'Behold,' the scripture says, 'He that keepeth Israel shall neither slumber nor sleep.' Jesus Christ is speaking to me, Diane, he is speaking to me now. He is offering his hand. Won't you pray with me? Let's pray together now."

Diane placed the phone on the kitchen table, lit a cigarette. She pushed the receiver against her fat leg until she heard her mother-in-law's voice vibrate clear through to her stomach. When the vibrations stopped, Diane thanked her mother-in-law, and hung up the phone. She was always polite to Mrs. Flannigan, although she would have loved to tell her to knock off the holy roller stuff, to maybe just shut up for a while. People were better off if they just shut up once in a while and took a look at what was happening in their own lives instead of feeding off the misfortune of others. Mrs. Flannigan was like that. A big-headed, empty-eyed owl, alert only in the darkness of others.

The next morning, Diane had an appointment with the hospital social worker. Mrs. White — she insisted that Diane call her Helen — was a pretty, middle-aged woman with the crisp voice of a radio announcer. She was preparing Diane for what everyone believed to be the inevitable: they were working on the funeral plans.

"You can't just passively sit there and wait for something to happen." Helen blinked frequently as she spoke; her eyes closed and opened lazily. A lizard daydreaming in the hot sun. "You've got to take your own mental health into consideration. Sitting in that little hospital room all day won't do you any good. Trust me, you've got to keep yourself active."

Today Helen took Diane to the cemetery where Dougie's ashes would be buried. Diane wanted to have him cremated. She felt that cremation would somehow put an end to things: no more sleep, just ash dissolving in the rain. She felt disappointed when she visited the site, under a willow on the crest of a hill, as the undertaker had described it, but the grass was parched, the willow small and tense. The view from the hill was of other small hills, other prickled, newly-planted willows, more acres of parched grass. A sign on the garbage can read, "No artificial flowers." A red lawn tractor circled the field. There were no headstones, at least not in this section. Only flat markers with names and dates and small hollows where visitors left flowers. Diane saw the mower clip the flowers as it rolled over the markers.

"Isn't it a beautiful spot? It's so . . . peaceful."

Diane nodded. I'll keep his ashes at home, she decided. I'll keep an urn in the kitchen on the ledge. Maybe I'll scatter his ashes in the bushes at the end of the yard.

That evening as Dougie slept, he moved and spoke. He rocked his head from side to side, then arched his back, drawing his arm slowly from his chest to above his head. Once, as he lay on his stomach, he straightened both arms, lifting his head and torso like a baby about to crawl. He turned his head to Diane, then yawned and smacked his lips. But his eyes remained shut. Like a newborn cat, Dougie strained to open his eyes, but they remained shut. Diane believed Dougie was trying. She sat rigid, afraid any movement would break the spell, would somehow make him aware of where he was and give up trying. His head was on the pillow for ten minutes before Diane moved again. He mumbled something, the words impossible to distinguish but the tone matter-of-fact, sincere. An apology, Diane imagined.

"This sleep is very much as if your boy is awake, yet he very deeply sleeps. We call this paradoxical sleep because the body both sleeps and wakes. Do you see what I mean?" Dr.

Sidhu doodled a crocodile on the back of the lab report. "We charac-terize this sleep with the rapid movements of the eye — the rapid eye movements — because the eyes move so." Dr. Sidhu rolled his eyes under closed lids. "The movements correspond to activities in the dream. As the sleeping dog fits and jumps, so do the boy's eyes as he sleeps. There is much other physiological activity in the body at this time: gross muscle movement, increased cardiovascular activity, vocalization, erection of the penis . . ." The doctor drew a firm line through his doodle. "I'm sorry to say, your boy still sleeps"

Saturday Diane almost passed out at the cash register. A customer came up with a few items — some plastic garbage bags, a generic shampoo the store had on sale — and asked for a carton of Vantage Lights. As Diane reached for the cigarettes she felt hot and weak, all the blood seemed to rush out of her head. She put her hand on her forehead, then bent over her register. The customer grabbed her arm. "Miss, are you all right?" He asked the question several times before calling out for help. Mr. Davis, the manager, sent Diane home.

"Don't worry about the time off. I'll take care of it." He offered to pay for a taxi.

"I'm all right now." She ran a kerchief across her forehead and noticed the sweat had made her mascara streak. "I'll be fine. I'll drive myself, I just need some rest".

The ride home took forever. Her head throbbed, the pain built up behind her eyes and echoed throughout her head. Traffic along the highway was slow: an ambulance and several police cars had stopped just before the lake turnoff, where a tractor trailer lay on its side. Diane saw the ambulance attendants carry a man on a stretcher. One of the attendants, an oriental man who looked no more than twenty, had a large bloodstain on the sleeve of his jacket. He nodded towards Diane as if he recognized her. Diane strained to get a better view of the stretcher. A man holding a fox terrier was talking with two boys on BMX bikes. They blocked her view. A policeman with an orange flashlight waved her on.

The lights of the yellow house were out as Diane drove down the driveway. She could see the cold flicker of the television. Big Doug was watching a movie and didn't hear Diane come in. He was sitting on the living room couch. His pants were undone, and his right hand rocked slowly, like a mechanical gear, under his shorts. "You're home!" Doug slapped the VCR on pause, freezing a woman's face, a woman with auburn hair and blue grey eyes, like Diane only much younger. The frozen woman was naked. A man reached from behind her, and she sucked his index finger as he squeezed her breast with his other hand. The box for the video lay on the coffee table: *Secret Friends. No one suspected the secret's they shared.*

"You surprised me." Doug picked up his t-shirt from the floor. "Is everything all right?" He turned the TV off. "You startled me. Is everything okay?"

That night they made love for the first time in two months. They lay in silence on the bed, then suddenly converged. Big Doug shifted and grunted for a few minutes, his black eyes tightly closed, then rolled off his wife. "I love you," he whispered. A moment later, he was asleep. Talk to him, act like nothing is wrong. Diane got up to fix herself some tea.

The phone rang. It was Mrs. Flannigan. "I knew you'd be up," she said in her rough hoot-voice. "I want you to turn on channel six. I've called the Huntley Street Prayer Line. They're going to pray for Dougie at twelve-thirty. I can't believe I got through! The holy spirit must be watching the phone lines tonight."

Diane promised to watch, but once she hung up the phone, she took her place at the kitchen window. Two gulls circled in the cold glow of the moon.

.   .   .

The social worker wore her hair in tight, permed curls. Barely red, almost light brown, her hair had been chemically treated and curling-ironed until it became unnatural. A handsome woman, Diane thought, with a slut's hair. And now Helen wanted her to join a group. She cornered Diane in the hospital cafeteria.

"I want you to meet some people, some friends of mine." She fidgeted with her hair as she spoke. "They're part of a support group I lead on Wednesday nights. We work on life skills and assertion . . ." Diane felt herself recoil as it dawned on her; Helen thought she was incompetent. The social worker put her hard fingers on Diane's shoulder. "Look, Diane, I don't think you realize how lonely you are, how sad and alone you seem to people. You're going through a lot. You need support."

Diane shook her head. No. I don't need your help, thank you, Diane wanted to say. No. Instead, she shook her head. She shook her head and smiled that stupid, empty, silent smile.

That evening, before visiting hours ended, Dr. Sidhu slipped a small plastic bottle into Diane's hand. Flurazepam. "I don't know if I can find how to wake your child," he almost whispered. "I hope these can help you find yourself some rest."

Monday Diane dropped Big Doug at the airport on her way to work. He was off till the end of the week, a purchasing seminar in Edmonton. He promised to take his wife to Hawaii "after all this blows over." Last time they went to Hawaii Big Doug drank seventeen mai-tais on the plane. He had to be escorted from the airport in a wheelchair.

At work Mr. Davis made a big fuss. He told Diane to take it easy. "We don't want our star cashier running herself into the ground," he said, loud enough so the other girls could hear. Later, while Diane was alone in the coffee room, Mr. Davis came in and put his hand on her arm. "I mean it." His voice was quiet now. "If there's anything I can do for you, Diane, please just ask. I . . . all of us realize what a very difficult time this must be for you." Mr. Davis sighed and shoved his hands into the pockets of his white lab coat. "This must be awful. None of it makes sense."

Near closing time a Chinese boy came into the store. He went straight to the magazine rack across from the sales desk. He seemed familiar; he did not notice Diane stare as he leafed through the hockey and bodybuilding magazines. Diane recalled the skinny, boyish face of the ambulance attendant; it was him, she was sure of it. After a moment, the boy reached for one of the adult magazines. They always did this, linger a while in the sports section before pawing the adult magazines. After looking at four or five, the boy selected one and moved towards the counter, trying to hide his erection with the magazine. He stopped on the way to select a bottle of cheap shampoo. They always did this. The boys never bought just a magazine. They always bought something else as a cover, an excuse.

When the boy reached the counter, Diane said "Hello," asked, "How are you?" The boy grunted. "Fine." He looked away. Diane could see that his hands trembled. She grabbed the magazine and turned it to read the price, her fingers scarcely an inch from the strip of bare skin between the waistband of the boy's track pants and the bottom of his t-shirt. On the cover was a picture of a young woman with auburn hair, just like Diane's. Her mouth was open a tiny bit, and she held her breasts with both hands as if she suddenly had to stop them from spilling out onto the floor.

"Goodbye," Diane said, as the boy turned to leave. He stopped at the door.

"Goodnight." His voice was calm. He did not turn around.

Diane thought about the Chinese boy on her way to the hospital. She imagined that his name was Ricky. He was twenty-four years old, although he looked much younger.

Ricky sat beside her in the car, and she ran her free hand along the inch of bare skin just above the waistline of his track pants, then she undid the string that held the track pants up and slipped her hand inside. His penis was slender but very hard. She imagined that she took him to the empty yellow house and that he kissed her by the big window in the kitchen, and that he held her wrists in his strong, small hands when they made love, he held her wrists away from her body so firmly that she felt she could not move. She was under his control. And as they made love Ricky growled obscenities at her: "This sleep," his voice was hesitant, "is a paradox. We sleep and wake. The eyes are shut, but there is much physiological activity: gross muscle movement, vocalization, erection of the penis . . ."

They lay side by side a long time in utter quiet. Diane believed that only in such silence could they communicate.

There was no doubt about it. Dougie's wrist was narrower, a good centimetre smaller all round. His index finger measured 0.5 cm shorter than on Thursday. Dr. Sidhu said it was to be expected, the boy's body atrophied. "The muscles and tendons, they get no work, see? They contract, they withdraw to give the appearance that the boy shrinks. He probably is in fact shorter than when he came to us."

Diane imagined her son growing smaller and smaller, his skin drying and cracking, mud in the sun, until he was a fragile insect tiny enough to fit in her apron pocket. She saw herself hop around the kitchen, tea in paw, a kangaroo mother and her larva.

"I'm sure it's for the best," Mrs. Flannigan said. "It's almost like a miracle, if you think about it. It's almost like a miracle in reverse."

Diane felt sick. Why do I even let her come with me? She excused herself and left the doctor and her mother-in-law standing in the waiting room. She ran to her son's room and dropped on the end of the bed. Diane was crying now, the tears just came. She shook her son by the shoulders, first gently, then with increased force until his head swung with such violence Diane feared she might snap his neck. "Wake up! Wake up, god damn it!" She let his head drop to the pillow. She put her hands to her throat and cried. Not loud, just the short, irregular breaths of a woman gasping for air.

Little Doug was looking at her, she felt it. If she lifted her head, his eyes would be open, silent emerald eyes, just as she remembered them. He did not speak, just looked at her, his eyebrows furled in a puzzled expression. Diane felt for his hand. "Hello?" she said. He seemed alert and calm, there was no mistaking that he was awake. Diane heard his head turn on the dry linen. He was looking out the window. Then his breath stopped, his eyes closed and his breath stopped. The mother opened her eyes.

Little Doug was awake. Little Doug was dead. Those were the simple solutions. Big Doug was fat and insensitive. Diane was adrift in her loneliness. Little Doug was awake or dead or something at least that was not lost somewhere in between, something that was not this shrinking energy, diminishing at every moment until it became invisible existence. Little Doug was awake or dead, those were the correct solutions, the perfect, disappointing conclusions; but still he went on sleeping.

Diane lifted her legs onto the bed, she lay on the bed, wrapped her arms around her son. She closed her eyes. Let me sleep, dear God, let me sleep. She reached in her pocket for the small bottle of pills Dr. Sidhu had left her. A moment later she felt herself drift away, she felt her skin retract as the slow air-conditioned wind blew across it. She imagined herself falling asleep, shrinking in half-lives until she was visible only to the eye of a seagull, an atom-woman entwined in the arms of her sub-molecular son, the invisible particle lost in the space of a secret lover's fist.

The Raindrops, Not Unlike Her Tears

When I last saw Marlene alive she said that everyone has a claim to fame, even if it's something trifling — she used words like that, "trifling" — it's righteous (righteous!) in the eyes of Our Lord. Perhaps that's why they rubbed her out. She thought too much.

Me, I hardly think at all, and if I do think, it's just about nothing. I'll try and guess the weight of someone walking by, a stranger. I'll remember the lyrics of a song popular forty or fifty years ago, when I was young and the world was my oyster. I'll speculate on the number of shovelfuls of dirt in a certain kind of pit or hole, say, a shallow grave.

I enjoy manual labour.

Me and Marlene were something, though, in those days, by which I mean in the days when she was still alive. We were two of a kind. Two peas in a pod, so to speak. Between us, we must have weighed . . . oh, twenty-three stone, which is I don't know how many kilograms. We met at public swimming. She sat down beside me in the whirlpool bath and just spoke up, saying that hot water was "a tonic for the soul" and that it "girded the loins." I do not hazard a guess at what she meant by that, "girded the loins." I replied only that I found the water very hot that day, very hot indeed. One hundred and three or four degrees. "Enough," I said, hoping to sound like a man who did not think too much, yet was of some intellect, "enough to perhaps, ah, boil an egg."

Marlene nodded and, under the cloud of bubble, slipped her hand into my shorts. She said nothing until a few moments later, when my stuff rose and swirled at whirlpool's centre.

"I believe that a man's substance is in that wad. A man's essence. With every squirt and shot a man's essence is depleted. Only so much at a time, but eventually . . ."

She meant to say, "it adds up," but didn't need to finish. I understood.

What a man does is important, it's a part of who he is: the outcome of your income is to become a someone, I always say. Myself, I am a service worker. I provide a public service, which is not to say I don't get paid — I get paid very well, thank you, for the service I provide. I'm only saying that my work is of benefit to others. I, in a word, bury things. Animals. Small things, mostly. Any thing. I should say I am retired, I'm a retiree, but in fact I am kept quite busy almost without end burying things. I have a truck, such as it is, which is one of the qualities Marlene liked most about me. "Gordon H. Fawcette, Inhumation Engineer," I think of writing on the door of my truck, although it reads in fact "Gordon H. Fawcette, Yard Maintenance." That is enough. I am known. I have a reputation.

Marlene shook her red hair and sort of sputtered like a sputtering thing when I told her what I did for a living. "What kind of a work is that for a gentleman . . ."

She was forever not finishing sentences.

"It's so . . ." she said.

"It's what I do," I answered. I said that one day, if she liked, I would bury her. "You have such delicate bone structure, such a lovely hunched posture, such beautiful, white, almost-translucent skin, slippery skin, I bet, in the right sort of, ah, climate. You'll bury well someday." I was only flirting, of course. But I meant it. I truly believed that she would bury well one day. Little did I know how wrong I was. She would not bury well. Not well at all.

Because I am known, because I have a reputation, people are forever calling me up. The evening Marlene died I was up at an acreage in the hills providing an estimate on the interment of a yellow greyhound. The owner had left the dog parked in the hot sun. "You can't think of everything," I said, by way of a comforting word, implying that man could not know in advance that dog would die if left in a car parked in the hot sun. "You can't think of everything." The fellow said, "Sure," and indicated that he wanted the job done quickly as possible.

"How much will it cost?" He looked me in the eyes. His face was very asymmetrical, the one eye round and awake, the other almost closed. Squinted. His hand gripped my wrist. "How much?"

"I don't know. I'll have to think. Thirty, hmm, maybe thirty- five."

"Thirty-five!"

"That's the going rate, sir. That's how much it costs to bury something these days."

The man huffed and counted out deliberately, "Five. Ten. Fifteen. Twenty. Twenty-five. Thirty. Thirty-five," as if each bill were his last breath.

"That dog's cost too much already," said the man (I estimate him to be five-foot-eightish, one-hundred and sixty-four or -five pounds, a muscular build, Marlene would say "sinewy"). "That dog's a hole in my pocket. Even dead. A hairy fucking hole in my pocket. Where are you fixing to bury it?"

"Hmm?" I had heard but wanted to seem uninterested, for there was something in this fellow's manner which didn't sit well with me.

"I said, where are you going to bury it?"

"Don't raise your voice at me, sir. No need to shout. I may be a retiree, but I am not deaf. And I am not your servant, either. When you address me I would appreciate it if you would keep a civil tone, sir. I expect I will bury this dog in the meadow by the gravel pit. However, this dog is not an easy one, not an easy dig at all. You've waited too long, sir, if you ask me. His body is stiff and all extended, all layered out, if you know what I mean. No, this one will not bury well at all." I gave a look, that look, you know, the one everyone has, the one that says, damn you, we're on my turf now. The man glared back at me. But it wasn't his look. I mean, I know that he was thinking, *stuff you, I'll bury the dog myself*, but in one tick I looked at his hands and he looked at his hands and we both knew that these weren't hands for dead things. These were not the hands to lift and turn soil. These were not the hands to cradle dead flesh like a suckling, carry the flesh from car to hole. These were not the hands to snap a rigored joint so that it would fit into that fresh-dug hole. These were not the hands to clasp in momentary prayer, to ask for blessing and forgiveness in the passing of another of God's humble things. These were hands for the opening of the wallet, for the counting by fives — five, ten, fifteen, twenty, twenty-five, thirty, thirty-five.

The last time Marlene and I made love she talked about the rain. "The thunder is God's wrath," she said. "The rain is Jesus' tears." I could hear the heart moving in the body beside me. I could feel through her ribs a heart thump like a cricket in a child's fist.

"You know the splendid thing about man, the wonderful thing? He's so incomplete. So full of absolute possibility. So dignified, so low." Marlene sighed. "But I'm not saying much. I'm not saying anything that hasn't been said . . ."

"I know what you mean," I said, my head laid neatly on her soft bosom, and I as snug as a trowel in a mound of fresh-dug earth. "I mean, there's just so many of them. Men, I mean. The world is so . . . full of them. Yes. I don't think you could count each and every person on this, God's earth."

Marlene kissed me several times, but she was like a distant thing, like a distant radio station, maybe, that keeps drifting in and out of tune.

Let me describe the gravel pit where I came to bury the greyhound. It is wedge-shaped, a parted-jaw-shaped pit on the edge of the forest. We call the forest "the forest" only by way of identification. It is in fact not a forest at all but a collection of yellowy shrubs and stunted birch trees. The forest is about two hectares long and one half-acre wide. The pit itself is perhaps three hundred yards long and only fifty-six feet wide, one league at its deepest point. The "meadow" is the grey field around the gravel pit, a field of mud, mostly, the colour of old writing paper. The meadow is cheerful the way rain is cheerful when you have nothing to do but sit around and watch it. I always bury my things here when I bury them. The ground is soft, once you crack the dry surface, and limey. Good for decomposition. That's the problem with many burial sites; they are so full of dead things that the soil loses its energy to break them down. The earth is of two minds: it can preserve or lay waste.

As I dug the hole for my canine client I started thinking, which, as I believe I said, is not my habit. But digging — manual labour — brings out the philosopher in a man, and if that be a sin, then let us hope it is not too great a one (more's the sin to speak one's mind in excess, I suspect). In any case, I was on my fifty-sixth or -seventh shovelful when I began, uncontrollably, to speculate on the density of man. Destiny, I should say. I'm not sure what brought on this particular topic, the destiny of man, although I suppose that burying the dead brings out that particular philosophical bent. So I began to speculate on the destiny of man, his purpose, if you will. I had a lot of digging ahead of me (circa fifteen thousand shovelfuls), for, as I explained, this dog was not to bury well. What tender rack of meat is man, I thought. What a globe, what a tedious globe, is man. He lives only to cause grief, for with every man who lives and dies, some, um, grief is caused. The only good is that a lot of bad soil gets good fertilizer. Alas, what trifling, righteous, tedious stuff is this planet man! Then I thought of an orange tabby I had once buried, on commission, in the back yard of a certain local alderman. Half-cut I was, for this was in my younger drinking days, and working quickly to capture the last rays of sun. When I returned the next morning to inspect my work I discovered a mound of fresh-turned earth and four stiff paws growing like cactus. The problem was quickly solved with hedge-clippers, but I remember thinking at that time, such is the fate of man, my puss, for what is man if not semi-decomposed, semi-interred, fifty percent this world, fifty percent the next? I can tell you with certainty that such thinking surprised myself, for in those days, my younger drinking days, I thought rarely, if at all.

As I was placing the greyhound in his pit and thinking of nothing at all but a warm bowl of soup, I heard the slow approach of a car. Out of prudence, I moved to the cover of forest and watched. (Black. Four-door. Stops. Two men get out, remove something from the trunk. Light cigarettes. Laugh, etc., then depart.)

I crept over. Here lay Marlene. Her body was naked. Over her head was a plastic bag, tied around her neck with a yellow nylon cord. Her blue face smudged against the plastic, and I could see that her lips were parted, as if she died mid-sentence. Hmm. She was dead. I did not stop to question why, for the answers were unthinkable, even for an aging man given perhaps to occasional rumination. Hmm. I really wasn't surprised to see her. Really. Like I think I said, she was always thinking. Always expressing herself on this and that. I suppose I had loved her, but — hmm. These were the ones the men in black cars got first. The men in black cars were attracted to people like Marlene. People like Marlene were electric light bulbs to people like the moth-men in black cars. People like

Marlene, who express themselves and whom you might have once loved. Meanwhile, people like me get left alone for the most part; we keep our thoughts to ourselves, buried under an acre of turf. Preserved.

I took it upon myself to give her a decent end. After all, such things are expected of me. I have a reputation. It is my claim to fame. And as I started to say, I think, some time ago, Marlene was not to bury well. She had the posture all right, and the inclination. But I'm afraid I had to snap some things to get her to sit right in the earth. The ground, too, seemed harder, each shovel heavy. Perhaps I loved her once. Rain, I think, began to fall. The distant sound of thunder. It was, um, God's wrath. The raindrops, not unlike tears I suppose, were my sorrow.

The Shulman Manoeuvre

Sarah had painted still lifes. Dripping sliced passion fruit, potted snapdragons, almonds and acorns, occasionally a coral or saffron feather teased from the tail of a cockatoo. Leave landscapes and sprawling portraits to the others. Sarah was interested in the things inside the things we see. She had often talked about doing a series: a porcelain bowl of walnuts and feathers set in the folds of a lace tablecloth. The series would consist of one large still life and thirty or so smaller pieces, details of the larger work, explored at different angles and magnitudes while maintaining the qualities of light, shadow, colour and contrast. Shulman believed his wife's paintings were beautiful, each a sensual meditation, medieval in its obsessiveness, almost erotic. She hadn't sold any yet, but that would change. He'd spoken to a friend who ran a gallery. He liked Sarah's work and would consider sponsoring a show. It would be a lot of effort, she'd have to start painting again, but it would be worth it. A show would bring her art to a larger audience, it would bring her the attention she deserved.

The encounter group was Sarah's idea. The young surgeon agreed to it because there was a certain strategic advantage. Yes, Shulman was curious, and yes, he loved his wife. And when she said it would help her scrape off the veneer of socialization and allow her to see the world in an entirely new light, he nodded as if he understood completely. There was, he noted, a hint of desperation in her voice which he assumed was related to the show. As yet, she hadn't painted a thing, and in fact technically she hadn't painted in seventeen months (there were a few false starts and a couple of phantom sketches, much discussed but never revealed). Shulman added up the evidence and came to the conclusion that the real reason for the encounter group was to help her in her work. She had, he assumed, the artist's equivalent of writer's block; she needed to find a way to get the creative juices flowing again. In chess, it would be called a *Zwischenzug*, an intermediate move, achieving little on its own but working toward an eventual improvement of position.

.　.　.

The encounter began at five-thirty precisely, in a rented suite at the Royal York Hotel. The suite was magnificent: two large living rooms separating three ornate boudoirs, each containing one of the largest beds Shulman and his wife had ever seen. They were connected by a short corridor to a conference room, in which succulent embroidered pillows and knitted rugs had been laid out for the occasion (Sarah made a note in the sketchbook David had given her; already, she'd had an idea), and a spa, which had been cleared of all its exercise equipment, leaving only the marble-tiled floors, mirrored walls, and there, purring in the middle of the room, the ceramic-tiled hot pool. At the sight of the hot pool, Sarah and David looked at each other just as the other couples who'd explored the suite before them had (and the couples yet to come would) with a certain mixture of anticipation and apprehension, a particular shade of titillation, and they wondered without speaking a word if they would actually have the nerve when the time came to take off all their clothes and enter the bubbling water with all those other couples. David panicked slightly: what if he got an erection when he wasn't supposed to? Or what if he didn't get one when he was supposed to, if, indeed, erections were at some point required? He deeply regretted ever agreeing to this. He would much rather be at home with his chess, developing his middle game. Sarah squeezed his hand. She was very happy to be here, the squeeze told him. And she was happy he was there with her. She kissed him lightly on the cheek and said that, no matter what happened, she would still love him.

"This is about breaking down walls," she said; he nodded vigorously, as if in agreement. "This will bring us closer together."

"They say these sorts of things only make your love stronger."

"It will, it will make our love stronger. Our love will be stronger, I'm almost certain of that."

Precisely at five-thirty was perhaps not the right term. The encounter started promptly at five-thirty, although people were still filtering in at quarter past six. And there was no formal opening ceremony; actually, one would hardly have known an encounter had begun. It seemed like any other cocktail party: waiters brought around trays of canapés and tiny sausages skewered with coloured toothpicks, while bartenders were kept busy in the main rooms serving wine and mixed drinks. People perhaps drank a little more than they normally would at this sort of affair, which Shulman figured was a function not only of their heightened state of anxiety, but also because each of them had shelled out $250 and wanted to make sure they got their money's worth. Shulman had to admit that he was taken aback when he first saw alcohol, but he quickly saw the sense in it. This was a different kind of science from what he was used to, a different kind of medicine. In this context, a martini or whiskey sour was no different from ether. He was also momentarily taken aback when he saw Dr. Barrymore enjoying a large glass of red wine along with everyone else. A definite *Fingerfehler*, Shulman concluded, regardless of the circumstances. This was his encounter, after all: he was morally, therapeutically and, most important, legally responsible. He should have his wits about him.

Sarah nudged him.

"There's Barrymore," she said, rather more excitedly that Shulman would have expected. Shulman looked at the group leader again. Barrymore was in his late fifties, completely bald, with a corked beak that made him look, to Shulman's mind, like a football coach or five-star general, the kind of man who, one would expect, would talk too loudly and laugh too often. The beige turtleneck was an attempt to soften his image, but the eyes gave him away. Little black holes, sucking in everything around them.

"He looks younger than his picture."

"Really? I thought he looked much, much older."

Zwischenzug. It was her move now.

. . .

Sarah had many peculiarities when it came to her sexuality, which, strange as they were on the surface, only endeared her to her husband. That she would undress in the dark like a biblical virgin was one (how she would handle the hot pool was anybody's guess). That she never opened her eyes during their moments of intimacy was another; she kept them shut, not in a fearful way, as if she was afraid to view what was going on, but in a dreamy way, the way of a woman who felt deliciously relaxed, concentrating fully on the pleasure she was receiving. More curious still was her habit of never directly referring to the act of love by anything but the most oblique of euphemisms. Like the patriarchs of old, who'd crafted cunning anagrams rather than utter the name of God, Sarah spoke of sex only in code. Expressions such as "making love" and "doing it" were far too graphic for her. She preferred the more rabbinical "congress" and "laying with" and even "applicated" — words which she managed to imbue with astonishing sensuality. It wasn't that she was a prude, but that she'd co-opted the veneer of prudishness for her own erotic purposes. Shulman recognized these habits as sadomasochism in its subtlest form, a kind of Indian Defence, the slow development of play, at once toward and in defiance of the endgame.

Shulman met her during his first year of med school. She was working in the day care at the Jewish Cultural Centre, where he frequently came to eat and socialize. Not that he was Jewish, although, because of his last name and his chosen profession . . . well, everyone assumed as much. At first, Schulman paid no attention to the misperception. He was essentially a polite young man and felt no need to put people in an awkward spot by correcting them. For example, when the woman in the registrar's office asked if he had any special dietary requirements, he shrugged and said, "Just the usual." And when the practicum advisor took him aside and asked in a hushed voice if Schulman needed to keep his Saturdays open for "religious observations," the young man replied with equal earnestness, "If it's not too much trouble." After a while, Shulman settled into the role, seeing its advantages. Toronto in those days was still a rigidly stratified Anglo-Saxon community: people liked their porters black and their doctors Jewish. Being one of God's chosen might not be such a bad career move for David Shulman. So he began to feed into the confusion in small ways. He'd say "mazel tov" when everyone else said "cheers," for example; he started to take his lunch at the kosher deli on Queen Street. Over time he developed a great affinity for Jewish culture and history, reading commentaries on the Torah and studying the meaning of Jewish ritual; he was something of an expert on the Holocaust. He identified with the Jewish sense of isolation and purpose. He wondered what it would be like to be circumcised.

What drew him first to the cultural centre was a group of Jewish students who'd formed something they called the Manhattan North Chess Collective. Followers of Nimzovich, Grünfeld and Breyer — the hypermodernists — the collective set about to revolutionize the Toronto chess scene, to free it from the strictures of centralization. They dreamt of turning the chess world on its big, brainy head, experimenting wildly (starting with brown square bottom right; random configurations of pawns and pieces), mapping solutions for intensely esoteric chess problems (which often included, interestingly enough considering the state of their collective sex lives, highly improbable queen captures) and playing, playing, playing. They even developed an opening gambit that received some attention in serious chess circles. Called the Toronto Defence, it involved the early sacrifice of pawns and bishops in an attempt to draw a positional advantage on the queen's flank. Unorthodox to be sure, but that was the climate of the collective.

Fittingly, it was her art that first brought Sarah to his attention. He'd noticed a half-finished mural on the day care centre wall, cartoon animals, large renderings of the Hebrew alphabet. From his seat in the card room, during a blitz marathon with the Hassidic core of the collective, Shulman watched the young woman working on her murals. Because of their relative positions, her back was almost always toward him; in the course of the two weeks it took Sarah to finish, he probably saw her face only half a dozen times. But her back, her back was enough. She wore white overalls (judging by the paint marks, the same white overalls) every day, loose enough to give her body a kind of amorphous sexlessness, an ambiguity which only heightened her mysterious attractiveness; Shulman began to appreciate the lure of the burka in Islamic cultures. She wore a short t-shirt under the overalls, and when she reached up, the overalls pulling against her buttocks to reveal, for only moments at a time, its strong contours, the shirt would slide up her back and her arms. Before he ever even knew her name, Shulman was in love with the row of muscles and eye of olive skin that surrounded the thin section of spine in the middle of Sarah's back. He'd always thought he'd marry an artist. He used to dream about it the way other adolescent boys would dream about playing in the NHL or going off to war. He already knew he'd be a doctor — his parents had prepped him since birth — and in his mind he could picture them, him and his wife, sitting in the study on Sundays, him, perhaps with a pipe, reading the latest issue of *Deutsche Schachzeitung* or perhaps *The Lancet*, she, in the corner by the window where the light was best, working on her latest piece. Sarah became the woman by the window. Within a month he'd asked her out (the beginning of the end of the collective); within the year he had proposed; and within another year, they were married in an orthodox service which only mildly surprised Shulman's family and childhood friends.

.   .   .

On their wedding night they made love for the first time. David Shulman lost his virginity. Sarah Shulman did not.

.   .   .

By eight o'clock almost everyone at the encounter was drunk, including Shulman and his wife. The first of the clothes had come off, jackets mostly, but some sweaters, ties, scarves and cravats (it was an age when men still wore cravats with impunity), and here and there a shirt or blouse. Shulman removed his coat and carefully folded it. By now he'd cornered himself in a side room with Kitty, an actress from Syracuse. She'd un- buttoned her top completely, and he, holding the folded coat across his chest, pretended to be interested as she told him, for the third time, how she'd recently almost been mugged in the shadow of the World Trade towers. Nearby, Sarah was talking at close quarters to a man with longish hair and fashionably ridiculous sideburns. As Kitty re-related the part where she screamed and screamed — now adding slurred and drunken screams for effect — Shulman noticed the man playfully tugging at one of the buttons on his wife's blouse. She pushed his hand away but let his fingers linger on her arm for a moment. Shulman's natural impulse was to interpose. But he'd promised her her space. He concentrated on Kitty's breasts instead.

A measured roar came from across the hall, and Shulman turned his head to see two women dancing bare-breasted in the middle of the room (although Shulman suspected they might have been more than innocent revellers; he'd noticed them arrive together and saw them stand off to the side together a few times. They seemed a little too detached, by Shulman's reckoning: professional dancers, probably, or prostitutes, hired to get the ball rolling). Everyone — men and women — strained to get a view of the dancers, and it wasn't long before other women were pulling off their tops.

"Dare I?" Kitty asked, her fingers on the front clasp of her bra.

"I wish you would." Shulman had hoped to sound less horny and more nonchalant.

Kitty kept her fingers in place, waiting for him to egg her on, but by now Shulman's concentration had returned to Sarah. She held her fingers on her top button for a very long time, five or six seconds, before finally pulling it open. She moved deliberately, almost mechanically, to the next button and repeated the process. Down and down she went, slowly, and so enraptured Shulman that he could almost hear her fingers scrape across the fabric, the buttons sigh as they slipped out of their holes. She was doing it for him. She was doing it to him. The tease. She knew it would upset him. She knew he would love it.

The first exercise was designed, in Barrymore's words, to "clear away the false images we project of ourselves." Participants were called to the front of the room one at a time to, in the case of women, ritualistically wash their faces with a small cloth to clear away any makeup, and in the case of men, shave off beards and moustaches (sideburns running to the bottom of the earlobe were accepted and, judging by Barrymore's mutton chops, encouraged); a couple of men were relieved of their toupees. Resentment was running high.

At the same time, everyone had to face the crowd and tell the audience one thing about themselves they hoped the encounter would help them change. It couldn't be anything superficial; Barrymore, with his studied badgering, made sure of that. One man, a real estate agent from Ajax, tried to turn the tables, asking Barrymore what he would like to change. The therapist, who'd been down the road a hundred times before, launched into a prolonged and rather graphic story about the sexual dysfunction he was currently experiencing, and how he hoped this challenging and loving group experience would help him overcoming the hidden hangups that were causing the dysfunction. The realtor from Ajax had to dig deeply indeed to top that.

Shulman was one of the last people to go before the crowd and figured he'd have a relatively easy time of it. "I really just came because of my wife," he explained. "We hoped it would help her painting."

"She's a good painter, isn't she, David?" Barrymore seemed genuinely interested.

"I think so."

"But you, you don't see any value in this experience for yourself?"

Shulman shrugged. "I'm willing to give it a try."

Barrymore looked at him for several moments, a cold grin spreading across his face. "Anyone can try, David," he said in perfect modulation. "But tonight we're not rewarding effort. Tonight, David" — and as he spoke Shulman's name he turned to the little mob — "tonight, we're rewarding achievement."

The crowd responded, madly clapping and whooping. Sarah seemed to slip a little further into the background. Most likely the crowd had pushed her there.

. . .

The pawn is much maligned in the popular imagination. Philidor, in his seminal *Analyse du jeu des échecs*, called it "the soul of chess." An overstatement perhaps, but he was urging us to recognize that pawns are more than expendable decorations. They are an integral part of any successful winning strategy. Their sacrifice should be contemplated as deeply as the loss of any queen or rook. It was the small game where Shulman excelled, the setting up of pawns to maximize the effectiveness of his strongest pieces. His father used to say that the greatest victories were the smallest, and every battle contained within it a thousand more, rules that applied as much to surgery — and marriage — as chess. Curiously, it was this advice that came into his head as he pushed his underwear to his feet and stepped out of it. He was not the last person to undress. An elderly couple who appeared somewhat Amish were still fully clothed (granted, they might have joined the group by mistake), while a terribly obese woman had stopped at her corset and was now broken down in the corner, having apparently regressed to childhood.

Shulman needn't have worried about the erection. Under the scrutiny of several dozen men and women, already waist-deep in the hot pool and anxious to move to the next phase of the therapeutic game, Shulman's member had recoiled and actually seemed to be retreating within itself. In retrospect, he saw the strategic advantages to not being the last one naked.

The game was simple. The men would stand in a line facing the women, all wearing blindfolds. When the music started, you let your hands explore the body of the person in front of you. You should touch everywhere — face, lips, breasts, genitals, feet — without disrupting the blindfolds. When the music stopped, you stopped and took two steps to the left. The music would start again. "It's a kind of sensual musical chairs," Barrymore explained, holding his own blindfold in front of his naked chest. The man was thirty years older than Shulman but in better physical condition than he could ever hope to attain. "But a word of caution. The point is not to arouse your partner or become aroused yourself. The point is to become more in tune with your tactile self — to literally *get in touch* with your feelings." His gestures were emphatic, like a TV pitchman's.

Shulman put on his blindfold and waited for the music to start. He sensed the house lights dim, as the sound of loud, slow rock music rose from nearby speakers. The music was sexy — soft horns and lingering guitar solos. Shulman reached out.

He intended only to touch his partner's hand and work his way rather purposefully up the arms and to the face. But his fingers almost immediately lit on the woman's breast, and in the moment between when he thought he should reposition his hand and the actual repositioning of that hand, the anonymous partner moved closer to him, encouraging him, and placed her fingers directly on his nipples. Perhaps it was the alcohol, but Shulman found himself instantly aroused, and more so by the second, as his partner's obvious arousal (her nipples puffed, her genitals pressed against his, one hand quickly slid to his buttocks, massaging, tickling . . .) grew stronger. She had begun to slide her hand down his chest when the music stopped.

Shulman took two steps to the left. As the music started, he wasted no time, moving his hands directly to his new partner's breasts, cupping them, tracing the outline of her nipples. She was taller than the last woman and slighter, with strong stomach muscles and taut breasts. She'd wasted no time either: both her hands went immediately to his genitals, running her fingers with glacial deliberation from the hard tip to the soft folds where his legs came together. She pulled him toward her, and he responded, grinding his hips into hers . . . just as the music stopped.

He moved on again, and again picked up where he left off. But his newest partner seemed rigid in his hands. She moved his hands off her breasts and placed them on her hips, pushing her own coarse fingers up his arms to his neck, where they lingered, encircling, almost on the verge of gentle strangulation. By the time he moved on to the next woman, his arousal was almost extinguished. But the new partner quickly changed that. Her hands went right between his legs and agitated his softened piece. Their lips met a moment later, and she sucked his tongue into her mouth. There was a familiarity to all this, and by now he was certain he'd found Sarah. He pressed his hips against hers and she directed him inside. There it was, the old compatibility. They came together within seconds, careful not to make a noise. And as they rested in each other's arms, he pushed his mask up with her cheek to see her face and find reassurance in it. All around them, other blind couples were in various advanced stages of intimacy, some having sex, some wildly groping, some resting in the afterglow. Only Barrymore and his partner were beyond arousal, or perhaps had reached a kind of hyper-arousal. His hands seemed to barely touch the woman, washing over her in the thin layer between the aura and the epidermis, while she stood, her head tilted, her arms outstretched like some art-film homage to the crucifix, her face radiant with something between anguish and delight. Shulman had never seen that look before, but if he had to hazard a guess, he would have described it as rapture.

He looked at his partner again. Kitty was still languishing. Not far off, he saw her husband vigorously mounting a women on the hot pool steps. And Sarah, standing two steps to his right, her arms outstretched, joy twisting off her face, as Barrymore — a naked, muscled sun — radiated around her.

.   .   .

There are men (and it's mostly men; chess is a masculine displacement) who see the game twenty, thirty, forty moves ahead. The Dutch Master Max Euwe is said to have been able to accurately predict the winner of a game ninety-nine out of a hundred times, based solely on the first two moves. That's because despite the outward appearance, chess isn't a random encounter between free-floating intellects. Chess is an unfolding of inevitabilities, always an approximation of life, never life itself. Mathematically, there are only a finite number of ways the game can be played out (it's an imponderably high number, but still finite), and as any mathematician will tell you, anything that is finite can be quantified and qualified. A chess player, therefore — and this may be the key to the attraction the game holds for some — is a kind of chess piece himself, an überpiece, whose function is to move, in some degree mechanically, the other pieces and pawns. And like any other piece, the Player (let's call him) is severely limited in his range of movement (the finite versus the infinite). But it's precisely these limitations — the ultimate predictability, or better, inevitability — of chess that appeals to the Player. The game is almost wholly objective and, despite appeals to the contrary, provides no quarter for such traditionally feminine values as creativity and intuition. There are, of course, Creative Players and Intuitive Players, but these are men who have committed a larger number of inevitabilities to memory and can work one off another. Chess tournaments, for example, regularly offer a brilliancy prize to the player who displays the most innovative moves in the course of his game, but this in fact rewards counter-intuitive behaviour, that is, play which rapidly shifts the game from one unfolding of the inevitable to another in a surprising but, ultimately, entirely predictable way. Shulman sometimes contemplated what the game of chess would have been like if it had been invented by women. It occurred to him that the finished product would no longer be an approximation of life but a game within which all the boundaries of life are contained.

And were brilliancy prizes to be handed out at this organized orgy, Barrymore would be taking all of them home. He had been studying Shulman for several moments. In the post-coital wash of the game, the room had gone silent, the men and women, many of them already unwrapped from their towels, bundled in identical silk housecoats (the word, Shulman thought, was "unisex"), all looking at Shulman's own little encounter group. He could smell Barrymore's minty breath and heavy cologne. "I said" — the therapist was emphatic — "you can go home."

"But —" Shulman tried not to look at the others, tried to catch on to where this exercise was leading.

The therapist continued. "You obviously don't want to be here, and we can't afford to have someone here who isn't committed to the needs of the group."

"But . . . but I've already paid."

Before Shulman had finished speaking, Barrymore had produced a chequebook from his kimono pocket. "I'll cut you a refund right now," he said, already writing. "And I'll tell you what, I'll add a hundred bucks for your trouble." The therapist handed the cheque to Shulman, then turned to the crowd again. "Now, is there anyone else here who isn't personally committed to this encounter?"

Shulman awkwardly shifted from one foot to the other. He held the cheque in one hand. Surely, he thought, Barrymore was joking. He'd merely suggested that perhaps the group could take a short break for coffee and maybe a visit to the bathrooms. Barrymore, who by now had taken to calling Shulman (with a curious biblical poignancy) the Uncommitted One, had barely been able to veil his contempt.

"I'm sorry, David," the therapist said, his voice rising slightly as he squared his shoulders. "I'm going to have to ask you to leave now."

"You're joking."

"Please, we need to move on."

"But —"

"Don't make me call security."

David hesitated, then took a step back.

"We'll get our clothes," he said quietly. Instinctively, he looked at Sarah. She began to walk toward him.

"Hang on, Sarah." Dr. Barrymore raised his hand. "You don't have to go. Clearly, you're the one who's committed to what we're trying to do tonight. You're certainly welcome to stay. In fact, I very much think you should."

.   .   .

"You stay, no, really."

Sarah was in his arms by now. "I can't stay without you."

"We came for your sake, honey. It's better this way, it really is."

"Really? Should I stay?"

"Really. Maybe that's what you need. A little time away from me. A chance to grow on your own."

"This will only make your love stronger."

"It will make our love stronger than ever."

.   .   .

Schulman waited until two o'clock in the morning for Sarah to come home. Finally, he fell asleep on the couch listening to classical music on the radio. Bartok. Music to not sleep by.

.   .   .

When he returned from work Monday evening, Sarah was in the bedroom packing her things. He did not enter the house immediately but stood in the driveway and waited. He knew she was in there, but he convinced himself that he needed to give her a little space. By the time he entered the front hall, she had stacked three suitcases by the doorway.

Each waited for the other to speak.

Shulman finally went to her. He wanted to hold her. He went to her with his arms open, and she accepted him in her arms. They embraced, and she held him very hard before letting go.

"I'm —"

"Don't."

"Dr. Barrymore says I need to grow, on my own. I need to be my own person."

"Don't go. Please."

"Maybe, in time —"

"Don't say it."

"He's a wonderful man. Brilliant."

"Is he?"

Sarah tried to pick up all three bags. The small one, the valise with the embroidered cover, kept falling. Shulman picked it up to hand to her; it was almost empty.

"This is just a phase, right? You're coming back, right?"

Sarah did not respond. She walked toward the door. "Don't worry about the car. I've called a cab."

Shulman grabbed her arm.

"This is just a phase, right?" He was squeezing her tighter now, and she was shaking his arm to get out of his grip.

"That's hurting, David, please . . ."

"You *are* coming back, right?"

"I need some time. I need to sort some things out."

She leaned forward and kissed him on the lips. They stood at the doorway for a moment, watching each other. David thought about grabbing her hair, throwing her to the floor. Then maybe she'd stay.

"I love you," he said.

"I know." She was already halfway out the door.

Shulman did not go to the front window to watch her leave. Instead, he went to the living room and sat in his chair. The fire was out now, and the flue exhaled a cool draft. That's when he spotted them in the corner, by the bay window, overlooking the willow and the sleeping hibiscus: her paints, her easel, half a dozen empty canvases. She forgot them all. Of course, it was her way of telling him that she would be back. It was her way of reassuring him. She left her painting supplies, her sketchbooks, the old shirt she wore (his old shirt), dappled with a hundred colours. This was *Zwischenzug*. She would be back. He was sure of it.

The Death of Carver

The front hedge was nearly buried in snow, and they were still arguing over who would play them in the movie.

"Brad Pitt?" April stubbed out her cigarette. "You've got to be kidding."

"Think about it." Boyd leaned back in the chair and raised his arms behind his head, playing with her now. "I'm a deceptively complicated man; he's a deceptively complicated actor."

"I don't know, Boyd. I can't get past the abs."

"In high school I —"

"Don't say it, Boyd, I'm warning you. Don't say it." April gulped the last of her Bacardi and soda. She'd started to do that lately, gulp the last of her drinks, whether to get it over with or to begin again, she was not sure. In any case, it was a bad omen. She'd read in *Ms.* that gulping was one of the Working Women's Warning Signs of Alcohol Addiction.

Boyd smiled. He had the cheekbones, that's true. Big high Brad Pitt cheekbones, and big thick lips like a male model or a cod. Imagine an older, shorter, chunkier Brad Pitt with bad skin weathered down by time and comfort, superimpose that on the face of a fish — one of your less fishy but more human fish, but a fish all the same — and you got a rough idea of Boyd.

"But what about you? Julia Roberts? Come on. It doesn't work, on any level. She's too," Boyd tried to think of the right word, "big. This is more of a . . . pastiche. It's an ensemble piece at best."

That was unfair, of course. He'd said himself she looked like Julia Roberts. An older, shorter, chunkier Julia Roberts, but slightly less cross-eyed and warmer in tone.

"I've changed my mind anyway. I'm thinking Angelica Huston. She has the range, the *compression* to pack a lot into a character who admittedly only dances on the periphery of the story."

Carver raged again from the back room. "God damn you, Ford! God damn you!"

Boyd and April hushed. She tried not to look at him; he tried not to look at her. But their eyes met momentarily, and that gid-diness overtook them. April had to cover her little mouth with both hands to suppress the laughter.

"If I've told you once I've told you a thousand times: I shot the bird, Ford. I shot the God damn bird!"

Boyd and April strained to hear Ford's reply. He spoke in a gentlemanly Kentucky fried accent. Very restrained. Well modulated. Polite. They could make out little of what he said, the odd word. "Bird" came up a few times; "sophistry"; "trousers" or a word that sounded very much like trousers; frequent expletives ("shee-it" seemed to be a particular favourite of Ford's). Then silence.

April tried the dip. It was a new one, pimento-chive, she'd picked up the recipe over the Internet. She'd gone a little heavy on the garlic and turned her head as her taste buds adjusted.

"And Carver?" Boyd smiled. He had his ideas.

April lit another cigarette and rattled her glass in Boyd's direction. He took it obligingly.

"Carver," she said. "That's a tough one. Ford's easy. I'm thinking that guy . . . you know, that guy from that movie?"

"What guy?"

"You know, *that guy*. From that movie. We just rented it."

"What was it about?"

"You know. A robbery."

"Well, that just about describes half the movies we ever rent."

"He's a character actor. Very good. Nondescript. Slips into his roles. Good ol' what's-his-name."

Boyd was nodding. He knew the man now. "That guy in that movie about the thing. Where he tries to kidnap his wife for the ransom money, but everything fucks up."

"That's it."

"That's right. He'd be perfect. Maybe not quite," he held out April's glass as he tried to recover the waylaid word, "debonair. Ford is kind of, you know, debonair."

April nodded. He had her there.

"Perhaps he could play it, though. Perhaps he could play it debonair. Proper lighting, the right costume —"

"A seersucker suit —"

"A seersucker suit. He's the kind of actor who could pull it off."

They sat in silence for a moment and sipped their drinks. Seersucker. Was that the right word? She wouldn't have minded arguing that point. But it sounded right, and if it wasn't right, it still fit Ford to a T. April was about to suggest Kevin Spacey when Carver started coughing in the back room. He coughed and coughed and coughed and coughed, then coughed some more. A thick, phlegmy, devilled-egg cough: sour, wet on the outside, dry on the inside, slightly oily.

April tried to say something when the coughing stopped. But Carver started up again, and this time he coughed so much that April was sure he would expire right then and there, just cough his lungs out on the guest bedspread and expire like every warranty she'd ever had. But then he stopped. Ford murmured some words of comfort. Boyd could make out only one of them: "puddle." It was a strange choice, under the circumstances, but he had to admit, it did sound comforting.

April looked out the window. The snow was still falling, falling. The car was buried, making a most uncarlike mound on the street. She imagined the view of the house from the road, snow stacked up against the screen door, snow drifting off t he front of the cantilevered roof, glazing the row of colonial pillars, completely obscuring the frieze work on the three load-bearing arches that supported the classical Grecian façade.

"Michael Douglas," April said suddenly, hoping, it seemed, to get a rise.

Boyd did not disappoint. "What? For Carver?"

April nodded.

"Too old."

"Then, Russell Crowe. He has the intensity."

"Too young."

"It's a movie, damn it, Boyd. It can take liberties. Besides, Russell Crowe can pull it off. Did you see *The Insider?* That man has chops, Boyd. That man has chops."

Gulp, gulp, gulp. She was finding she could handle her liquor a lot better now, which wasn't actually a good thing if you took the editors at *Ms.* to heart. *Enhanced capacity for alcohol*: another Working Woman's Warning Sign of Alcohol Addiction.

"Do you like them, then? His books?"

Boyd shrugged. In truth, he never read them.

"It's not my thing, really. I'm into more traditional stories. You know: beginning, middle, end. You?"

April shrugged right back. "I don't read much anymore. Articles, on the bus sometimes, when I'm not sleeping. I saw the movie."

Boyd raised his eyebrows — a signature move — conveying that he saw the movie too and that he had a generally favourable opinion of it. "He's a minimalist, I suppose," he added, as an afterthought.

April shook her head. She'd never been one to characterize writers. She shifted in her seat. Her back was acting up again. It hadn't been the same since the breast reduction surgery (a small price to pay for perfect breasts, however). It was the sciatic nerve. The chiropractor said it was because of the operation and because her chair at work didn't offer enough support, enough, that is, of the right kind of support. She leaned back, tipping the chair slightly. That was better.

"So. Do you want to get a video or something?" Boyd was getting bored.

"Do you think we should? I mean, it doesn't seem quite right, what with Carver in the next room . . ." Now it was her turn to hesitate. She had never actually said it before, not in this context anyway. Boyd just looked at her, daring her to finish. "Not with him in the guest room . . . passing away." She took a gulp from her drink, sucking on an ice cube, one of those machine-made ones with the divot in the middle. She bit the ice cube and danced the pieces across the roof her mouth with her tongue. Usually Boyd didn't like it when she drank, but he was drinking himself tonight and had started things right with a fat spliff. He hadn't smoked up in years; it seemed to take the edge off him. She wanted to ask him, Boyd, how'd we get this way, how'd we become a middle-aged married couple with nothing good left to argue about, when Carver started belly-aching again. At first it was impossible to understand a single word (Boyd's eyes froze in a half-roll — another signature move). Carver's voice was unusually high, and April was sure that he was crying, or at least trying to speak through great anguish. Her father did the same thing when he was dying. A great anguish came over him. The context all but eluded her now — it had something to do with a business deal he'd made years before, when he bought out a partner or had a partner

buy his shares — but the subtext still resonated. He wanted ab-
solution. He wanted to die with an easy conscience. He wanted
to forgive himself. April couldn't really help him. She held his a
hand and said, There there there, that was a long time ago. You
just rest, Daddy. You just let yourself get some rest. And he did.
He closed his eyes and slipped gently into that good night.
But Carver wasn't going anywhere just yet. He began shouting
again, at first incomprehensibly. But soon they could make out
the words.

"I'm telling you, Ford, you have to tell the truth! The truth,
Ford. The truth! You didn't kill the bird. I killed the bird! I killed
the God damned bird."

This time they didn't giggle, they didn't even feel like it.
Boyd was rolling another joint. He was pretty good at it. Dex-
terous. A craftsman-in-the-works. April was chugging her
drink. She felt a little guilty about it (guilt: another Warning
Sign for Working Women), but she did it anyway. She wanted
to be drunk. She wanted to be drunker than any one person
had ever been drunk before.

"What's with the bird, Boyd? What does that mean?"

Boyd shrugged as he licked the edge of the rolling paper.

"Maybe it's an allusion."

"Well, duh. Obviously he's alluding to something."

"I mean, like, a literary allusion. Maybe there's a bird in a
book or something."

"I suppose. Or a symbol." Her father told her once, years
ago, that birds frequently had a symbolic function in literature.
"Maybe it represents freedom —"

"— or some kind of abstract notion of life —"

"Yes." April started to get excited now. "Or the human spirit?
Maybe it's a comment on the indomitability of the human
spirit?"

"Or the domitability," Boyd said.

"Do you think?"

"He does kill the bird, right? That seems to be the whole point. That he killed the bird."

"But you could read that, again, as a triumph. We assume that he's speaking in anger, imploring Ford to set the record straight. Maybe it's defiance. Maybe he's asking Ford to tell the world that he, Carver, beat the bird. He beat the bird before the bird beat him?"

Boyd sat back in the couch and lit the joint. He took a deep, deep toke that went straight to his eyes. "It's possible," smoke leaked from his mouth as he spoke, "that it's just a bird. Maybe they have nothing else to talk about except that bird."

That was a good point. April shifted in her seat, struggling to think of something meaningful to do (hence — and she understood this very clearly — the alcohol, which neatly filled the empty spaces between meaning).

"You know, I was a pretty good actress myself, once."

"Actor."

"Actor?"

"Yeah. They call them actors now. Male, female, it doesn't matter. It's a gender equity thing."

April sighed. She liked the world when it wasn't post-feminist.

"Anyway, the point is, I used to be a pretty good little actress."

"I know. I saw you. Your Blanche Dubois, that was good."

"I struggled with Gabbler."

"Who didn't?"

"I'm not saying that I was a great actress —"

"I understand."

"— or that I could play the part."

"I know. It's just talk." The words faded in the grey light.

"No one's better qualified."

Boyd coughed. "It could be an . . . emissary."

"Huh?"

"The bird. Maybe it's an emissary from God or from some other Higher Power. Some kind of go-between between heaven and earth, between the possible and the drearily obvious."

Boyd paused.

"And maybe Carver's saying that by killing the bird he's cut off the link between the high and the low, he's forced us, the high and the low, to come together, to meet on equal terms."

"I like that."

"It's a standard motif."

"Still . . ."

See. That was why she hung in with Boyd after all these years, why she still loved him. When you scraped off the layers of varnish and bullshee-it, there was still a decent man inside.

"So, what about that video? The new Russell Crowe is in. We could check it out, audition him right here on the couch." Boyd smiled wide and stretched his arms wide apart to suggest that their couch went on forever in either direction. April did not res-pond. She picked up the movie offer and thumbed through it. It was almost too good to be true.

"I wonder if we should get an agent or something. Or at least let our lawyer go through it."

"It'll all work out in the end, dear. It always does."

"It's so — you know. You wait your whole life for something like this, and when it finally happens . . ."

"It is a lot of money."

"And we didn't . . ."

"We didn't do nothing to earn it. It came looking for us."

"We're just really on the edge of the story here . . ."

"We're furniture, honey. We're the back-story. We're white noise. But you know, maybe our time has come."

April read the offer through again from the beginning, the thick yellowed vellum scratching her fingers as she turned the pages, her eyes straining to read the infinitesimally small small print, hand-written in a fine hand, almost Lutheran in its pained, beautiful precision. Boyd put on a Mingus CD and played drums with two swizzle sticks, a red one and a green one, both shaped like little swords, both effortlessly mutilating the air in perfect time. Right bang in the pocket. And so they sat, each one resisting destiny, until April realized that things had gotten pretty quiet in the guest bedroom. A moment later, she heard someone stirring, then the door opened slowly and Ford emerged. He was holding a small lap dog that looked like one of those knitted dogs you'd put over a Kleenex dispenser. April had never noticed the dog before.

Ford stood in the hallway for a long time, not speaking, his eyes watered over although he was not actually crying. Every once in a while the little dog looked up and licked his face. It had a goldy yellow bow in the middle of its forehead, a bow the same colour as Ford's tie. They looked quite comical, the two of them together. The dog kind of resembled him, with its narrow eyes close together, its nose that hadn't quite been grown into yet.

"Well . . ." Ford said finally, drawling the word into extra innings. "It's finished. I'll be going now."

April got his coat from the coat rack by the front door and helped him put it on.

"You've been most kind."

"Think nothing of it," Boyd said, and he meant it.

"It's been an awful imposition."

"Nonsense," said April.

Ford closed his eyes, his lids fluttering quickly for several seconds, the little dog lapping his chin, before he finally re-opened them.

"It's a far, far better —"

"Yes, yes, yes." Boyd deftly nudged the writer out the door.

Ford thanked them both quietly, then left.

"He's a very polite man," April said.

"Yes," Boyd said. "Almost too polite."

"I'm glad he's gone."

"Me too."

"I wonder why his wife never showed. Carver's, I mean? You'd think she'd of been here."

"Maybe he wasn't married, April. Or maybe he was, but she got stuck in the snow."

That was a good point. It had been snowing for days.

Boyd got up from the couch and moved to April's chair. He put his arm around her. He snuggled up to her, almost bored into her like a tick in a deer's ass. You can only get so close. There there there, she wanted to say. You get some rest, Boyd. You just let yourself get some rest. April put her hand on his shoulder, and at that moment she looked at Boyd and Boyd looked at her and it hit them: Carver was really dead. Now he was their problem.

Gris-Gris Gumbo and Mrs. Charles Bukowski
at the Mardi Gras Detox Centre

THEORY I. *A body at rest tends to remain at rest*

Six weeks. The doctor was clear. David Plumber would be in a coma for six weeks, then die, just like that. Kaput. Maybe that started his latest binge. It was ugly news for any man, and Plumber took it particularly hard. He'd never seen it coming. He'd just signed a new contract, two years with a two-year option. He wasn't ready to die. He'd rather move to Siberia.

The clinic had been his father's idea. Dad had struggled on and off with booze for years and knew the signs. Dad insisted, Dave resisted. He was too handsome to be a drunk. But then when he got the death sentence — six weeks — he relented. It was the mechanical inevitability of existence. What could you do?

Plumber quickly understood why actors were always checking themselves into these places. First of all, the coverage was great. Lilly really did a great job there. She must have been working the phones 24-7. Every major tab did something, and the stories were uniformly sympathetic.[1] *People* was talking cover. They'd already sent a guy round to shoot it: Plumber nearly unconscious in a hospital bed,[2] Dad posed grimly in the back-

---

[1] Sample headline: *Curtain Call for Drunk Hunk?*
[2] Not his. The private rooms at the Mardi Gras Detox Centre were beautifully appointed. Plumber's room featured an antique pine four-poster with a silk canopy and a state-of-the-art entertainment system built into the headboard.

ground, holding his son's hand. Both looking haggard and handsome,[3] an effect produced with harsh cross lighting and a special filter, which added a curious grainy texture to the final print. Kudos to the shooter, he really knew his stuff. But it wasn't just the coverage; the atmosphere suited Plumber. It was actor heaven, everyone paying attention to him all the time. Talk about falling into a part. He was intuitively into it. All he had to do was show up, say some lines, whatever came into his head, really, and everyone seemed tremendously pleased. Dad was a bit of a pill — he always was, you'd almost think he was the one with six weeks left to live — and of course all that stuff with Nancy. But all in all things were good. Life, in fact, couldn't get much better.

THEORY II: *A straight line is the shortest distance between two pints*

The last binge started like this. Plumber out for a walk, completely innocent. In fact, he'd left his apartment to get away from all the temptations it contained: the liquor cabinet (empty but inviting), the phone (Dad could be calling again at any minute to check up), and the general air of nothingness — that nameless boredom that Plumber could not stand. He was the kind of person who just couldn't sit there alone with himself, with his thoughts, with his memories. It left him in a panic. He had to do something, and over time, through a process of trial and error,[4] he'd found that booze filled the void

---

[3]   David Plumber Sr. was also an actor of note, best remembered for his work as the Kissing Bandit in those old Colgate commercials and the voice of Gris-Gris Gumbo, cartoon spokescrawdaddy for the Louisiana Hot Sauce Company.

[4]   He'd discovered early in life that you could only masturbate so many times a day before it actually began to hurt.

quite nicely.[5] So when Goldberg called Plumber to tell him he had six weeks to live, Plumber looked at the liquor cabinet, the phone and the void and decided that a stroll was in order, if not to deliver him from temptation, at least to delay it a little. Everything was fine until he took a wrong turn and passed a bar offering Glenmorangie eighteen-year-old highland single malt for five bucks a shot. Obviously fate was interceding; he'd have been insane to pass it up.

The first drink was no problem. He ordered it calmly, as a man only passing through for a single social single malt might do, and accepted it with such nonchalance that the waitress might have thought he'd changed his mind about a drink after all. Plumber tried to sip, God knows he did, but found himself gobbling the drink down, as much as any man can gobble a drink. The warm wave washed over him and covered him like a comfortable watery blanket, and Plumber was on to the next drink and the next before he knew what hit him. That's when the camera shut off. The director in his head called cut, and his brain took five for who knows how long. Days? At least.[6] The next thing he remembered was waking up in Goldberg's guest bedroom, the door bolted from the outside, in a pair of pee-soaked pyjamas, in the clutch of a pee-soaked

---

5   Let's be more specific. For booze read scotch, and for scotch read vintage single malt. If he weren't a real drinker's drinker, he was at least a real actor's drinker.

6   In fact, the sequence ran like this: Plumber finished the evening at the Welsh Rabbit, downing tequila shooters with two college students who later joined him in the men's room for a couple of lines. At closing time, Plumber made his way home, where he found his factory-condition TR-6 waiting for him. He climbed into the car and drove with the semiconscious hyper-clarity that only a Stage Two drunk with a secondary cocaine dependency can summon, making his way almost to Bel Aire before pulling over to rest. Two emergency fifths later, he wound up on Nancy's doorstep and was halfway though a raucous apology when the Jewish Cavalry showed up.

mattress, covered with a ragged pee-soaked quilt, feeling deeply, if not urgently, the need to pee.

He'd made it to work, Goldberg had seen to that, and had apparently done quite well. All that was asked of him was that he lie in a bed looking hideous and fitful, but still, he pulled it off with unconscious aplomb. In fact Plumber's popularity seemed to have soared. The phone lines had been jammed by viewers concerned with the state of his health. This was Plumber's greatest fear. They didn't want him to go. Maim him. Cripple him. Leave him a living vegetable. Just don't kill him. The dying he could handle, it was the lingering he wasn't keen on. He had a friend who'd played Blaise, the evil twin on *Santa Clara Nights*. The producers had him run over by a horse-drawn carriage; the doctors gave him two weeks to live. It was the longest two weeks of his life. He lingered for four full seasons before suddenly, miraculously regaining consciousness. Four years of dragging his hump to work, punching the clock, getting paid for pretending to be on death's door five minutes a week. It was work. It paid the bills. But it wasn't art and it wasn't even craft. The poor bastard left the show the following year, depressed and disillusioned.[7] In Plumber's case the worst part was that the producers must have known it was coming. Levitz and Sherwood must have offered to renew his contract early because they wanted to lock him up on *To the Ends of the Earth*. They knew that other soaps were calling, and it's a cinch Goldberg would have bolted in a second if he knew his client would be spending six weeks — an eternity, surely — unconscious and drooling, growing older and less marketable as each week-long second ticked past.

---

[7] In fact, Mischa Petersen now runs a pet store in Albuquerque, New Mexico. He is "happily married" to a weight loss counselor; they have three children. "Hollywood was an experience," he says. "But I wouldn't go back. I've got all the money and fame I can handle right here."

Dad arrived mid-stream as Plumber was enjoying what might have been the most satisfyingly, bladder-soothing pee of his life. Dad had a stuffed duffel bag in one hand and a large bottle of Evian in the other. "Any blood?" Dad moved closer to inspect Plumber's urine. "All clear." He sounded upset. He was the kind of man who thrived on crisis, who in fact could barely function unless there was a crisis to react to, who in fact, not to stress the point too finely, would go out of his way to create chaos with almost biblical precision out of the day-to-day nothingness of existence. Simple example: Dad moved more often than some men[8] changed relationships. On average, three times a year. He'd be in one apartment or another and then, without warning, give notice. A few weeks later, he'd be setting up house in a new place, subconsciously plotting his next foray into the void. On the one hand, Plumber understood this as a kind of quasi-spiritual quest, or rather, an anti-quasi-spiritual quest, an example of his father's ongoing search to find peace of mind in his surroundings. But just as important, the moves ensured that Dad's life was in constant flux. So the What, the chaos, was easy to figure, but the Why — the Why had Plumber puzzled. And there was no sense asking Dad about it. He was a walking recessive gene, emotionally speaking, who'd evolved past the alcoholism and then hit a brick wall.

> Plumber: So, Dad, I want to ask you about the chaos.
> Dad: What chaos is that, son?
> Plumber: You know, the overwhelming chaos wherein you live your life.
> Dad: I'm not sure I follow you.
> Plumber: Okay, let me put it this way. If you were to live your life in a constant state of chaos — theoretically

---

8   Dad, for example.

speaking — do you think you'd be doing it out of a sense of comfort, because maybe you grew up in a chaotic home and longed to return to some kind of blissful, familiar disorder? Or do you think you'd be doing it as a kind of distraction, to take your mind off higher matters of philosophical importance — life, death, the meaning of existence and so forth? In other words, do you think you'd be trading one addiction, alcohol, for another, chaos? Or is it possible that you'd be extracting a certain sense of power from it, the desperate machismo of the self-generated messiah, leading yourself from the wilderness of complacency into a funhouse-mirror promised land? Or could it simply be that you wouldn't know any better? This is how you've always lived your life — theoretically speaking — and this is how you will continue?

Dad: Sorry. I'm still not sure I follow.

Plumber: Then answer this: why did she leave?

Dad: *Le cœur a ses raisons que la raison ne connait point.*[9]

The purpose of the stuffed duffel bag was quickly explained. Dad was doing an "intervention" with Goldberg's blessing and support.[10] Dad had been to more than one intervention in his day[11] and knew the drill. Confront the victim with his problem, give him the ol' man in the mirror routine, offer an empathic word or two, hug (required), cry (optional), then hand the poor sod his bag[12] and push him into an awaiting limousine. Failure

---

[9] Pascal. *Eds.*

[10] And, for that matter, the blessing and support of Levitz and Sherwood, who had enough footage of Plumber unconscious in hospital blues to last through a covey of comas and perhaps an autopsy or two.

[11] For a while, after he'd sobered himself up, he'd been a walking intervention.

[12] The bag is critical. No one, it seems, can argue with a packed suitcase.

— which in this case meant measured response and careful consideration — was not an option.

Fast forward to Plumber, showered and dressed, strapped in the back of a stretch limo, packed bag in lap,[13] Evian in hand, airport bound. He'd succumbed willingly, all things considered. Of course, he'd resisted, everybody does. Dad's hugging and crying[14] did little to undermine his resolve, and even Goldberg's tough love ("I can't spend all my time baby-sitting you, I have other clients" [15]) failed to move Plumber. The young man wasn't arguing with the facts. He knew he had a problem, although he did dispute how that problem was characterized and even maintained that, at this precise moment in his life, his problem was as much a solution. And maybe he never would have gotten in the limo if it hadn't been for a timely phone call from Nancy, who said that if he got treatment maybe, just maybe, she'd talk to him. Isn't love strange?

THEORY III. *The acceleration of an assumption is directly proportional to the force exerted on that assumption*

So, we go through life burdened by false assumptions. Plumber, for one, had some odd ideas. His unattractiveness. That's a curious bit. Practically the entire world telling him how handsome he was, strange women[16] stopping him on the street and offering to perform unsolicited and, in some cases,

---

13 Shrink-wrapped, factory fresh jammies and gonches, courtesy Grandma Plumber.

14 Even at the time Plumber suspected that Dad's need to alleviate his own guilt was at least as strong as his concern for his son.

15 True, but Plumber was the only one of Goldberg's collection of shoe models, voice-over artists and animal acts to have made the crossover to the small screen.

16 And men, for that matter.

truly complex sex acts on him, and still nada on the self-perception scale. The child psychiatrist[17] had pegged him early: low self esteem. Go figure. Practically the entire day-time-TV-watching country thinking Plumber was one of the finest pieces of man flesh ever to strut across the face of the earth, while inside he seeing himself as a repulsive smudge with a seashell lip and asymmetrical eyes and ears too big for his too-small head. Maybe that's why he drank, to mask the ugliness he felt inside. Or perhaps to wallpaper over the unresolved conflict of his parents' divorce and his mother's subsequent and o'er-hasty suicide. Of course, this is just another assumption, the belief that people — you and I, say — do things out of emotional need. Certainly Dr. Prock assumed as much when he treated the young David Plumber, years ago. Back then, alcohol wasn't the problem. Back then, Plumber was addicted to school, or more precisely, Plumber was addicted to not going to school. Maybe it happened gra-dually, Plumber couldn't remember exactly now, but he does remember a point when he was going to school and then a point when he wasn't going to school, and nothing anyone said or did would make him go. The shrink pegged it as an emo-tional problem, which to David's young mind was about as useful as saying the night sky was black. Dad had handled it all right, though. Dad had learned that while time didn't necessarily heal all wounds (in fact, David Plumber Sr. would tell you the inverse was true), there was never a bad excuse for a holiday. He took young David on extensive bus trips, to folk festivals in the Ozarks and Newfoundland, to arctic-circle fish camps with nonsense names several dozen syllables long. Mostly, he took his son to the movies. Lots and lots of movies. Dad said he was studying. Dad said he was the luckiest man in

---

[17]   Dr. W.T. Prock, author of the best-selling parenting manual *The Competent Child.*

the world because to learn his craft he didn't need to study textbooks; it was all up there for him to learn, on the silver screen. So there Plumber the Younger sat, fifteen going on sixteen, inwardly ugly, unattended and unattending, diagnosed Paranoid Neurotic School Phobic with Underlying Depressive Tendencies, assumed by most everyone[18] in his little town to be wildly fucking up, alone in the dark but surrounded, studying and learning too, and slowly working his way to becoming the most famous, handsomest man ever to come out of Bradenton, California.[19] The irony was lost on everyone.

THEORY IV. *All objects are accelerated equally by the force of authority*

The Mardi Gras Detox Centre had three rules etched in a bullet-proof, shatter-proof window that separated the guest foyer from the clinic per se.

1. Everyone gets out alive.
2. To forgive is holy; to forgive yourself, divine.
3. One day at a time.

This last rule had achieved corporate sponsor status at the clinic. The counsellors (jeans, sneakers and, as a rule, earth-tone sweaters) and nurses (jeans, sensible shoes and, as a rule, pastel smocks) used the expression compulsively, leaving Plumber to wonder if they weren't all part of some complicated royalty sharing scheme. Within the first hour after admission, Plumber heard the phrase used to admonish a teenaged girl who was refusing to make her bed[20] ("Someone's

---

[18] Except for his father, who chose the irrational but perhaps more productive assumption that everything would work out fine in the end.

[19] A town whence, it was widely assumed, no one famous would ever come.

[20] Everyone had simple chores to do at the Mardi Gras Detox Centre.

not feeling very one-day-at-a-time today, is she?"), calm two prepubescent dotcom billionaires arguing over a disputed line call in table tennis ("You can't respect your one-day-at-a-time unless you respect other people's one-day-at-a-time") and praise an old bum[21] who'd successfully swallowed his medication ("See? One pill at a time and one day at a time. It's that simple"). Plumber was a quick study.

> Counsellor A: We treat a lot of celebrities here. I just want you to know that you can't expect to be treated differently from the other patients.
> Plumber: I understand. I just want to take things one day at a time.
> Counsellor A: That's the right approach. You've got your work cut out for you, but if you just take it one day at a time, it'll go a lot easier.
> Plumber: One day at a time?
> Counsellor A: Yes. One day at a time.

The first days of treatment were not bad. Plumber was put on a strict diet — lots of water and fresh fruit — and confined to his room and the exercise yard. The sudden abstinence didn't hit him, a career binger, as hard as it might some. He'd glimpsed the worst of the lot,[22] those patients in the cheap seats, the semi-private rooms and wards in the east wing of the centre, strapped to their real aluminum hospital beds, frothing and howling and crying like the worst Emmy-conscious hack in the cheesiest made-for-TV MOTW. Plumber was amazed to see real drunks act this way. They must have been the hard

---

21 In fact, a former bank president, who over a couple of decades had slipped from the occasional liquid lunch to the upper reaches of alcoholism, a place from which few, if any, ever returned.
22 Seated on his stationary bike, he could look directly down onto the east wing.

core, the superdrunks, who'd transcended ordinary drunkenness and addiction and landed on a higher lower plane, the mythic realm of the DTs. Plumber silently applauded their tenacity. In a world organized to help them, a culture which in fact orbited the diseased and miserable like an obedient, dependent satellite, these drunks had persevered. Kudos all round.

THEORY V. *For every inaction there is an equal and opposite contraction*

One the third day, the nurse stood with arms folded, blocking Plumber's exit. She'd just appeared, an uncouth vision. It had been his refusal to go to group that seemed to summon her from the depths of the darkest nurses' station. Group was mandatory, she informed Plumber. Option was not an option.

She stared for a long time without speaking. Plumber couldn't tell if she was really angry or simply reaching into her patient-motivation bag of tricks. It was effective in either case; Plumber enjoyed watching a professional at work.

"I'm not going to pick you up and carry you there."

"Try again tomorrow. I'm, like, too one-day-at-a-time today." Plumber smiled and shifted on his bed. It was basic physics at work. An irresistible force coming up against an immovable object.[23] The nurse stood in place, breathing deeply, trying, Plumber supposed, to calm herself. She was taking her role much too seriously. What were her options? Would she kick him out? No. The clinic needed high profile cases like Plumber to keep the cheap seats full. Would she cut off his privileges? Not likely, since it was the privileges that

---

[23] Rendered mathematically, it might look like this: $(N^1)(P^1) = -(NP^1)\chi$.

kept his cute butt in the centre, helping to drum up business. A vicious circle.

"I don't want to have to call the orderlies." She spoke with the empty authority of someone who had survived a lifetime of assertiveness training seminars.

"Good. I don't want you to have to call them." He wasn't being cheeky,[24] although it no doubt sounded that way. He really didn't want her to call the orderlies.[25] Almost as soon as he said the words, though, he regretted them. He'd painted both of them into a corner. You learn this kind of thing at theatre school,[26] how to pace a scene to move toward an end-point. The key was listening, always listening. If you weren't listening, truly listening, to the other actors, if you were only paying attention to your own lines, then you wouldn't react properly. That was the key, reactions, because despite the name — acting — the craft was really all about reacting. Clearly, then, Plumber hadn't been listening; he'd been too I-focused and not eye-focused.[27] He'd been acting, not reacting, and now he was nine-tenths through a scene without an ending in sight. He wanted to start again, but life, as the counsellors were wont to tell him, was not a dress rehearsal. So

---

[24] Then again, maybe he was. He was aware of his reaction to female authority figures. They were "the red cape to the bull of his anger," as Prock had so obtusely put it. More useful was the psychiatrist's explanation that anger was a typical, healthy reaction to suicide. The way Plumber had applied this anger to women in general, and particularly to women in positions of authority, was also typical of the male (and especially the adolescent male) ego.

[25] He'd promised autographs for their girlfriends but wasn't in the mood to sign them right now.

[26] It would be wrong to assume that just because Plumber had no formal education he therefore had no formal training. He spent two years with the Actors' Development Project in NYC before signing on as an apprentice at LA's American Academy of Theatrical Arts.

[27] To steal a quote from Mr. Addleton of the AATA.

there they sat, neither giving an inch, the nurse growing angrier as each second sauntered past, and Plumber — Plumber even more handsome than usual, noticeable more thirsty, wishing that he'd begun better so he could end well, but most of all impatient. When was Nancy coming? She should have been there by now.

THEORY VI. *Beauty is skin deep, but ugly goes right to the bone*
They called her Mrs. Charles Bukowski, Plumber and Roy.[28] Not to her face. That would have been rude. Plumber and Roy were not rude. Roy[29] was an actor too, and he'd sort of latched onto Plumber in the way that less successful actors (lawyers, dentists, writers) tended to latch on to more successful actors (lawyers, dentists, writers).[30] Maybe they hoped that some of the magic would rub off, or that they might catch the financial and emotional drips? In any case, Plumber didn't mind. Roy was okay to talk to, just one of the guys. Maybe a little too skinny to be trusted, with bit player features: big head, small black eyes, thin lips. Not too handsome. A good side-kick. Plus, he'd somehow[31] smuggled some smoke into the centre and was disposed to sharing it in the exercise yard.[32] That's where and how they first met, in the exercise yard over a joint. They soon had the giggles. And then they spotted her,

---

28 That sounded like an act. Plumber and Roy, from the old vaudeville circuit.
29 Plumber was never certain if this was his first or last name.
30 Prock, in a widely read monograph, refers to this as UFS (Ugly Friend Syndrome).
31 Up his ass, frankly.
32 Yard here is a misnomer, designed to make the centre sound more thera-peutically Spartan than in fact it was. It sat on four or five undulating acres of woods and meadows, and all sorts of indiscretions took place in those hidden nooks and crannies.

seated in a folding lawn chair by the fountain. She wore a pink housecoat with pink pyjamas underneath and pink furry slippers like the ones Plumber's mother, God rest her soul, might have worn. They giggled some more. Who said it first? Plumber was not sure. Maybe they both said it at the same time — certainly they both thought it at the same time. *Mrs. Charles Bukowski.*

The resemblance was breathtaking, which only made it funnier. Not that she was ugly. Just that she was the kind of woman who'd never once been beautiful in her life, not even for a second.[33] Halt. Maybe once. Maybe for a moment some days after birth, after the ugly-inducing trauma of that event had washed off and before the dissymmetry of her young life had begun to weigh on her face, pulling it apart, separating her countenance forever from the land mass of beauty. It wasn't so much that she'd never been beautiful, there were entire English villages which shared that burden without apparent ill effect, but more that she'd never *felt* beautiful. Every woman on earth deserved that, if only for a moment. Every woman on earth deserved to feel beautiful, which means, Plumber supposed, feel themselves an object of beauty, feel themselves gazed upon — by a parent, a friend, a lover — with adoration and, where appropriate, stylized lust. Even in the least relative terms, beauty was fleeting, and eventually every woman[34] was reduced to mourning lost youth, lost beauty. This woman — she would never know that sad charm. Never, never quite ugly, never beautiful. An entire life on a folding lawn chair, in pink slippers, by a fountain.

Then there were the boils. Plumber thought that was the word for them. Bumps on her face and her hands. On a much

---

[33] She was opposite to Nancy in that respect; Nancy had never once been not beautiful.

[34] Everyone.

older woman, a grandmother, they wouldn't be worth a second look, in fact they'd add character.[35] But on her, so young, so unbeautiful, they were painful. They puffed up her already puffed face, casting little shadows on her pale skin. The boils boiled even along her hairline, where the skin ridged the bright red hair.

So one of them said it first. *Mrs. Charles Bukowski.* Then they both laughed. They laughed and laughed and laughed, laughing so hard that Plumber actually slapped his knee, again and again, and finally snorted, just like his mother used to snort whenever she laughed too much. That made them laugh some more. They laughed until Roy fell off his chair, fell off his chair and onto the ground, where he lay curled up, holding his stomach from laughing so hard, and laughed and laughed until he farted so loud he scared off a couple of pigeons that had lighted on a branch nearby. Roy farted so loud Plumber's chair shook. Then they laughed some more.

THEORY VII. *The length of a body contracts as humiliation increases*

The woman knew they were laughing at her.[36] Plumber could tell by the way she shifted in her seat, uncrossing her legs and crossing them again. She probably wanted to get up and leave. But that would signal defeat. That would acknowledge that the assholes were winning.

---

[35] Character: the booby prize of the formerly beautiful.
[36] You could argue that Plumber and Roy weren't laughing at her but because of her. This distinction, however, is too subtle for the human heart to make.

THEORY VIII. *The mediocre are the message*

Life? Now was that a cool medium or a hot one?[37] Plumber had read *Understanding Media* from start to finish six times and read it again when he got into the Mardi Gras Detox Centre. In truth he never understood it,[38] but little things, useful tidbits, he picked up. Television. Was that cool? *Never be hot on a cool medium*. A good rule of thumb. Film. Hot, as he recalled. Direct to video (it could be assumed): cool. Books — literature — were surprisingly hot, were they not? But what of sex?[39] And love?[40] What of truth and beauty?[41] What of life? Where did life fit into McLuhan's scheme? He'd planned to ask Nancy that, but her promised visit never materialized.[42] Instead he had Dad. Dad, overcome with the sudden urge to impart fatherly wisdom.

> Voice A: The secret to life is not a secret. Simple blind acceptance, that's all that's needed.
>
> Voice B: Did she say why?
>
> Voice A: It's funny, but all that square stuff you hear

---

[37] Nancy, in truth, had started this debate. When they'd met she was a communications major at UCLA. She maintained that life was hot in that it demanded a "dynamic engagement" from its audience. Plumber never followed the logic but went along with it in hopes that he eventually might sleep with her and perhaps, ultimately, cause her to fall in love with him.

[38] Suggested alternative title: *Misunderstanding Media*.

[39] Hot, obviously, Plumber assumed.

[40] Surprisingly cool, it seemed.

[41] Hot, according to Nancy. Beauty required involvement, ugliness demanded it.

[42] Plumber agonized for an hour over the razor. The scruffy facial hair thing wasn't a bad look. It made him seem darker, slightly gaunt in a sexy, desert-island-survivor way. And vulnerable, but maybe she'd had her fill of that. An argument could be made for shaving. Less dramatic, for starters, and Nancy was never one for the drama. More presentable as well, more like a man who had got, or was certainly in the process of getting, his shit together once and for all.

growing up? It all turns out to be true. You Get Out
of Life What You Put In. Respect Yourself. All Things
Come to Those Who Wait.

Voice B: She's been saying all week she was going to
come.

Voice A: But the worst thing you can do is blame yourself. You can't turn back the clock. You Can't Turn
Back the Clock. Everyone makes mistakes. It's time
to take action. It's time to move on.

Voice B: I don't understand. You'd think a woman, a
wife, would visit. Why wouldn't she visit?

Voice A: Sometimes you just have to move on.

Voice B: What's wrong with me?[43]

Voice A: *Le cœur a ses raisons que la raison ne connait
point.*

Voice B: That's your answer to everything.

Voice A: *Le cœur a ses raisons que la raison ne connait
point?*

Voice B: No. Moving on.

Dad patted his hand as he might have done when Plumber
was a boy. "There, there, there, son. One day at a time. You've
got to take things one day at a time." Dad stood up, he looked
around like a man looking for his hat.[44] Then he left.

THEORY IX. *The distance between two bodies is directly
proportional to the previous intimacy*

Day fifteen. Plumber does not get out of bed. He spends the

---

[43] Plumber had recently reached the conclusion that he was cursed. Every
woman he'd ever loved did not love him, and vice versa.

[44] David Plumber Sr. did in fact wear a felt hat during the summer of 1965.

morning throwing up into a bucket and the afternoon in his four-poster unable to budge. The nurses see this as a good sign. The body throwing off its poisons, the cells, chemically altered by the ongoing exposure to alcohol, realigning themselves, dutiful planets. In the evening, Plumber cannot sleep. Eventually he has to be restrained by orderlies as the night nurse injects him with Valium. Still Plumber wards off sleep. He lies strapped to his bed, moaning. He expects hallucinations, but they never come. He closes his eyes and hopes to dream of Nancy.[45] But when he finally falls asleep, he dreams of nothing at all.

THEORY IX, restated: *Gravity is directly proportional to mass and inversely proportional distance*

When Plumber finally came to his senses, he was strapped to a metal bed in the ICU. He mouth tasted like a raccoon's nest, his brain had a charley horse. His lips were so dry he had to pry them apart with his tongue. Mrs. Charles Bukowski was strapped to the next bed. She looked like Death with an attitude. Like Death on a bender. Like Death after losing the Daytime Emmy for Best Performance by Death to some young upstart Death for the seventh year running. Like Death after His wife and mistress had just run off together to set up house in Iceland: cold, cold Iceland. Snot oozed along the tube in Mrs. Charles Bukowski's nose. A white paste of spittle surrounded her mouth. Each time she inhaled, her body was shaken by a thunderous

---

[45] Nancy has by now sold the condo. Under the advice of the police and her lawyer, she is on her way back to her parents' house in New Rochelle. She is driving the red Mustang she bought with the settlement money. In the back seat are six boxes full of books, clothes and shoes. The rest she'd either sold or given away: the furniture, the appliances, the art, everything. She did not need it, she did not want it anymore.

snore. Imagine waking up to that every morning.[46] The folds of her hospital PJs had fallen open, and Plumber could follow the vein-splattered contour of her skin from her neck to her belly. One large boob hung out, artfully arranged across her arm, the huge, huge nipple engorged in sleep, her silver-dollar-pancake-sized aureole, her truck-tire-nipple-sized nipple engorged asexually, artfully. Even aroused, she was not arousing. All subject, no object. Plumber studied her. He was

---

[46] Nancy herself was just waking up on the other side of the country. She woke up gradually, restfully, and her thoughts turned almost immediately to him. Something in the room, the book perhaps, the Rimbaud poems he'd given her — faintly smelt of him and brought him to her mind. She imagined him beside her and immediately allowed her fingers to linger across her breast. She thought of fucking him again, there was no other word for it, the way they took to each other and took each other, great, interlocking attracted opposites. She thought of fucking him and immediately felt herself grow wet. She moved her hand between her legs and pressed her legs together and moved her hand and let sensation swallow her, gulp her. Maybe this was simple distraction. She'd fallen into it suddenly, quickly, only after promising herself that she wouldn't let it happen like this again. She'd promised herself that next time she'd take her time. But the next time was now and she was letting herself go. Call it an indulgence — surely it was stupid (*Don't call me Shirley,* that's what he'd say). But love was a cold medium, and all the more so when the sex was hot.

Nancy came quickly and quietly, then got out of bed and dressed. She wanted to be on the road by nine o'clock. She had to be in the city by three o'clock if she wanted to be at JFK on time. He'd offered to meet her at Grand Central, to save her the drive (or on top of the Empire State Building — an incurable romantic). Nancy put on a yellow cotton sundress, it was warm enough already, and wrapped a yellow scarf around her head. Most American woman could not wear a scarf like that, but Nancy could; she'd studied in Italy.

He'd bought her pantyhose. Normally she didn't like them, but they turned him on no end. He loved to run his hand up her legs and rub his fingers along her wet lips — you could see how hot it got him. And that's what this was about, Nancy wasn't kidding herself. Maybe it would become love, one day. But right now it was all about getting off. She gone too long without that. She didn't blame Plumber completely. He just couldn't cut it in bed. That was no one's fault.

thinking about inner beauty and wondering seriously if it was true, as the ancients believed, that the surface was a genuine reflection of the depth. Was an ugly woman ugly inside? Was her heart ugly? Was her soul ugly? Did she, as the ancients believed, have ugly thoughts and ugly corpuscles? And conversely, were beautiful people really beautiful inside and out? But no. Surely our inner life registered our reaction to circumstance rather than simple circumstance. Beauty, he reasoned, could be found in even the least beautiful objects: Arbus's freaks; Mapplethorpe's plundered assholes.

Plumber wanted to scratch his lip, but his arms were gently strapped to the bed.[47]

It was the scar. The shell-shaped scar in the middle of his upper lip. The only reminder of an incomplete palate, surgically repaired in infancy. Plumber wriggled his lips, trying to scratch the half-vortex, the parenthetical mark, with his teeth. He managed to raise his shoulder to his mouth. Everything has its imperfections. Even beauty.

Mrs. Charles Bukowski gasped suddenly and opened her eyes. Plumber smiled wanly. She stared at him for almost a minute, perhaps allowing her eyes to adjust to the light.

"Where the fuck am I?"

"We're in intensive care, I think."

"Who the fuck are you?"

"I'm —"

---

[47] He'd never understood why this was such a turn-on for Nancy. She liked the feeling of helplessness, which was perhaps some curious Catholic guilt thing, a rejection of the responsibility for sex. Nancy, despite her protests and apparent ambivalence, was still a closet Cathoholic. But those sex games were relatively subdued and had never done anything for him. He wanted more than anything to hold and to touch. She'd tied him up more than once. She'd spend hours tickling him and licking his nipples and softly squeezing his balls before climbing on top of him. She'd come several times before slipping off him. Then he was expected to reciprocate. Frankly, it was exhausting.

"And what the fuck are you looking at?"

Plumber turned his head as the woman started screaming for the nurse. Perhaps they'd sedate her, she seemed nearly hysterical. Perhaps they'd sedate him. There were rules, he supposed, about looking into the soul of the person beside you.[48]

HYPOTHESIS A. *If love is blind, then lust really needs glasses*

Plumber was having a lucid moment. In the exercise yard, the sun setting right on time, waiting for his father, already late.

"We were talking about anger."

"No. We were talking about men."

"Same thing." Roy took a big toke, enjoying the role of devil's advocate. "The point is that the emotional entry —"

---

[48] Nancy had made one promise to herself, and so far she'd kept it. No more pills, no more booze. Hell, she'd even sworn off coffee. She was going to take on each day on her own; she was going to look at each day through two clear eyes. She was surprised how easy it was. Making your mind up, that was the hard part.

Don't look back. That was the other promise she'd made to herself. The past is past and there's no changing it. She'd already taken steps. She'd applied to a few colleges and was ready, finally, to get her degree. He'd been a real help there. He said you only live once. It was a cliché, but it's funny how all the clichés were turning out to be true.

Nancy had her yellow sundress on, with the buttons undone. The wind scooped in through the open sunroof and washed her face and skin, the scarf holding her hair perfectly in place. The warm wind washed her clean and tugged and bit her neck and breasts. Her nipples had been hard through four states. She turned up the tunes. It was something Creole, incoherently fun, the music of the uninhibited: hot. She spread her legs and ran her fingers up her pantyhose. She'd be inhibited again. But today — now — she was free, and freedom was the best revenge. Already the bruises were healing.

"What the hell is that?"

"The emotional entry, you know, the context. The place where emotions begin and end. It's always hot for a man. For a woman —"

"Cold?"

"Precisely."

"Which means?"

"Men are a hot medium. We demand engagement."

"And women are a cold medium?"

Plumber nodded.

"Well, my girlfriend is demanding engagement, and she's definitely hot."

"Now you're mincing words."

"I thought that's was the point."

"We're having an intelligent discussion."

"Same thing."

"I'll give you an example. My wife says I don't know how to express my quote unquote feelings. She says that's the problem with me, with men. That we don't know how to express our quote unquote feelings. But I say I do know how to express my feelings, but it just so happens that most of the feelings I want to express are not the ones she wants me to express. I get pissed off. I get angry. I get horny. I get happy when the Dodgers win, I get unhappy when they lose."

"It's an old story."

"Timeless."

"But what has it to do with relative temperature?"

"Well, that's my point. My quote unquote feelings are dependent on circumstance. I have to look outside for my emotional . . ."

"Cues?"

"Thank you. Cues. While women, most women, evaluate the world solely on what's going on inside . . ."

"Women's intuition."

"That's part of it. But I'm talking more about the shape of their emotional substance . . ."

"You're losing me here."

"You know: what informs their emotion, or better, what informs their interpretation of their emotions."

"Huh?"

"For example, I say 'I'm going out,' and she says 'Fine, go out.' But when I come home she says, 'Where the hell were you?' and I say 'Out,' and then she shuts up and goes to the bedroom and closes the door. I find her there a few minutes later, crying. It's got nothing to do with external circumstance, it's just that I happened to go out at a point when she was feeling vulnerable, and when I said 'I'm going out,' she heard 'I don't love you anymore.' The point is, their emotional context is cold because it is completely internal and is almost entirely dependant on whether or not a woman is feeling particularly loved at a given point in time and space. Our emotional context is hot because it is external, based on our reaction to an observable, for lack of a better term, reality. That's why all the greatest scientists are men, and the great sex therapists are women."

Roy took a long toke. The cherry glowed red hot in the darkness.

"Plumber, you're a genius," he said, after much consideration.

"Thank you, Roy. I try. In my humble way, I try."

A wave of nausea washed over Plumber, and he barfed into his own lap. Roy called for the orderly. Plumber dropped to his hands and knees and barfed again, spewing almost nothing but air. Roy called for the orderly again as the woman in the bushes, hitherto unnoticed, shifted slightly to get a better view.

.   .   .

HYPOTHESIS B. *If object a orbits planet ß, then ß really has its work cut out*

"Why did you leave Mom?"

"Why?"

"We've been discussing our families in group."

"Really? What did you say about me?"

"I said that you were handsome. I said that you once played the voice of a fish . . ."

"Crustacean, actually."

"I said that you were indecisive. In fact I said that you were positively definitive in your indecisiveness. And I told the story of how, when I was ten and first came to live with you, you made us both sleep on the pullout couch even though there were two perfectly good, albeit unfurnished, bedrooms in the apartment. And how we moved in two weeks later with that woman in the Marines . . . "

"An actress, really. She only played a Marine on TV."

"Well, she might as well have been a Marine, the way she barked commands at us. I told group how she used to make us line up by our beds in our underwear for inspection, and how the coin had to bounce off the bed before we were allowed to move on to breakfast, and how she wouldn't let you drive to work because she thought you needed the exercise, and how her mother with the limp and the moustache came to live with us, and you and I wound up sleeping, again, on the pullout couch, and how three weeks later we were on the move again. I told them how that's not your real hair, and how you spent your entire inheritance getting your teeth capped, and about the time you decided to save money on a Christmas tree and took me up north to cut our own, but then how the cops caught us and you had to pay a five-hundred-dollar fine, which wound up being the most expensive Christmas tree you ever bought, so instead of moving like we planned, we slept in the car for the next two months. And I told them how we moved to

Seattle with that woman with two gold teeth and an enormous teenaged son who dressed in a yellow sarong and cried whenever anyone mentioned the last episode of *M*A*S*H**, and how the son fell in love with you and used to follow you around and moon over you, and how we woke up one morning in the pullout and he was on top of you trying to force his tongue into your mouth, and how that same afternoon we caught a ride with that lady trucker who drove us all the way to Salinas, in part because she felt sorry for us but mostly because you were feeling her up and didn't think I'd noticed."

"You covered the bases."

Plumber shifted from one hip to the other. The leg bindings were loosened now, but his wrists were still strapped to the bed. A protective measure only, to stop him scratching his eyes when the giant blue spiders crawled across his face.

"I thought the details were relevant. Like the time you left me at your mother's place while you went to work down south on a series of commercials . . ."

"I was a crustacean. I was in demand."

"And how your mother . . ."

"Your grandmother . . ."

"— used to wash my hair every night with lye soap and vinegar, and how she kept an autographed photograph of you in every room and gave one to everyone who came to visit her, and how when you came to get me you gave her a stack of autographed photographs and borrowed a hundred dollars from her. I told group a lot of things because that's what we do in group and because I am coming to realize that these little details, these tiny particles of my life, collectively define who I am, while the larger arc, let's call it the narrative or even orbit, really only establishes my relative position in space. My counsellor suggests I try to live more in the here and now: the particles. I am choosing to follow that advice. So, Father, you've never told me why you left her."

"You see, I was working on a pilot with Jan Michael Vincent."

"Father."

"There were rumours swirling of work for out-of-work actors with Golden Globe potential . . ."

"The truth."

"The truth?"

"Please."

"The truth is that one morning I woke up and looked at your mother. She was still sleeping, and I looked over at her and thought how beautiful she was. She was the most beautiful woman in the world. And as I lay there looking at her, it struck me how I didn't really know her. Really, we were man and wife, but we were strangers. And that frightened me. Not so much the fact that we were strangers — you get used to that — but the thought that we were perhaps growing less strange, that in fact over time we might no longer be strangers at all, but intimates. Not that the idea of being intimate with someone frightened me. It was the thought of becoming something other than what I was. That's what frightened me. I never wanted to become anything. I wanted only temporary. I am, after all an actor. That is my fate. *Le coeur a ses raisons que la raison ne connait point.*"

"That's your answer for everything."

David Plumber Sr. looked at his watch.

"To become something, that's too much like death."

Dad looked at his watch again.

"Well, I must be going."

"Goodbye, Father."

"Goodbye, son."

.   .   .

THEORY X. *The speed of a heartbeat increases as its distance from the sun decreases*

In line for dinner at the commissary that night, she was staring at him from behind a mound of mashed potatoes. She had an almost heavenly look of disgust on her face. Roy said, if looks could kill . . .

Plumber had been at the centre for five and a half weeks. He hadn't had a drink for five weeks, and he'd never felt worse in his life. Plumber and Roy took their dinner in the solarium. Afterwards they went for a long walk in the exercise yard. They played volleyball by the pool until bedtime. And every time he looked around, there she was. The woman. Mrs. Charles Bukowski. Standing there, in the shadows. Watching.

COROLLARY TO THEORY X. $E = MC^2$

I'm having an out-of-body experience, I think. I am asleep on the bed, or rather watching myself asleep on the bed. The woman is there. She's strapped my arms and legs to the four-poster and begun to remove her pink housecoat. "You're an ugly man," she says. No argument here. "You are ugly inside, you're ugly outside." I couldn't agree more. She removes her pink pyjama top. Her giant breasts sag to her belly. She takes off her bottoms, her belly hanging over her pubic hair. I feel myself getting hard. She climbs on top of me and plugs my cock inside her. Her breath is putrid, like onions and rotten eggs, her flabby body covered in oily boils. She rides me bitterly, joylessly, scowling, grunting, digging her dirty nails deep into my shoulders, and I wake up screaming from the pain, with her on top of me, riding me, her dry box holding onto my cock like an angry fist, and just as I'm about to come, the orderlies peel back the doors and enter. "Fuck you!" she screams at me as they carry her out. "Fuck you, you ugly, ugly man!" I couldn't agree more. Fuck me. Fuck me, I'm an ugly, ugly man.

SUMMARY. *All things are relative; conversely, all relatives are things*

Understand, Plumber wanted to die. What he didn't want to do was linger.

The Mardi Gras Detox Centre was a case in point. After six weeks — the recommended course of treatment — he was clean and sober. The alcohol had had time to work itself out of his system. He was saved but not cured. Every day would be a struggle. He was ready to go home.

They gave a party in his honour. Plumber was asked to say a few words. He declined.

Goldberg picked him up at the front door. A photographer snapped his photo stepping into the agent's SUV. Plumber smiled and waved; Lilly had done it again. Plumber got in the car.

Goldberg had good news. He'd landed Plumber a plumb job on *Santa Clara Nights*. He would play the Contessa's good and evil twin sons. It was a field day for an actor of his calibre. Meanwhile, he would still stay under contract to Levitz and Sherwood, who had no immediate plans to kill him off.

Plumber nodded. "Where's Dad?"

Goldberg revved the engine of his BMW SUV. The giant station wagon lurched into action.

"I said, where's Dad?"

Goldberg smiled and looked in his side-view mirror.

"Dad's moving, baby. He's going places, just like you."

Plumber looked out the window. Rain had begun to fall, streaking the glass. He looked at his watch. He'd been out of the clinic five minutes, and already he wanted a drink.[49]

---

[49] Cut to Dad, settled in his new apartment. He thought of his son as he watered the Indian rubber plant in the bedroom. The plants were his responsibility. She ran her finger across his bare shoulders.

"Do you always do housework in the nude?"

Dad shrugged.

"If you've got it, baby . . ."

She gently pulled him to the bed, pulled him down and pushed him onto his back. She took him in her mouth, soft, just the way he liked it, building him up with her lips and tongue.

He wanted to say *Fuck baby, you're amazing*, but all that came out of his mouth was "fuck." He said it over and over again, to let her know how hot she made him and that, no matter what, he would never let himself love her.

Nancy's face contorted as the intensity increased. Her eyes were closed now as her head bobbed frantically, like a novelty dog in a car window, and her fist pounded up and down his cock like a pneumatic bureaucrat — Death's own bureaucrat — rubber-stamping summary orders. He was almost ready to come, she could feel his balls and legs tighten, feel his belly contract. She looked up quickly to see his face contort, his eyes squint, his mouth stretch as if in pain (the emotional pain, say, of a heartbroken man at the grave of his only son), just as a stream of obscenities spurted from his mouth like hot semen, and it struck her that nothing in the world — nothing — was more beautiful than the act of love.

Sunshine Sketches of a Rat-Infested Shitbox

Wonnacott had locked the door from the inside and placed the papier-mâché bust of Canada's greatest literary criminal in the barred window. He pictured the police snipers, strategically positioned on rooftops along Park Street, taking aim, mistaking one dummy for another.

Wonnacott removed his shoes and then the ancient Robes of State. But the mortarboard stayed. A nice touch. He went to the bed and pushed it to one side, quickly stripping the mattress. This was much better that the authors' dinner, better by half than all the authors' dinners in the world.

Wonnacott pushed the mattress to the floor and lay down on it. From here, he could see out the window, past the vacant lot across the street and over and through the houses and off to the shadows of Lake Couchiching. He lay the Indian gun across his chest like an olde tyme sheriff.

It had been easy enough to get back in. After he blew off the conference, he drove back to the Park House. Turner met him at the door in pyjamas, clearly impatient but not willing to appear impolite to a man who, let's face it, was a minor celebrity in the country. A simple ruse ("I'm afraid I left my chapbook upstairs") and a furtive glace at the Indian gun and that was it.

Wonnacott stood and whipped off his pants.

He found the switch to the overhead light, turned it off, then lay back on the bed again. He could hear the front door creak open and the irrational chatter from the street below as the Turners brought their neighbours up to date. Who knows what this man might do, they were saying; he was, after all a writer, and capable of anything.

The lamp beside the bed illuminated the room, casting monster shadows on the walls. Wonnacott reached up and shut off the lamp. The room went dark. He could just see the flames rising from the Mariposa Belle.

Go big or stay home.

He closed his eyes and waited for the rats to come.

.   .   .

They'd spent the summer here together just after they first met. She worked as a cook in a day camp; he'd landed a job as a provincial enumerator. It was nostalgia that brought him back and nothing else. By now, Wonnacott had had his fill of these literary conferences: grey-haired men with last year's soup on their ties, leaning too close with their coffee breath to make hideous puns or ask him if he'd ever actually met Pierre Berton. This one promised to be more odious than most — *The Muse of Laughter: Sunshine Sketches of Stephen Leacock*. It was inevitable; a middle-aged male writer with some reputation for wit could go only so far before being asked to deliver a lecture on Leacock, Canada's official dullard laureate.

Wonnacott had wondered if the rooming house on Park Street was still standing. The Park House, they'd called it twenty years earlier, when it had been a curious hybrid, a cross between a firetrap and a dump, a dirty, peeling friend to woodworm and carpenter ant, the kind of place that only a pair of twenty-three-year-olds in love could find romantic. There were mice (every so often they'd find one floating in what passed for the kitchen sink with last night's soaking dishes) and rats (the first night Thérèse caught one climbing out of her boot; she impaled it on a bread knife when it tried to hide be-hind the icebox) and raccoons (a nest in the attic, beside the wasps' nest, not far from the covey of bats that daylighted upside-down on the cross-beams). The entire house death-rattled whenever someone flushed the ancient commode (rumoured to have survived the Peloponnesian Wars) or turned on the hot water without first turning on the cold or opened a tap on the top floor without shutting down the outflow valve for the storm sewer in the basement. The house death-rattled whenever the wind blew west from Lake Couchiching or north from Lake Simcoe or down from Washago, Muskoka or North Bay; when someone threw a rock into Shannon Bay, the sewers backed up; when someone had a glass of beer on Grape Island, the whole house teetered in sympathy. But it was summer and they were in love.

The landlady's name was Grace, but they called her dis-Grace because her own squalid room was filled with cat shit and bags of garbage, and she herself was half-cut on rye by lunch time and passed out in her housecoat and nylons by supper. They cooked their meals, canned soup, mostly, on a Sterno hotplate they stored in the clothes closet (no cooking in the rooms, Grace was firm on that), and slept on a pile of sleeping bags on the floor with one or several of Grace's cats keeping them company, and made acrobatic love in every conceivable position, on every conceivable stick of furniture, at every conceivable time of day, taking special care that their screams of ecstasy could be heard no further than four blocks away. They were impossibly happy.

·   ·   ·

Friday night. Wonnacott had checked into his room at the Mariposa Belle. Like Leacock's famously unfunny ship, the hotel had seen better days, half sunk, half run aground, the embodiment of middle age. Beside the reception desk, behind a glass case, a marbly bust of the great man sat on a wood pedestal, adorned with a black mortarboard, while inexplicable judicial robes hung as backdrop. In the corner was a cracked blunderbuss; "Leacock's Indian Gun," read the handwritten caption. There was a picture of the great man himself behind the desk, a rather too brown-and-blue portrait that bore the stench of commission. In one hand, Leacock held a book, a leathery, reptile tome; his other was hooked on his vest in that jaunty pose academics sometimes affect. His wispy hair writhed in grey and black serpents, more like the real-life Mark Twain than the real-life Stephen Leacock: perhaps the artist was trying to draw a comparison. For Wonnacott, the painting was a reminder of kind of failure that had come to define his country: Canada, the second-rate sketch writer, puffing and preening in the hope that it would be mistaken for a first-rate novelist.

But his room was clean and quiet and afforded a decent view. He'd plugged a little hotplate, just for old time's sake, into the octopus outlet behind the TV, and lay on the super single. He could see the wharf at Centennial Park and Veteran's Park beyond it and beyond that Pumpkin Bay. He could see the rock at the tip of Heward's Point, where he and Thérèse once made love, stopping only momentarily as a convoy of paddle-boating tourists flustered by. He got up and stepped onto the little balcony and looked north. He was too close to the water to see Park Street, but there, across the road in Couchiching Beach Park, was the Champlain Monument, commemorating a brief visit the Father of New France had made to the area in the summer of 1615. Once upon a time, under the light of an August moon, Thérèse stripped naked on its steps. She brought herself off, not allowing him to touch her, not allowing him to touch himself. If he so much as moved, she stopped, and would not start again until he promised to sit dead still. It was the single most erotic moment of his life. Wonnacott checked his printed itinerary. He was expected in the Lakeshore Room at six-thirty for a No-Host Reception. That gave him a little less than an hour. He lay on the bed, he quickly undressed.

. . .

He'd promised himself to save Park Street for Saturday afternoon. There was an Authors' Breakfast in the morning, and he wasn't needed again until he gave his keynote speech at the formal dinner that evening. That left the afternoon free. But the reception had been all but unbearable and he'd drunk too much. The walk would do him good.

For most of the reception he'd been pinned like a collected butterfly to a back wall along with the other authors, none of whom he liked or respected or, for that matter, had ever even bothered to read. There was Humphries, an unpleasant Upper Canadian in his mid-hundreds who'd written a scathing exposé on Dieppe (apparently, a lot of young men had been slaughtered needlessly), whose place at the conference was never satisfactorily explained, and a floating, perch-like academic who, between his doubtlessly fumbling attempts to seduce eighteen-year-old dowagers and his all-consuming habit of cultivating dandruff, had managed to find the time to write a humourless monograph on the function of wit in the academic writings of his honour, Lord Leacock. The crowning dung on the heap was a middle-aged woman in a knitted shawl who repeatedly referred to herself as "a poetess," although, as near as Wonnacott could tell, she was a high school English teacher who'd once been banged by Irving Layton. She was Official Laureate of the conference, which meant, Wonnacott suspected, that the local paper would inflict one of her turdy little poems commemorating the event on its readers. Let's see, what rhymes with flatulent?

Wonnacott fielded the usual questions as Dutton, the beagle-faced administrator — who ran the conference with military precision — fed him scotch and ice. Yes, he'd been to Pierre Berton's house. No, he didn't know Margaret Atwood. Some-one, a gentle former grad student named Mervin or Morris or something, even launched into a detailed appreciation of Wonnacott's earliest and most deservedly obscure work, *Flowers for the Sewer*, elaborating on the book's conflicting themes (love *and* death) and commenting on the challenges of char-acter and narrative (female first person) and repeatedly refer-ring to the title of the work until Wonnacott could no longer cower under the cover of indifference and good manners and practically screamed, *"for the Steward*, damn it, *Steward."* Then came the inevitable hit-on by the woman with big tits and glasses, who'd offered to show him around the sights of Orillia ("Sights, plural?" he'd asided) and then mentioned, as if to lend the clan-destine nightmare an odour of probity, that her husband was a volunteer driver for the festival. Her name was Luellen, and by that time Wonnacott was so drunk that he al-most took her up on the offer. He did let her press up against him as the conversation persisted, with one of her larger breasts doing serious damage to his yellow and blue boutonniere, a gift from the festival sponsors, Granite Garden Lilies. When she excused herself to go to the bathroom ("Number one or number two?" he'd asided), Wonnacott slipped out the back door, grabbing a tray of finger sandwiches as he went. There were red sandwiches, blue sandwiches, yellow sandwiches and green sandwiches, and they all tasted the same. Some kind of fish-like thing. Fishy. Fish.

.   .   .

The route had not changed. The buildings were done up or undone, but mostly they were the same as they had always been. Orillia resisted change. First, he walked to the beach, intending to piss in Lake Couchiching for old time's sake, and by the time he'd reached the wharf he'd made up his mind to swim. The cold water would wash out the cobwebs. But it was barely half-past nine when he reached the lakeshore, and the mild night air had drawn the locals out. He was forced to take his commemorative piss on the steps of the Champlain Monument. Then it was, as it always had been, west up Brandt Street (always "west up," they'd said) and north on Park.

The house was smaller than he remembered. And cleaner. The roof had been reshingled, and the dormer window, where they'd lain and watched the summer tick past like the last three minutes of math class, was significantly smaller than the dormer window of his imaginings: a portal, not a vista. He could see a couple, upper-middle-aged like him, sitting in the front room where Grace used to bathe in self-pity and filth. The man was reading a paper; the woman was knitting. A swing set rusted in the corner of the yard where the willow, upon which he'd carved their initials, once stood. Wonnacott realized that the heel of his shoe had fallen off. He wondered if he was too drunk to drive back to Toronto.

. . .

When he got back to his hotel room, he found Luellen sitting on the very corner of the bed.

"I let myself in," she said. "I have a friend who . . ."

"Would you please leave."

She did not respond but instead removed her beige overcoat. She wore a leather bra and panties and garterless stockings.

"Please. Don't make me call the manager."

"Yes. Of course."

She pulled her coat back on and seemed neither offended nor the slightest bit upset, as if the episode was simply a matter of course. All in a day's work.

Luellen stopped at the door. "Good night," she said, her voice rising at the end. Her tone was familiar. Comforting.

"Good evening," he replied, bolting the door behind her.

. . .

Wonnacott was depressed. He tried to ring Thérèse but the line was busy. She was talking, forever talking. He put a can of Campbell's chicken noodle on the hotplate, right on the element, just like they did for forty days and forty nights on Park Street, then opened the mini bar. He took out a tiny bottle of Canadian Club, or perhaps, he thought, it was a regular-sized bottle and he'd grown to gigantic proportions. Drink me, the bottle said. Drink me.

The woman depressed him — Luellen — and the poetess and the academic and Mr. Dutton and General Montcalm and the earnest, hardworking grad student who'd only wanted to please him. But what depressed Wonnacott most was Wonnacott. He'd thought his trip to Orillia would take him back to happier times (not that times now were particularly unhappy or happy; they were simply times). But the town had changed just enough to remind him that it was no longer the same. In fact, the town looked younger and fresher, with new sidewalks and well-paved streets and rows of modern houses and a supermart where the grocery once stood. The town had gotten younger; only his memories were old. Time was the enemy, he liked to say. In fact, time had already won. It had sacked the present, injecting him with nostalgia, the morphine of the vanquished, as it marched on.

Wonnacott had finished the Canadian Club and worked his

way through a bottle of Smirnoff's that seemed like a child's toy in his gargantuan hand. The beer was next, and then the other beer and then the other . . .

This time, Thérèse picked up the phone and answered in a dreamy voice.

"Did I wake you, love?" he asked.

Thérèse yawned, then lowered her voice. "I was waiting for your call . . ."

"The line was busy . . ."

"But now I can't really talk. I have a man here."

"Really? Who's that?"

"Mmmm. Just an old friend."

"I see."

"I'm just about to fuck him, do you understand?"

"Yes . . ."

"I've got his cock in my hand and I'm about to put it in my mouth."

It was an old game. Whenever he went away, he would call her. They would make love from a distance with people they'd only just invented. Go big or stay home. That's what Thérèse called it.

"Just a moment." Wonnacott kicked off his pants and hopped onto the bed.

"Are you comfortable, now?"

"Yes. Go on."

"Are you sure?"

"Yes, please."

"Good. Because he's slipping his hands up my dress, and I want to tell you all about it . . ."

.   .   .

They had met on the bus to Orillia. By chance, he'd found himself alone in the back row with Thérèse and an old woman whom he mistook for her grandmother. Soon the old woman got off, leaving the two young people virtually alone. They had barely spoken up to this point, and both pretended to be engrossed in their reading material, when Thérèse subtly shifted her leg. Now, if he looked — and he did — he could see the edge of her panties. At this point, she began talking to him, as if she'd always known him. She wondered about the book he was reading (*More Poems for People*, by the radical poet Milton Acorn) and asked him if he liked Leonard Cohen and if he was going to Orillia and why (not so much why Orillia, but more a general why, why anything? Why not?). She had some beers in her backpack, and he had a couple of joints, which they smoked with their heads close to the window, carefully blowing the smoke outside so as not to alert the bus driver. Not that he really gave a shit. He probably enjoyed getting high on the job. Soon Wonnacott let his hand slip onto her knee, and she was asking him if he had a place to stay in Orillia and he already answering no. He moved his hand up her leg slowly. Until, that is, she grabbed it and slipped it inside her panties.

"Maybe we could find a place together," she said.

He took another toke and tickled her pubic hair. It was a classic case of lust at first sight.

.　　.　　.

They used to stay up late and listen to the rats. At first she'd been afraid of them. He'd been afraid of them too but hid it better, using her fear as his camouflage. After impaling one of them that first night, she'd slept sitting upright with a cast iron frying pan in her hand. Both of them were wrecked for work the next day; she'd fallen asleep and burnt the macaroni lunch, he got into an argument with the second woman on his list, then packed it in early and got drunk with some Indians in Couchiching Park. In time they grew more comfortable with their roommates. They'd leave out bits of leftovers — there wasn't much; it would have been fairer if the rats left food out for them — and it got to the point where a couple of the bigger, braver rats would eat right out of their hands. Not that any of them were tiny; on average, they were roughly the size and shape of a shoebox. Even the cats, great mousers in their own rights, mostly left the rats alone. By the end of the summer, he and Thérèse had come to see them as friends and more, gnawing, scurrying, voracious gods who watched over them as they slept.

. . .

If misery were a rainbow, the Authors' Breakfast would be at the highest end of the spectrum, a special kind of invisible, ultraviolet misery that only particularly sensitive and habitually mistreated bats could detect. Before the wet eggs and undercooked bacon were served, an asthmatic canon read a meandering prayer, along with several of the longer verses from the Book of Deuteronomy. Then Dutton, standing at attention before a portrait of the Red Ensign (which, to the best of Wonnacott's recollection, hadn't been the country's flag for eleven years) led the group in a rousing chorus of "God Save the Queen." Wonnacott did not join in, although he stood up exceedingly slowly and remained on his feet, shifting his weight from one leg to the other, for the duration of the anthem, just to be polite (and even then, only polite enough). Next the ill-used poetess rose and read a seven-hundred-line epic narrative entitled "The Death of Wolfe," for which she was apparently quite famous locally and, most deservedly, completely unknown everywhere else.

The horse, that steed, the Captain held
Before the mighty General fell'd . . .

And on and on in thumping iambs, until the poem surpassed mere annoyance and entered the realm of almost hypnotic irritation. By the end, Wonnacott's neck hurt from nodding the measure. And just when it seemed the morning could not get any worse, the academic arose. "I have been asked to read one of my favourite of Dr. Leacock's pieces," he said, offering no hint of the plague that was about to descend. "I have selected his master's thesis, *The Doctrine of Laissez Faire*."

It was lunch by the time breakfast ended.

.   .   .

He had the feeling he was being watched. Not looked at, which was to be expected — he was, after all, the conference's star attraction, a best-selling author who'd twice been long-listed for the CBC short story competition (it was a very long longlist, Bob Weaver assured him) and once very seriously considered for a Governor General's award. But this was different. Not captured schoolgirl glances, but burning, clicking, sucking eyes, taking him in, taking him on. When he tried to return eye contact and smile and nod, they (many of them at least) looked away, frowning. Clearly they did not approve of him. He spotted Luellen in the back, a bald husband latched to her arm. She turned her head quickly. But he did not, only grabbing his wife tighter and fixed his eyes on Wonnacott.

After the breakfast, Wonnacott stayed on the podium. Not that he wanted to talk to any of the attendees, or worse, let any of them talk to him, but because he did not want to face the ambush that seemed to wait for him by the doors. Luellen and her husband stood there, he with his arms folded, staring directly at Wonnacott, she cooing, it seemed, to get him to leave with her. Finally Wonnacott decided to escape through the kitchen, but as he pushed his way through the yellow room divider and toward a narrow corridor, Dutton grabbed his arm.

"A word, Mr. Wonnacott, if I may . . ."

He had that familiar look publicists and conference organizers get whenever they have to deliver bad news to writers, a drawn-out, pained smile that would not look out of place in a Edvard Munch painting.

"Ah, Dutton. Great breakfast. Thank you so much."

"The eggs were a little overdone, don't you think?"

"I hardly noticed."

"Excellent. And the room? It's to your liking?" Dutton still held onto his napkin and twisted it obsessively as he spoke.

"I like it fine. It has a fine view of . . . everything."

"Oh, that's fine. Fine!"

"Yes, fine."

"Fine, indeed. I know you used to live here, and thought, you know, the view."

"Yes. Indeed. The view. It really hasn't changed. When I wrote the book . . ."

"I love the book, by the way. *Sunshine Sketches of . . . a . . . Little . . .*"

"*Sunshine Sketches of a Rat-Infested Shitbox.*"

"Yes. Wonderful book. Memoir, is it not?"

"After a fashion."

In the long pause, Dutton twisted his napkin ever more vigorously. Wonnacott was not about to make his job easier. There was an undeclared war between writers and conference organizers — or not a war so much as a destructive dependence. Like mutual parasites, they had to feed off one another to survive.

"Excellent. Lovely. Anyway. There is a small programming change I think you should know about."

"Programming change?"

"Programming change. We'd like to add Humphries to the reading tonight."

"I'm not sure I understand."

"Tonight, at dinner. Humphries is going to read as well."

"But —"

"I'd really hoped to get him more to do this morning, but I couldn't very well interrupt Miss Davis's poem, and everyone else ran on a bit."

"I'll be honest. I'm not sure we'd compliment each other. He's rather more —" Wonnacott struggled for an acceptable euphemism for "dull."

"I know, it's all of a sudden."

"I'd prefer if . . ."

"You'll still be keynote speaker, of course. Everyone will be expecting that."

"I'm . . ."

"We'll just save him for later. An after-dinner treat."

"I'm reading *first*?"

"That would be more appropriate, don't you think?"

"Look, I could see him saying a few words before me, to sort of warm up the crowd. But I am, as you say, the attraction here — in all modesty — and it would be highly unusual — unorthodox — for the keynote speaker to go before . . . someone else."

"I see your point. Perhaps, then, we should make him co-keynote speaker?"

"What?"

"Let's give it some thought, shall we?"

That was that. Dutton had made up his mind. They could stand there for another hour pretending not to argue, or Wonnacott could simply let it go and hope he'd never be asked back.

"It's your call, Dutton."

But there was something else. The grimace, the twisting continued.

"Is that it?"

"There's just one more thing."

"Yes?"

"I'm not really sure how to broach this, so I'll just say it."

"Please."

"I . . . I try to run a tight ship. We — myself and the organizers and volunteers — it's like a family."

"The point being?"

"It's just that, well, frankly, you people blow into town and do your business, and that's really none of my concern, except that I'm the one left standing here to pick up the pieces." Dutton had become quite animated during that last bit, punctuating every other word by pecking his finger in the air. He was intimating some darker purpose, but his point was lost on Wonnacott.

"I'm not sure I . . ."

"I'm talking about Luellen Dupris, Mr. Wonnacott. And I'd appreciate it if you kept your filthy hands off her."

.   .   .

After lunch in his room — soup — Wonnacott had returned to the old house on Park Street. He parked in front of the vacant lot where he and Thérèse used to hunt for garter snakes. The rats, as it turned out, were particularly fond of snakes. Thérèse would cut their heads off, leave them bleeding on the kitchen floor and watch the room fill with rats. She'd named most of them, the regulars anyway: Pratt, PK, Leonard, Archibald, Uncle Milty, Miss Johnson, Purdy. She liked them exactly because other women would have found them repulsive. She liked to be contradictory. One night, after Grace's son had come and set traps in the gutters and attic, killing perhaps a dozen rats in one sortie and ending their nocturnal visits for the summer, Thérèse smoked almost an entire bag of weed on her own. "You know," she said, "youth is a trap that only catches you when it's not there."

"What?"

"I said, youth is a trap that only catches you when it's not there."

"What the hell does that mean?"

Thérèse paused to take another long toke, then started to laugh. She laughed and she laughed and she laughed and she laughed. Wonnacott laughed too. It was, indeed, the stupidest thing she'd ever said.

She would come to say far stupider things than that, and so would he. As the summer came to its close, it seemed that one stupid thing only followed another. And that's when Wonnacott said the stupidest thing of all. Goodbye. One afternoon he'd left her in the Park Street house with their rats and future memories and found a train home on his own. The summer was over. Go big or stay home.

.   .   .

Enter Birdie. They'd started off as friends. Maybe that was the problem. They started off as friends and drifted into lover-hood, quite the opposite of the natural progress of things, in Wonnacott's estimation. Eventually they sank into marriage. And thus they floundered.

She had been his brother's keeper. Literally. She tended to Morgan all through his final illness. Not through the goodness of her heart — although surely her heart was good enough — but in a strictly professional capacity. She'd worked as a home care attendant to put herself through college. Morgan was her attendee.

Birdie and Wonnacott would chat as she wiped or rolled or medicated Morgan. The conversation was pleasant enough: books (she had a distressing interest in the "novels" of Ayn Rand), amateur theatrics, Italian cooking. He'd asked her out once, but even that was platonic: a music recital featuring, as he recalled, several dozen student cellists murdering Bartok. The sex thing started almost by accident. Morgan was asleep, and Wonnacott had called for Birdie with some urgency. He only wanted her to hold a picture while he hammered in the tack. Birdie came running, and when he explained his simple request, she said, as a joke, "Thank God. I thought by the tone of your voice you wanted to kiss me." The veil of friendship was lifted. He looked at her again, took her in his spindly arms and looked some more. She must have been as horny as he was, for when he kissed her — and he must admit, he wasn't a bad kisser — her lips parted like the Red Sea. Clothes were quickly shed and parts of people were pressed into parts of other people. And so they continued as absent lovers, remaining cordial for great stretches before lapsing into another bout of perfect, vicious sex. When Morgan finally died, Wonnacott had no choice. He asked Birdie to marry him. With Morgan gone and several months of sex behind her, Birdie felt obligated. They were friends, after all, and the sex was more than adequate. Yes, she said, yes. Yes.

Yes.

· · ·

Birdie left him on Christmas Eve. She left him passed out under the neighbour's tree. When he came to early in the morning, he found his house missing exactly one wife and one son. He cooked the turkey anyway. He had cold turkey sandwiches for breakfast lunch and dinner till the day after New Year's.

· · ·

Her name was Lee, and she had been the back story in *l'affaire de Wonnacott et Birdie*. A student in his Comparative North American Fictions class at York, she had taken unfair advantage of his weakness for sex with another human being (by this point in their relationship, the Birdie well had pretty much run dry). To be fair, he'd gone into it with his eyes wide open: he knew the young woman had a crush on him, but he accepted her offer of a drink. He knew the risks, although he didn't wholly believe them. Drinks were drunk and drunks were drinking, and Wonnacott accepted a blow job in the front seat of his car. If it had ended there, it might have been manageable. Wonnacott could have lived with the guilt — in its ever diminishing orbit — and persevered. But blow jobs take on a life of their own, and soon *a* blow job became the odd blow job, which soon gave way to the where-the-hell's-my-blow-job. Lee plunged further into infatuation. This particular voyage ended, as these particular voyages do, with a phone call from student to wife. The student declared her everlasting fidelity; the wife, in the difficult position of defending herself by defending her husband (for in these sorts of situations, proprietorship is the key), wholly rejected in the abstract what she knew in the concrete to be true.

.　　.　　.

Wonnacott parked in front of the vacant lot where he and Thérèse used to hunt for garter snakes. He got out and went directly to the front door. It was answered by a thin man who appeared to be almost exactly the same age as Wonnacott. The writer wasn't exactly sure what he was going to say. All he really wanted was to see the room or, to be precise, the view from the room. He'd fixed in his mind a certain picture of that view and associated it with all manner of gnawing nostalgia: the smell of potato peels boiling in an old soup can; the taste of rain and pencil lead; the sound of apples tumbling into a sink; mosquito bites on the back of his hand and that moment of sensual perfection when he finally gave in and scratched. This is what the view meant to him.

Luckily, the man knew of Wonnacott and his work. His name was Turner — Roger, Wonnacott thought, and Beth, or if not Beth, something very much like it. They'd bought the house not long after Wonnacott and Thérèse had moved out.

"It was a mess when we moved in. Of course, no one knew how long she'd been there."

"The police figured six weeks." Beth had entered with coffee.

"We thought it would be perfect for . . ." His voice trailed off. "We always wondered if this was the house." Roger was scouring the bookshelves in the living room. "We knew it was, we just weren't sure."

"I love the scene where the roof collapses, and you spend the night sleeping under the stars." Beth had entered again, carrying a dog-eared copy of *Sunshine Sketches of a Rat-Infested Shitbox*. Hard-cover, first edition. Signed, it might be rather valuable. "I thought it should have won the Governor General's Award." She handed him the book and a fountain pen.

"Politics, you know. It's all politics."

They chatted for a little while, with Beth producing some small cakes and date squares and later fresh butter tarts. "No Canadian on earth can resist," he muttered, taking another.

Eventually, Beth remembered she had another of his books and excavated a tiny volume from under a rubble of old encyclopedias. *Singing with Brambles in My Mouth*, his first chapbook, printed on the mimeograph machine at Thérèse's summer camp.

"We found it in the closet when we moved in. You can have it if you want."

Wonnacott thanked them and put the booklet in his pocket.

And then he asked, if it wasn't too much trouble, if he could just see the room upstairs, for old times' sake. Beth and Roger looked at one another.

"It's a bit of a mess," she said.

"I don't mind, really. It would mean a lot."

"It really is a scramble." His hosts looked at each other again.

"Please?"

Roger slowly rose.

"I'll get the key," he said. "But just a quick look."

The stairway was narrower than Wonnacott remembered, but he instinctively ducked at the corner to avoid hitting his head on the low ceiling. The body, he told himself, never forgets.

The top floor was cold. Not that sweet coolness of a basement in summer, just stale and damp and cold. Roger put the key in the lock.

"We don't come up here much. Not since Jimmy . . ." He looked again at his wife.

"Left. Not since Jimmy left." Beth pushed the door open and turned on the light. The room was immaculate. The tidy bed (the linen seemed fresh), a boy's hockey gear stored neatly in the corner, a shelf of books with the spines ordered in an even line.

"That's where the kitchen was." Wonnacott pointed to a little alcove past the bed, which now housed a walnut armoire. "Of course, it wasn't much of a kitchen." He stepped toward the closet. "And that's where Michele Ferrie slept for . . ."

Both Beth and Roger quickly stepped in front of him. Roger put his shoulder against the door.

"This is locked," he said. "We . . . we don't have the key."

"I'm afraid you'll have to go now, Mr. Wonnacott."

"We have to go out."

"We're going to visit friends."

"It was so nice to meet you."

Wonnacott looked at the small window above the bed; they had covered it with an iron grate. Roger followed his gaze.

"There's been a lot of break-ins around here," he explained. "Now — oh, look at the time. We really have to get moving."

Wonnacott nodded and thought to mention (but did not) that if they were going to bar their windows they better be damned sure they never had to get out.

.   .   .

And so Birdie had been Wife Number One, and not long after that, not counting the two months he waited for Lee to move out after tersely moving in, Wife Number Two (Delores, a real estate agent, don't ask) had come and gone, along with ten years, and then a few more women whom he'd taken a serious run at. At about this time, just as his daily alcohol intake was reaching that of a small Finnish mining enclave, it occurred to him that what he really wanted wasn't a wife, per se. What he really wanted was summer. And not just any summer. The Orillia summer, when love and sex were simple and the same, when the boy was more of a girl and the girl was more of a boy, when anyone with a drink or a toke was his lifelong pal, and where even God's wild creatures (rats, but still) were his friends. The natural, the unnatural and the supernatural merged into one. It was his Summer of Love; his Summer When He'd Conquered Time. He recognized he could never get it back, but he committed himself to the closest approximation possible. The first step was quitting his job at the university and giving himself up fully to his writing. The second step was to sell his share of the house to Wife Number Two and take a funky apartment in an old house near High Park. Toronto wasn't Orillia, but on the other hand, Orillia wasn't Toronto. The third step was much harder. The third step was to recreate Thérèse, or rather the relationship he'd had with her. He started by sending her anonymous postcards of Orillia. Then he moved to sending her a little chocolate rat he'd found in a candy shop on St. Claire. He sent her another, then another, then another — all by special delivery, every one in an unsigned gift-wrapped package. When she finally figured it out and called him (she was surprised how easy it was to find him, she just opened the phone book and there he was), Wonnacott could not speak for a very long time.

"I just wanted to tell you how very, very sorry I am," he said finally, chewing on emotion.

"For what?"

"For . . . for going away."

"Going away?"

"For leaving ."

"Leaving? You didn't leave. You just haven't come home yet."

Two hours later, they were naked on his mattress, on the floor by the fireplace near the window. She was heavier and jaded; he was bonier, with hair where once there'd been muscle. They gnawed into each other's soul and promised never to come out.

·   ·   ·

The dinner was not sold out. Almost half the tables sat empty. Dutton made a valiant effort to convince the guests to move to the tables near the front, in hopes, perhaps, that then the hall wouldn't seem so empty. Most people were content to stay in their places. Humphries had arrived early and sat at a table in the back, frantically marking his book; it wasn't clear whether he was identifying the parts he would read or the parts he wouldn't. Wonnacott leaned against the back wall and smiled, silently composing.

*Most of the things I hate about this country can be summed up
in two words: Stephen Leacock . . .*

It would be, quite literally, the speech to end all speeches;
they'd never ask him back. With luck, no one would. Leacock
was Orillia's favourite son, a writer who, for a brief time after
the First World War, could lay claim to being the most famous
humorist in the world, although by the 1970s, he was largely
forgotten outside of Canada and, inside it, remembered mostly by middle-aged schoolmasters with toast-crumbed beards
and bad breath. But he was routinely presented — and this
was the irritating part — as a paragon of literary excellence,
a shadowing of our primordial, collective summer, when the
world decided we weren't so bad after all. Wonnacott resented
Leacock, true, but not for his success. Rather for his legacy of
diminished expectations. The Eternal Present.

Wonnacott checked his watch. Just enough time for a
quick phone call to his wife and a pre-victory shower.

.   .   .

This time, Luellen hadn't even bothered to remove her coat.

"That's it," Wonnacott declared. "This time I'm calling the
manager."

"Just one minute, please. Just give me one minute." Luellen
shifted her weight, barely making a ripple on the hard mattress.
She sat silently, almost hypnotized by her own breathing.

"Well?"

"Shh."

The leather bra and panties bound her flesh in all the
wrong places.

"I'm waiting."

Then there was a knock on the door.

"Luellen," a voice called from the other side. "I know
you're in there. Come out here this instant."

The woman held her finger to her lips and smiled at Wonnacott. He smiled and fell into the chair.

"Luellen." The man was desperate now. "Open this door
right now, or I'll break it down." There was a pause, then a
loud crash as Luellen's husband fell upon the door.

Wonnacott sighed, enlightened. "Have you ever thought of
counselling?"

Luellen shrugged.

"You have to forgive my husband. He's not very worldly,
you understand. He's at that age; he's afraid that life has
passed him by."

Her husband threw himself against the door one more
time and then slipped to the floor. He was whimpering now
and muttering her name with each breath. Luellen stood
up and pulled her coat close to her shoulders. She thanked
Wonnacott and left, walking headlong, Wonnacott realized,
into an Orillia summer of her own.

. . .

Somewhere the sun was rising. Somewhere young lovers were
lying together in the net of summer, licking the dry salt off
each other's tanned and perfect skin. Somewhere, maybe, a
bird was singing, although, to be truthful, who listens to
birds any more? They were irritants, mostly. Perhaps even
somewhere in that fine little township of Orillia, a man and a
woman were now coming together, holding onto one another
in defence of history, in defiance of time. For all he could tell,
Luellen and her husband were screwing right now in the front
seat of their car, parked down by the lakeshore, basking in the
conspiratorial shade of Champlain Monument. Wonnacott
could not know and did not care. He sat on the bed, naked
except for his t-shirt, the receiver still to his ear, the dial tone still
buzzing like a crowing bee, his finger still holding down the

switch, stuck between hanging up and putting down. His face was probably quite comical, halfway between a smile and a frown. A fmile. A srown. That was it. A bemused srown.

.   .   .

The encounter had begun like this.

Wonnacott sitting on the bed, soup on the boil. "Did I wake you, love?"

Thérèse yawned, then lowered her voice. "I was waiting for your call . . ."

It had ended like this.

The sound of a man coughing. Then the sound of a man trying to suppress a cough. Then the sound of a man, comically no doubt, stumbling to the floor as he fell out of bed trying to suppress his cough as another man, on the other end of a phone, tried not to listen to the sound of the man stumbling to the floor as he fell out of bed trying to suppress his cough. Then a man hanging up the phone abruptly, pushing the switch down with his finger and lifting it again. Then the sound of the dial tone, buzzing like a crowing bee.

Go big or stay home.

.   .   .

The Mariposa Belle was on fire before Wonnacott had even been booed off the podium. It had started, the Fire Marshall would later conclude, on an unauthorized hotplate in a guest room. But Wonnacott had already left the hotel by the time the alarms went off. He had liberated Leacock's bust and gown and mortarboard and Indian gun from the display case, employed a little ruse to borrow one of the volunteer drivers' cars, and used another little ruse (and, okay, a threat) to gain entrance to the Park House.

From below, Wonnacott hears the chief of police hail him on the loudspeaker. He wants to know Wonnacott's demands. *Let's not do nothing foolish*, he says.

Wonnacott laughs. A double negative. Perfect. *Come and get me, copper.*

Wonnacott stands up quickly and pulls off the Robes of State. But the mortarboard stays. A nice touch.

He gropes for the switch to the overhead light and turns it off.

The lamp beside the bed illuminates the room, casting monster shadows on the walls.

Wonnacott lies back on the mattress again. In the distance he hears a siren wail like a heard of crowing bees. A fire truck for the Belle? Or maybe more cops, cops from as far away as Bracebridge, Barrie, Collingwood, Wasaga Beach . . .

Outside he hears muffled voices and the shuffling of troops. The Turners are still at it, agitating the neighbours. Telling tales out of class. *Who knows what this man might do? He is, after all a writer, and capable of anything.*

Wonnacott reaches up and shuts off the lamp. The room goes dark. From this vantage he can see the flames rising from the Mariposa Belle.

He closes his eyes.

In the distance, he hears a faint sound, beyond the gossip and organized silence. It might have been a child coughing, or the soft scratch scratching as, a very long way off, all the rats of the world are joining together to burrow into the maw of a perfect, sinking summer. He sighs and gets to his feet, and lifting the Indian gun he moves to the window to take aim and give the nearest police sharpshooter a lesson in history.

The Man with a Thousand Wives

Dimitri noticed his wife deliberately not looking at the man in the booth. He pretended to flip through the book she had given him to celebrate her promotion: an antique Grimms' fairy tales in mint condition. The pages, although yellow along the edge, were still white, and many were not cut.

"Nobody likes a fat accountant." Dimitri rubbed his thin belly, carefully watching his wife's eyes to see if they would betray her. "You always let me eat too much."

"Sorry, dear." She talked through her nose, imitating the whiny wife of his imagination.

Outside the Funky Chicken Dimitri pretended to blow his nose in a twenty dollar bill. "I saw you looking at him."

"At who?"

"'At who?'" Dimitri exaggerated her innocence. "Don't give me that. At Dumbo in the booth across from us."

"Now I forget, which one was Dumbo?"

"Dumbo, the one with the ears in the booth across from us."

Dimitri's wife shook her head slowly. "No, you'll have to be more specific. Which one of my secret lovers was it?" She was very good at this.

"I said, it was Dumbo. The one with the ears. Wearing a grey jacket. Smoking a cigarette with just two fingers, you know, waving his cigarette like a magician, holding it between two little fingers and flicking it with his little thumb. In the booth across from us."

"What booth? The one by the ceramic mule?"

"What booth? You know the one I'm talking about. Right by the bathroom door."

"Ah yes, where my lovers always sit, in case they have to beat a hasty retreat or retire to pluck some offending hair from their nostrils. Remind me again, what did he look like?"

"How should I know? He's your lover. I could only see him from the back. That little bald triangle at the point of his tiny head, those big, galumphing ears that flap when you kiss them. Tell me, what's it like to kiss a man with a trunk?"

"Jealous?"

"Ah-ha!"

"Ah-ha what, Dick Tracy?"

"You can always tell when a woman is cornered. She attacks your masculinity, it's a sure sign. Come, tell me, where did you meet him? At the health spa, jiggling around in his little circus tights? At Safeway, pinching tomatoes and stealing peanuts?"

"How much did you drink tonight, anyway? I think you're sufferings from the DTs."

"Don't try to change the subject. I want to know, for reference. Where did you meet him? Was it one of those ads: 'Horny chimpanzee with large ears, etcetera, seeks well-endowed companion to service. Discretion assured and expected.'"

"How did you know? Did you read it in the paper?"

"I didn't have to. It's written all over your face."

"Still? I thought I washed it off last night."

"Make jokes if you want to. She who jokes confesses."

"That's deep, Confucius. Now give me the keys. You're not driving anywhere."

Dimitri held the keys up to the streetlight. "Look," he rattled them. "The Star of Bethlehem." His wife grabbed the keys and unlocked the passenger door. Dimitri fumbled in his coat pocket. "And don't think I haven't forgotten your lover. Don't think you're fooling anyone, I know the likes of you, young

— have you seen my keys? — young lady. You're not the first wife I've had, you're only one of many. Hundreds. Thousands." Dimitri tried to open the car door with his left hand. "I've studied the feminine psyche. I know how it works. Ah . . . you have them. A clever ploy."

Dimitri's wife started the car in silence. She craned her neck to check for traffic coming up from behind before she slipped onto the road. Her grey and black hair was pulled into a bun; she looked old and severe. Dimitri tapped the bun. "I love it when you look nasty." His wife smiled. Dimitri closed his eyes and tried not to think of his stomach, too full and upset with alcohol. "Just tell me one thing." Dimitri realized he was slurring. "What did you find so attractive about this lover of yours? He looked like a pineapple with ears and sideburns." His wife smiled again and did not speak. Dimitri wondered how she could still love him.

Waiting for them at home was a large bouquet of red and white roses. "Ah-ha!" Dimitri pointed to the flowers, then wagged his finger at his wife. "An elephantine gesture if ever there was one. Let's decipher . . ." He opened the card buried at the bottom of the bouquet.

"Congratulations, Winnie, on your promotion. Yours, Frank."

Dimitri thought for a moment, scrapping the card across his thin beard, the kind of beard that some men grow to hide their bad skin but Dimitri wore in a vain effort to look debonair.

"Hmm. Obviously it's in code. What do you think it means, honey?"

His wife said, "It beats me," and Dimitri thought, she's humouring me now.

"That's one thing about your lovers: they're so . . . sensitive." Dimitri got the bottle of scotch from the shelf above the fridge. He filled two mismatched tumblers with ice and poured. "I propose a toast." He handed one tumbler to his wife and held his glass aloft. "To your new job: Vice President, Employee Relations."

"And congratulations to you. You got the title right for once."

"Thank you." He took a gulp, then put his tumbler on the coffee table. "I just need to know one thing. Does that mean you have relations with every employee, or just some?"

"That all depends on what day of the week it is."

Dimitri sat down on the couch and tried to undo his shoes. The laces kept slipping from his fingers as he swayed from side to side. Finally he gave up. He sat up straight and tried to cross his legs, succeeding instead in kicking the coffee table and knocking over his scotch. "It's official." He held one arm up in victory. "I'm pissed." Dimitri bent forward and wiped the spill with his jacket sleeve.

"Frank, Frank, Frank," he said. "Do we know a Frank? It's not our old friend Frank Furter of Frankfort, is it? He's a diabolical dog. I can't believe you'd sleep with him."

"I believe, unless I'm mistaken, that Frank is that brother you've had for forty-one years."

Dimitri covered his ears. "My own brother. Is nothing sacred?"

The black cat, Adolph, paraded into the room. He stopped by the coffee table, spread his paws and stretched to the end of his tail. "Precious," Dimitri sang, smacking his lips to call the cat. "Hi, kitty. Hi, precious." His wife, too, saw the cat. She knelt down near the kitchen door and scratched the carpet, smacking her lips. The cat rolled towards her and rubbed his head on her thigh. She picked him up and hugged him.

"You know, he likes me better." Dimitri picked up Grimms' from the coffee table and opened to the title page. *Grimms' Tales, from "Kinder und Hausmarchen."* Thomas Lloyd McKenzie & Son, Publisher, 1883. "He only pretends to like you because you feed him. In the army, we used to call people like him brown-nosers."

"You were never in the army."

"Is that so? Oh, of course, I'm *married*. I always get the two mixed up."

Dimitri ran his finger down the table of contents. "You know, I've always wanted a book. Really, ever since I was a young man. A book like this is a good investment, look after you in your old age. When your cat is dead and buried and the rest of the world has left you to rot, a book will remain by your side. True blue. Dependable." Dimitri flipped the pages. "I'm looking for a story called 'The Man with a Thousands Wives.' Do you know it? It's about an accountant who has a harem of women at his disposal. He changes women like other men change ties, depending on weather, social occasion and mood." Dimitri put the book back on the coffee table. "It's based, I think, on a true story." He looked up. Adolph sat on the floor near the kitchen doorway, staring at him. His wife was nowhere to be seen. The cat jumped onto the coffee table, then into Dimitri's lap. Dimitri stroked the length of his back. "You're lucky," he said. "A cat has only nine wives. A man has a thousand, each more deceitful and troublesome than the next."

Adolph looked up and mewed. Dimitri was certain the cat understood.

He was falling asleep when he wife came into the room and declared, "Well." On its own that single word suggested more to follow, which always meant bad news to Dimitri. Coming from his wife, it was even more alarming. She always spoke in complete thoughts. Simple noun-verb-noun sentences, like they teach in a foreign language class.

"Well, what?"

"That was your brother."

"Well, what did he say?"

"He's just been to the hospital."

(Noun-verb-noun). "Again?"

"Again."

"Is he coming over?"

"No. He just wanted to talk."

Dimitri looked at his watch. Ten-thirty. "It's getting late."

Dimitri's brother had the unbelievable number of seven children, which included two sets of twins. He did not live in a shoe, as Dimitri often expected, but in a very nice house on the edge of the woods that circled the university. Frank, a lawyer, made more money than even a man with seven children could use. Once, three years ago, Frank's wife was supposed to do the laundry. Instead, she decided to drink what was left of a bottle of bleach. Now his oldest daughter was in and out of hospital all the time. She was, the doctor said, schizophrenic. She heard voices, voices that suggested she kill herself.

"Frank has just been to the hospital, ergo we can conclude that Kitty's hearing voices?" Dimitri said to no one.

"Do you want another?" Dimitri's wife shook the scotch bottle, a mute bell.

"Well, I really shouldn't. It's getting late. Just half a cup." Dimitri took a sip, then shivered. "That'll warm me up. You know, you never told me about the man in the restaurant. Who is he?"

"Dumbo? He's been my lover for six years now. I met him while you were at a linguists' conference in Montreal. Don't let his big ears and pointy head fool you. He's very hot in bed."

"Well, you know what they say about men with big ears."

"No. What?"

"I don't know, I thought you knew." Dimitri's wife sat on the piano bench, her body on the edge of a corner, barely touching it seemed. She held the tumbler of scotch in her lap with both hands, her head bowed, her eyes lightly closed. Was she meditating or fighting back a migraine? Her red lipstick smeared at one corner of her lips, and she looked like a cartoon drunk, although Dimitri believed she was very likely sober. She looked old and tired. "You know, you remind me so much of my first wife."

"Really?"

"Yes. She was a bitch too."

Dimitri's wife smiled for a moment, then sighed. "He has so many children."

Dimitri woke shivering. He had slid off the couch so that only one leg, the one with the shoe at the end of it, was elevated. His tie had folded onto his face. He pulled himself to his knees, then pushed up to his feet, using the couch and coffee table for support. His head throbbed, and he wondered for a moment if he might not vomit. This is why he never drank. He picked his jacket and Grimms' from the floor and stood tottering. He saw the light on upstairs in the bedroom.

Dimitri's wife lay facing the wall, the down comforter pulled over her shoulder. Dimitri slipped onto the bed and softly shook her, realizing at that he was still elegantly hammered.

"I want to know the truth. If you had any secrets, you'd tell me, right?"

"But then they wouldn't be secrets. Besides, even if I told you any, you'd forget them by morning. That's why I love you."

The wind blew against the house. The floorboards creaked. "Did you hear that?" Dimitri asked, his voice hushed. "I believe there is a presence in this house trying to communicate with us."

"Yes. And it's saying, shut up and go to sleep."

Dimitri removed his tie and dropped it on the floor.

"I have a confession to make. I threw the book you gave me in the fire. I'm sorry. I don't know why I did it. I can't believe I would do something like that. Sometimes I can't believe the things that go on in my head, almost on their own. Almost without me being aware of what they're doing.

"Really?" She was very tired.

Dimitri nodded. "I'm sorry. It was a lovely gift, it really was."

"I didn't know the fire was plugged in."

Dimitri shrugged. "Perhaps I stuffed it down the Garburator, then. My recollection is hazy at best."

She turned her head to get a better look at him. "That's all right," her voice was dreamy. "I'll get you another. Chapters had a sale on limited first editions."

Dimitri sat on the edge of the bed and undressed. Sometimes he wished he had a thousand secrets he could tell his wife. Sometimes he wished that she did not know him so well, that maybe she did not know him at all. Instinctively, she knew the number of hairs on his back, the weight of his breath, the sound of his spine when he turned his head.

Dimitri lay down and turned off the lamp on the bedside table. "I think there is a presence in this house trying to communicate." He spoke in a whisper.

He closed his eyes and imagined himself sitting on a tropical beach, surrounded by antique books with perfect, uncut pages.

"Honey?" Dimitri's lone wife rolled over and put her arm around his waist.

"Yes dear?"

"Surprise me."

Dimitri lay very still for a long, long time, then reached over and touched his wife very gently on the cheek.

"Once upon a time," he said, "they all lived happily ever after."

Mitzou

Sometimes you chase the stick; sometimes the stick chases you.
— Canine proverb

Mitzou, the bichon frise, began growing shortly after Kevin moved out. Psychologists have noted that perhaps the unusual developments were related to the move. It marked a significant change in the family dynamic; with Kevin gone to the New York School of Divinity, Paul and Deborah Wallace were officially empty nesters. Kate had moved out two years before, having taken a job as a telephone repairperson in Albuquerque, and Rosalita hadn't been seen since the night she left in a huff in her boyfriend Joaquim's yellow Ferrari. There'd been pictures, sure: Joaquim and Rosalita at the Grand Canyon; Rosalita and Joaquim on the observation deck of the Eiffel Tower (which Deborah always called *la tour Eiffel*, much to Paul's annoyance), with Joaquim comically, and rather dangerously, hanging from the railing by one hand; Joaquim, Rosalita and megastar Jack Nicholson taking in a Lakers game at LA's Great Western Forum. But while pictures spoke a thousand words, they never said quite the right words, and this, in all truth, left a bitter taste, a chocolate-covered espresso bean minus the chocolate coating, in Paul and Deborah's emotional mouths. But that didn't explain Mitzou, the bichon frise, despite what some mental health professionals whispered to one another behind closed and bolted office doors.

It began simply enough. Paul and Deborah noticed something was up. Nothing they could put their fingers on, mind, but something. A kind of lethargy perhaps, but lethargy wasn't exactly the right word. Reluctance. Yes. A kind of reluctance to get on with it, whatever it was that a bichon frise might get on with. Mitzou no longer wolfed her dinner down, taking on, instead, a mewing disinterest. They tried different brands — of course they did — and switched from dry to soft to straight-from-the-can to butcher fresh and back again. But the spark, the Itness with which Mitzou once enjoyed, once attacked her din-dins was lost. And the malaise didn't stop at dinner. The old tricks, she was not up to them. Her "sit" (or "*zitz!*" as Deborah coyly, annoyingly preferred; he had come to loathe her fluency in Eastern European languages) was half-hearted, more a free-form expression of a sigh than a sit; her "speak!" ("*mówi!*") was alternately guttural or whiney, lacking its usual — and here's that word again — spark. Paul could still hear her bark in his mind's ear, sharp and thick, like a little electrical shock, the kind of shock he got from the bedroom door handle on a cold morning when he wore his socks instead of his slippers, only magnified two hundred times. Once she was fetching, now it was out of the question. Paul might throw a stick or Mr. Tinkles, the plastic postman toy with a bell inside, her favourite chewy, but Mitzou would barely raise her eye. Before — well, before there'd be no stopping her. But after the . . . reluctance set in, there was no getting her going.

"Maybe she's just overtired," Deborah said in the evening as they lay on their heated king-sized waterbed.

"That's your explanation for everything," Paul said rather tersely, then added, "lamb chop."

"I know. I was just thinking. Maybe she's not sleeping well. Maybe all she needs is a good sleep." Deborah rolled over and shut her eyes. A moment later she was snoring loudly. Paul looked over at her and thought, for just a second really, how easy it would be right now to kill Deborah, smother her with a pillow or put his hands around her neck and squeeze. She'd struggle, of course, Paul had seen enough TV to know that. He leaned over and kissed his wife and returned to his book: Churchill's massive *History of the English Speaking Peoples.*

"She's not overtired," he said under his breath, and he repeated the sentence once more in his own head, just to be certain.

And then Mitzou grew. At first Paul and Deborah were encouraged by the change. It provided a rational explanation for her . . . reluctance. She had been storing up energy, banking her reserves; what dog — what person — would not have done the same? The growth itself was odd, to be sure, but not unprecedented. Her grandfather, Ovid, added ten pounds and six inches from tip to tail when he was six years old, while her maternal great-great aunt Magellan, if the rumours were to be believed, had extensive growth spurts at age four and again at age twelve (bichon frise are an exceptionally long-lived breed; sixteen or seventeen years is the norm, and twenty-three-year-old specimens are not uncommon). But Mitzou didn't stop at a few pounds or a few inches. She grew and grew, like an unchecked credit card debt or some cursed pet in a comical, cruel folk tale. Soon she was the size of a mid-to-big-sized dog, a standard poodle, say, or a fuzzy sheep dog, the kind that used to figure prominently in Disney films and other family pictures.

The vet assured them it was biochemical. "The hormones are out of balance, and this is causing her unusual growth." He had a deep, quite voice and several diplomas on his wall including, Paul noted, a baccalaureate from the New York School of Divinity; surely this was a good sign.

"When will she stop growing?"

Dr. Tomlinson ran his hand through his beard. "It's hard to tell in a case like this. Days? Weeks? Years?"

And over the coming days, weeks and years Mitzou grew

and grew and grew. They tried a range of remedies: hormone therapy, vitamin therapy, laser therapy, behavioural therapy, acupuncture, obedience school, even, in a fit of desperation soon regretted, exorcism by a disreputable-looking priest who had demanded payment in advance.

Nothing helped.

Paul and Deborah did not enjoy owning a big dog. Besides the obvious problems (food bills, waste disposal, etc.), there were serious personal consequences. At first their friends tried to be supportive, making humorous remarks about food bills and waste disposal, referring to her — at first jokingly but, over time, less so — as Clifford and consoling Paul and Deborah whenever they expressed concern for the mental health of their "li'l Mitzi." But gradually, almost proportionately in fact, their friends grew distant. Hostile. It was a kind of frightened hostility, Paul reckoned, not unexpected in the face of something as unusual as this, as unprecedented. Mitzou was a big dog and getting bigger all the time, like a boil on the face that wouldn't stop growing or a heartache that expanded exponentially each day. Mitzou's breeding didn't help, her bichon-friseness. A snappy breed at the best of times, affectionate, yes, and intelligent, but stubborn and high-strung (they'd known this going in) and, if the truth be told, almost impossible to housetrain (this had come as a surprise). Paul had hoped that the essence, the bichon-friseness, would dissipate as she grew larger. But she remained a little dog in a big dog's body — yappy, snappy, snippy, hyper — if not more so, as if her essential bichon-friseness grew along with the rest of her. And who could blame her if it did? She certainly hadn't asked to become a big dog, and it must have been terribly frightening for her. (It was Kevin who reminded everyone that this whole experience was just as stressful for Mitzou as it was for the family, and as Paul nodded in agreement he realized that perhaps the move to the New York School of Divinity hadn't been such a bad one after all.) In any case, this expanded, exaggerated bichon-friseness (Mitzou was drifting dangerously close to self-parody, Paul admitted to himself) did not sit well with Paul and Deborah's friends and acquaintances. In a small dog these little quirks were one thing; they were, well, little. In a big dog it was a whole nother story: they were big quirks. Paul was no longer certain who was the master of the house.

Paul had never wanted a bichon frise in the first place. There was something . . . unmanly about the breed. Not that manliness was an ongoing issue for him (at least he hoped it wasn't). It's just that he felt — what was the word? — silly. Walking that little tiny dog, and he such a big man himself, something of a sportsman still, a wrestler in college, a big man with big hands, wrestler's hands. A hound dog was more suited to him, or a black lab. That was it, a black lab with a red bandana round his neck, with a soft mouth for collecting birds and a laid-back attitude for lazing by a fire or sleeping in the Sunday sun. The bichon frise, that was Deborah's idea. And why? If the truth be told, Paul had always suspected that the dog was nothing more than a status symbol. He hated to say so, but his wife was in many ways a shallow person (of course, that's what you get for marrying a beautiful woman, some might say). They'd got Mitzou when the breed was popular in certain circles, just as it reached the apex of its popularity, in fact, despite Deborah never having expressed the slightest interest in owning a dog before. Paul tried to appear happy when she brought the dog home, at least tried to not appear unhappy for the sake of the kids, but he almost shit his pants when he saw how much she'd paid for the thing.

"Twelve hundred dollars for a lousy . . . I'm not made of . . ."

It was one of those conversations.

But in time Mitzou grew on him, metaphorically speaking. He accepted the inherent comedy of their relationship, the amusing size difference often accentuated by the tiny raincoats and mufflers Deborah insisted the dog wear for walkies in inclement weather. In time he grew fond of the pet, quite fond, and not despite her foibles but, to use a cliché, because of them. She was like a glacier or the military-industrial-congressional complex: never changing, or changing so imperceptibly over time as to be more a comfort than a concern. But now, of course, she was changing all the time, changing in an unpleasantly predictable way: getting bigger.

At first, Paul and Deborah talked about it. A lot. In fact, for a long time — months and months — it was practically the only thing they talked about. And when they weren't talking about it, they were talking around it or towards it or to avoid the topic altogether, which is not much different from talking about it. Of course, other people talked about it too, at the start. Politely, at least when Paul and Deborah were in earshot. The press also took an interest: an article in the local paper, and a television news crew had come down from New York to film Mitzou, who uncooperatively licked herself the entire time the cameras were there. The report never made it to air.

But in time everyone simply stopped talking about the situation. Mitzou the bichon frise grew and grew and grew, reaching unheard of dimensions without remark. Paul and Deborah went on — persevered — as if nothing had happened. They'd speak to her — "No!" ("*nej!*"); "Hurry up!" ("*požurite!*"); "Come" ("прйезжаю") — assuming an air of normalcy, but they would not speak about her. In fact, in time they barely spoke at all, particularly to each other, because everything they could say or would say or might say would have somehow, in either a positive or negative sense, brought them back to a discussion (or non-discussion, which was just as bad if not worse) of the big dog. Paul, desperate, wondered if Deborah felt the same. At night, alone together in their king-sized waterbed, that enormous heaving tongue between them, Paul sometimes tried to reach across the gulf of dog and hold

Deborah's hand or a strand of her hair, for even a strand of her hair was warm in his fingers, vibrant, like a high vibrato note from a gypsy cello, and comforted his big, big hand.

And then Mitzou was gone. It happened shortly after Kevin returned from the New York School of Divinity. They did not check the kitchen or the back yard, they did not post bulletins on telephone poles in the neighbourhood, they did not check the lost and found ads in the paper. They just quietly held their breath, for days it seemed. They did not want to dare to believe that the big dog was gone and awaited her return at every moment. But they did not see her again. "I miss the big dog," Paul thought of saying once or twice. But he never did.

Kevin took up his old quarters in the back bedroom. He brought word of Kate, who was doing well keeping the good people of Albuquerque connected, and a long, long letter from Rosalita, with whom he'd spent several wonderful months on a motor holiday in the south of France. Of course, psychologists suggested that Kevin's return to the family nest triggered the end of the big dog. But Kevin speculates that the dog had not disappeared and in fact had not stopped growing, and that perhaps she only reached a particular critical point at which volume and density and mass and light converged to render the object (the "dogject" as Kevin jokingly called it) too vast to contemplate, invisible to the naked eye, although perhaps visible through sophisticated X-ray, gamma-ray or ultraviolet-light sensing equipment. Paul, in keeping with his newfound respect for the intelligence and insight of his youngest, tended to agree, and at night, for months afterwards, he clung to his wife like death in case the big dog came back and tried to nuzzle her way between them again.

The Medusa Project

Étienne's hands were trembling. He'd come to rely on their steadiness, his ability to control them. He was a heart surgeon, after all. And now he'd lost his composure like a stupid school-girl.

His hands had let him down.

.   .   .

Paul Antiphon says hello.

That was it. Nothing really, a trifle. And the Pole had trifled with him before. So why did it strike a chord this time? Perhaps it was the surgical precision with which he threw out the name. There was a Paul Antiphon, at least there had been (although the chance of his saying hello was negligible). Clearly the Pole just threw out the remark to see his reaction. He had a name, but at this point it was just a jumble of sounds. Madrn needed Étienne to translate. Madrn needed Étienne to make sense of the sounds.

They'd seen each other on and off for years, perhaps ever since Étienne had come to Toronto. There was something quite unlikable about this fellow, something mostly about the eyes. Small eyes, dark but not pleasantly so, placed too close together, lending the journalist an air of imbecility. They said Madrn had escaped his country through a daring midnight flight in a hand-made hot air balloon; they said that, for a time, he'd worked for the Polish branch of the KGB, building up the confidence of the state as all the while he plotted his escape. None of this played in his favour. Étienne did not trust this cultivated air of mystery. A man with something to hide does not advertise.

"We should talk sometime, hmm? We should get together and talk about the old times in Quebec City. I'll bet you have some stories to tell . . ."

Étienne arched his eyebrows and smiled, feigning fond remembrance of those Quebec summers.

"I'm a very busy man, Mr. Madrn," he said, in a perfectly modulated tone. But his hands — his hands were trembling and trembled still as he rode the subway home.

"Let's talk, hmm?" he says. His French is a tad too cultivated. "We can talk, comrade, can't we?"

He could smell jet fuel now, they must be near the airport, must be heading east.

He takes that to be a good sign.

The van brakes sharply, sending Madrn sliding forward to the front of the box. He can taste blood in his mouth and feels his lip with his tongue. He is cut, all right. But it is nothing.

He tries to peek out of one of the air holes to get a sense of where he might be. They were the first thing he'd noticed, the air holes. That meant they wanted to keep him alive.

He can see nothing outside his box. They are on the highway, that is clear. The road is too straight; they are moving too fast. He'd drifted in and out of sleep a couple of times, so it is impossible for him to tell how long they've been driving. But it is still dark. That is a good sign. They couldn't have gone too far, and it would be light soon.

. . .

In 1959, Maurice Duplessis, Quebec's autocratic premier, died after sixteen unbroken years in office. A Jew-hating, anti-union, anti-communist despot, Duplessis clung to his position by graft, patronage, and the support of a corrupt clergy that, in comparison, made him seem saintly. But he made the trains run on time, as the Italians say: the province's schools and roads doubled in number; hospital beds tripled; electricity was brought to even the most remote corner of Quebec. Besides, he was not so out of place. He came from an age where people still believed in gods, still entrusted themselves to marble men. People then were comfortable with demi-despots.

Within a year of Duplessis's death, the Liberal party slunk into power in Quebec, and the province became acquainted with an enlightened mix of young intellectuals — Quebec nationalists of a sort — and older, devoted federalists, who rejected the tyranny of Duplessis and the church, in that order. Étienne had known many of this second group personally, not that they would admit it now. After the war, they'd opened their homes to him, they'd sought his opinion of the Liberation, which they spoke of with more disdain than he could muster, Laurentia, the Terror (which they humourlessly parodied in their own vision of the Duplessis years as *La Grande Noirceur*, the Great Darkness) and the politics of Rome. As nationalists, they shared to a degree Étienne did not an ideological sympathy with fascism and, in particular, National Socialism of the Vichy variety. Looked at in its most charitable light, ultranationalism seemed the perfect antidote to the ills inherent in internationalism. These Quebec nationalists could never understand that for Étienne collaboration (a term, by the way, Étienne was comfortable with, although they would never use it) had been perfectly pragmatic. His uncle, a provincial mayor, had had friends in Vichy; Étienne's conversion was a matter of course, and, if not a pre-requisite to survival, it certainly offered the family a level of comfort and security scarce in those times.

No one mentioned Vichy anymore. The war years had been swallowed whole. Étienne was forgotten too, more or less, which suited him fine. Not long ago, he'd run into one of the *action français* men, a federal cabinet minister, at a fund-raiser for the new clinic. Once they had regularly drunk together at the Kerhulu. Now they shook hands as impervious strangers — statues — and chit-chatted about sports. Their eyes twinkled a little, of course, although at this point in their lives, laughter was beyond either of them. Their joke, and quarrel, was with history, and there it would remain.

"Quebec City? I also spent some time there, after the war," the minister said. He wore a silver chain around his neck that held a small medallion depicting St. Christopher, the patron saint of travellers.

"Yes. After the war."

"That was a long time ago."

"A long time."

"You were a student too?"

"I was an . . . émigré."

"Ah, yes. A long time."

For a split second they stood frozen, partially impressed with their own shadow play and partially afraid to go on lest they say something they might regret. They shook hands and parted, but the exchange was not lost on Anna. Exchanges never were.

"Who was that?"

"A cabinet minister, I think."

"You didn't know him?"

"No."

"You seemed to know him quite well."

"How so?"

"I don't know. There was something in your manner. It seemed familiar."

"We might have met before, at Laval. We could not be certain."

Anna knew there was more to the story — there was always more. But she did not push it. She never did. She was the perfect wife. An afterthought.

.   .   .

Étienne saw another statue at the fundraiser, posing by the artist's rendering of the new Toronto Cardiology Clinic, talking to Dr. Blair, chairman of the hospital board, and that slithering journalist Madrn, holding on to her champagne glass with one hand while girlishly tracing a line in the condensation with a free finger. She may have been flirting with one of the men, or both. It had been twenty-five years. Predictably, Thérèse's wonderful, youthful voluptuousness had lost the battle to time and gravity. She was still pretty, he supposed. Handsome. But the size . . .

Étienne ducked into the atrium. He did not want to see her, or rather, he did not want her to know that she had been seen by him. It would be embarrassing for both of them. He'd aged well enough: slim for fifty, greying in a distinguished way, like an actor or an existential philosopher. But Thérèse would no doubt be self-conscious about her weight; how could she not? He would be looking at her through the eyes of youth, and she would feel naked and ashamed for having transformed, in an instant of sorts, into a very old, very large woman. Étienne positioned himself behind a potted palm and peeked again. Had he really been in love with her? Had she really been as beautiful as he remembered? They'd been together only months or weeks and made love eight or nine times. But Étienne had revisited each encounter a thousand times. Could he ever go back to it?

"Tell me, who is that woman there, talking to Blair?" Étienne had grabbed Shulman's elbow. The intern apologized for not having his glasses and strained to see.

"That's what's-her-name, the alderwoman."

"Alderwoman?"

"Yes, I think."

"Thérèse?"

"Yes. That's it. Her husband's a writer or something. Lefty, you know — a socialist."

Shulman said something else to continue the conversation, but Étienne had moved on. A kind of panic had seized him, and he decided that he and his wife should leave at once. Anna was standing where he'd left her, talking to the reeve about flowers. A passionless man, the reeve had ensnared Anna in a Gregorian monotone that barely subsided as Étienne took his wife's arm and led her in the general direction of the door.

"We really must be going . . . tremendous event . . . the clinic . . ."

Étienne tried to think of some triviality to add but could not. So he smiled and nodded, implying something deeper.

Anna came quietly. Parties she could take or leave. If her husband was ready to go, she was ready to go with him. She was so uncomplicated, this sturdy Upper Canadian.

Then the statue appeared again, placed now by the doorway, talking loudly to the director, who was holding her coat. The sleeve was inside out, and had tangled. The slack muscle and fat of Thérèse's arm had bound with the fabric somehow and pinned one arm behind her back. She did not stop talking. This was the last thing Étienne wanted — to come face-to-face with this former lover at the doorway, his wife in tow. It would have been too horrible, too awkward. They would have to be introduced and coyly remember each other, then

Thérèse would see Anna, already so much younger than Étienne, and start to feel self-conscious, and that, *that* would be enough to let everyone know (the director, Anna) that he and Thérèse had once slept together. It was an embarrassment they could all do without.

"Drink, my dear?" He piloted Anna toward the bar counter, and not a moment too soon, as he heard the director calling his name from behind.

"Dr. du Chatelait? Doctor?"

"I thought you wanted to leave." Anna was perplexed.

"No, my dear. I was merely saving you from that awful drone."

"He can go on."

"He certainly can, my dear. He certainly can."

Étienne signalled the bartender with one finger, then called for two gin and tonics. They'd barely started their drinks when he had the curious thought of making Thérèse his lover again. He smiled a little, and Anna, thinking he was smiling at her in that adoring way husbands sometimes did in laundry commercials, smiled back. It was a private joke, of course: Thérèse did nothing for him. Anna was vastly more attractive, not to mention Dr. Cole. An occasional affair was one thing a wife could always forgive. But to cheat on Dr. Cole . . . to cheat on his mistress? It seemed almost too wicked to contemplate.

Every negotiation is a shared lie that starts when one party tells the other, "I will not negotiate." Every negotiation, every marriage vow, every death begins this way.

How did they know? No doubt someone in the RCMP had ratted him out. It was never a good idea to make deals with the cops, it was never a good idea to make deals with anyone. But life was a series of deals and deals within deals, with new ones coming up always to replace the broken promises and lies. That was the nature of his business: survival. Information was Madrn's currency, and it required considerable investment to keep him going.

That he'd double-crossed the Front — the FLQ — well, it was expected of him. Now they would want something in return. Madrn was ready to negotiate.

The van turned sharply, sending Madrn and his box skidding across the floor. The crate jammed into the side panel, smashing Madrn's ring finger. He swore quickly in Polish, realizing that this was the first time he had spoken his mother tongue in — what? — four years?

"You should be a little more careful," he said, good naturedly. He could tell now they were off the highway. The road was bumpier and had many curves. He folded his arms across his chest as the crate skidded around this way and that. "Maybe I should drive," he said, laughing to stress that his remark was a joke. He wanted to show them he was a good guy. He wanted to show them that he was on their side.

So he saw an old lover at a party, and now he was upset. It would be easy enough to dismiss the queasy feeling as Étienne's vanity, the dilemma of the middle-aged man who did not wish to acknowledge that time was conquering even him. But there were more practical concerns. After his arrival from France, Étienne hadn't just flirted with fascism, he embraced it wholeheartedly; they'd set up house together. Not out of a driving political sense, although that grew with time, but mostly because it so very much pleased the people around him. The students, the politicos, the priests (particularly the priests — Abbé Groulx even paid him the honour of a visit) all wanted to meet the elegant young man with the curious accent, almost

Swiss, and the intimate ties with Vichy. They treated him as a true relic, a fingernail of Christ, and let's be clear: he was only twenty-five. It went to his head, of course it did. Thérèse was intimately tied to that moment of his life, and here lay the root of his greatest worry. While he was largely protected from the others, who cowered with him behind the same veil of secrecy, there were no guarantees with this woman. She had been attracted to him because he was handsome and silent and young and foreign and seemed to be a man of rank within the intelligent circles of Quebec City. But she herself had no political interest at the time and therefore was invulnerable today. Étienne could not say the same. If word of his past escaped, everything from his good name (bought and paid for from a Parisian passport forger) to his surgical practice to his Rosedale home, everything he'd struggled to acquire in the years since he'd come to Toronto could dissolve. He'd seen it happen before his very eyes. Himmel was head of cardiology when Étienne first arrived at the clinic back in 1958. Within a year, stories began to circulate about Himmel's activities during the war, eventually publicly confirmed by a woman who'd been his acquaintance in Austria. To hear Himmel tell it, he'd been some office functionary for the Nazi Party in Vienna, "collecting names for lists." But the clinic, which depended heavily on the benevolence of the local Jewish community, could not tolerate the whisper of such scandal. A Nazi among us? Himmel lost his post and almost went bankrupt fighting the extradition case launched by overzealous immigration officials. Last Étienne heard, this doctor — a gifted surgeon, really — was working the night shift at a local asylum, dispensing tranquilizers and carrying the bedpans of lunatics.

It would be foolish to think that things had changed very much in ten years. Certainly the hair was fashionably longer, the clothing looser, and a vine of joyless sexual and moral liberation had crept through the garden of society, but Étienne would not to be fooled. Thérèse was to be wooed and seduced and thus her silence bought. It was a different sort of veil from his own but cut from the same cloth. This silence could be won.

But how to win her body?

.   .   .

One of Étienne's pet theories was that, while the fastest route to a man's heart was through his stomach (emotionally speaking, of course, although some of his experiments with less invasive surgical techniques suggested that the adage might have genuine medical applications), the fastest way to a woman's heart was through her husband's chequebook. The meeting was easy to arrange. A writer was always looking for commissions, and when Shulman, under Étienne's auspices, suggested that the board approach the alderwoman's husband to write a series of promotional articles on the cardiology clinic, the members immediately recognized the political and public relations benefits.

Lunch was at the Royal York. The writer came prepared. He opened his clipboard, clicked his pen and adjusted his tie in a manner that led Étienne to suspect he was not accustomed to wearing one.

"It's quite a coincidence, really. I've only just finished an article on heart disease for *Readers' Digest*." His name was Wonnacott, and he was a likeable enough sort. A little dull, perhaps. But in another time and place, Étienne and he might have been friends, if there were no worthier company around. "I think the world of cardiology is about to explode — if you'll excuse a bad joke. And as I understand it, you folks here in Toronto are leading the advance guard . . ."

He needn't try so hard. The job was already his. But Étienne said nothing, it wasn't his place, and Dr. Baird of the board let the writer go on, contributing the odd encouraging interjection here and there. Perhaps even the writer knew that no one was interested in him.

The idea was simple enough. The *Globe* was a long-time supporter of the clinic. They had agreed to run a special eight-page insert to promote the clinic and its activities. Dr. Baird had even cooked up a title: "Heart to Heart."

"Of course, there could be some travel involved." It was the first time Étienne had spoken since the introductions.

"Of course."

"A couple of weekenders: Ottawa, New York."

"The Mayo Clinic?"

"Exactly. My office will make the arrangements. I'll have Shulman set it up."

"Of course."

"Excellent."

"Excellent."

The subject of money was tactfully broached, with Baird offering a sizable retainer with per diem. And there it was, before the coffee had even arrived, the husband was bought and paid for. The wife would soon follow.

. . .

Let us permit Étienne to indulge in a little fantasy. He has taken the train to Marseilles — it could have been yesterday (like any good fantasy, this one seamlessly blends past, present and future) — and, by chance, found himself alone in a compartment with Thérèse and her doddering grandmother. Of course, as far as he knew, Thérèse had never actually been to France, let alone Marseilles. But at seventeen, her chubby beauty and unsophisticated charm — a gorgeous, uninhibited hedgehog — would not have been out of place in the south. Of course, the grandmother would fall asleep some time into the trip, leaving the two teenagers virtually alone. They would have barely spoken up to this point, and both would be pretending to be engrossed in their reading material, when Thérèse would subtly shift her leg, offering Étienne a glimpse of her school-white panties. Of course, it could have been an accident, there was no way of knowing for sure, but Étienne found that if he moved in his seat just so, he could find a spot where a triangle of panties was in full view, and, with a slight tilt of his head, he could make out the line of her brassiere peeking through an undone button. And so they would continue for the rest of the train ride, Thérèse shifting ever so slightly (a small, planetary motion) and Étienne adjusting himself accordingly. Occasionally, her hand would brush up against herself here or there, seemingly signalling her desire, but nothing definitive. That was the attraction for him: the uncertainty, the endless erotic possibility of the uncertain.

In truth, she'd been twenty or so when they'd met and he twenty-five, already a veteran of the sexual wars. But where he was reserved in his advance, she went on the attack (they *did* meet on a train, a train from Montreal, and she did wordlessly seduce him across a crowded compartment in a manner not dissimilar to his fantasy) as only colonial Catholic girls — convinced they were protected by God and society — could do. She'd come to Quebec City that summer to stay with her widowed aunt (a vivacious teacher in her early thirties; Étienne had made a play for her too) but wound up spending most of her time — sleeping, eating, drinking and making love — in Étienne's bedroom. There were tears when she left to go back to her parents, but not too many. Pleasure was the only stake; that they were doomed from the start only sweetened the pot. Still, Étienne preferred the Marseilles fantasy, the endless tease in a train that would never reach its destination, to the real-life memory. He tried to imagine how things would work out with his newly rediscovered Thérèse and what sort of effect this would have on his fantasies. Would the experience of the present erase the memory of his non-existent past? And how would it all transpire? Perhaps he would telephone her when her husband was away (the telephone was the perfect tool of seduction for Étienne: no eye contact, no body language, every nuance of intent packed into the voice), suggest they go for a drink or a walk in the park (she'd been something of an exhibitionist, and on one occasion had pleased him forcefully in the grassy moat surrounding the Citadel as dozens of tourists wandered close by). Perhaps he could arrange an accidental encounter (women were pushovers when they believed fate was involved); this might take some doing, but it was easy enough to imagine them running into one another on the subway. The symmetry was appealing.

The How was one thing, the How Could He was another. It wasn't Anna; she barely concerned herself in his affairs beyond the usual social and domestic duties. As long as the social order wasn't challenged, Anna, the good old Canadian, remained docile. But Dr. Cole — Sondra really, but he loved the pretentiousness of her full title, and it underscored that she was a professional, a New Woman in the New World — she kept him on a short leash and seemed to know everyone in the city. He had to be discrete, or word would get back to his mistress. Of course, discretion was just what he wanted. Discretion turned him on. The other part of the equation, though, was difficult to work through. How could he bring himself to kiss her? How could he bring himself to make love to a woman so old and so . . . expansive? It may seem a vanity, but he was certain of his powers of seduction, particularly in this case. He was well kept, again for his age, sophisticated and successful — these things mattered more than almost anything to a woman. But most of all, he would represent for Thérèse that moment in time when she had been so much more than she is now (in being much less), when she had been (and this is

critical) an object of desire. Here lay the key to the whole seduction. Whereas in a man's fantasy, the woman was the
subject of desire (the subject, that is, of erotic fulfillment), in
her own mind, she needed to feel like a sexual object. Not in
the utilitarian sense, something to be used and discarded (that
came afterwards), but almost in an iconographical sense:
something greater than what it was; something steeped in
meaning; something venerated and desired, but always with
the understanding that while it could be approached, it could
never be fully possessed. There was something mythic about
this kind of love — about seduction. Something very Greek.
So, from that point of view, the seduction was easy. But what
about him? How could he do it? How could he love her again?
How could he make love to her again?

.   .   .

He almost blew it. Sunday morning, and Anna had asked him
to walk along Lakeshore. The weather was unusually tem-
perate for this time of year, and Étienne thought nothing of it.
Of course, just past the public pool (still open this late in the
season), who should the fates decree would walk towards them
but Thérèse and her husband with a young child, no more
than a toddler, whom Étienne concluded must be their grandson. Étienne considered leading Anna off the pathway down
toward the water, on the pretext of looking for birds. But the
writer had already seen them. An encounter was unavoidable.
  "We have to stop meeting like this. People are started to
talk."
  "Mr. Wonnacott, how good to see you. I was just telling my
wife about your work. Anna, this is the author I was telling you
about. He's going to be helping the clinic . . ."
  Introductions were made all round, and when it came time
for Thérèse to shake his hand she played the scene perfectly.

Barely a flash of recognition in her eyes, but when he permitted his hand to linger a moment in hers, she did not repel it. He could feel the warmth transferring between them. And that was it. A moment of doting upon the child (whose particulars were never fully explained), some pleasant "good afternoons," and the meeting was terminated. It could not have lasted more than three minutes. But Étienne believed he'd turned what might have been a small disaster to his advantage. He'd definitely made a connection with Thérèse, reinforced by their spontaneous pact of secrecy. Perhaps she'd been embarrassed — no doubt she had — but kept it to herself well. Another woman might have been flustered, which would have aroused suspicions in the husband, even a dullard such as this. But she conceded nothing. She was better at this than Étienne ever expected. So potential disaster was turned into gain. The gods had brought them together and tickled her interest. The next time they met, she would be ready.

. . .

It was not who he thought. When the receptionist told him there was a writer in his office, he expected to find Wonnacott waiting there. But it was that journalist. The Pole. Madrn.

"Just a few questions, *monsieur le docteur*. If I may . . ."

He always had just a few questions. He'd always bring up names: Georges-Benoit Montel; Raymond Chouinard; Abbé Pierre Gravel. Antiphon.

"I'm just trying to put together the facts, *monsieur le docteur*. There are so many missing pieces to the puzzle, yes?"

You'd think Madrn (a dissident himself with a dubious past who still courted extremists of both the right and the left) would let well enough alone. He had been one of the first people in Canada to write about Oswald Mosely's Blackshirts and had also interviewed key members of the FLQ and even introduced them to visiting celebrity radicals and rock stars. When Pierre Valliers showed up at John and Yoko's Bed-In for Peace at the Queen Elizabeth Hotel in Montreal, Madrn was there, slouching in the background.

Mostly, Étienne had been able to keep Madrn at bay. The journalist had approached him several times with an interest in doing an article or book or something on the roots of French Canadian radicalism. Étienne demurred: he'd been a student only; he knew nothing of radical politics; having spent only a few years in Quebec, he had very little to add along the lines of cultural or social observations. Once, at a party for the Belgian consul, Madrn tried to bait Étienne into confessing . . . something or another. That he'd been a fascist or had befriended fascists or spoken to someone who knew a fascist, Étienne was never sure. The consul himself came to Étienne's defence, saying that he knew of the doctor's family, that they'd comported themselves during the war no less nobly than his own (the consul, a charter member of the Fellowship of the Veil, was being perfectly truthful). The Pole was playing the odds. He knew that every man, and certainly any man who'd safely come out of Europe in the last thirty years, had a shadow in his past, and he took it as a personal affront whenever anyone tried to keep his private business private.

"It was a long time ago, sir. I'm sure it's a time many would rather forget."

"And you, *monsieur le docteur*? Would you rather forget? Hmm?"

"I, Mr. Madrn, I have nothing worth remembering."

.   .   .

These are the facts as Étienne did not remember them, exactly as they were never reported to that journalist. In July of 1940, mere weeks after the aging Marshall Pétain had signed the armistice agreement (not out of cowardice or a particular fondness for Hitler and his politics, as some maintained, but because he very rightly perceived that capitulation under the Nazis would be vastly more palatable than defeat), Étienne and his family moved from Rhône, that ancient Roman city where his father had worked as a general physician, to Verrière, where his uncle was mayor and where his father was granted an administrative post with the local hospital council. Here, Étienne (né Paul André Emmanuel Étienne Boussat-Antiphon; he'd added du Chatelait, rather uncleverly, because it was his grandmother's maiden name) began his internship, having already completed his formal studies. Here, at his uncle's insistence, he also took nominal membership in the Legion of French Volunteers against Bolshevism and, after that, the Legionnaire Security Service, pledging to fight democracy, Jews and the Resistance, in that order. Eventually, he was pressed into service of the Franc-Garde of the French Militia, a fervently anti-Gaullist organization whose main objective seemed to be the systematic denunciation of every French man, woman and child who was not a militia member (and many who were). Étienne satisfied the mandate by providing key militia officials with an endless supply of names taken from the hospital death rolls. That they were dead only enhanced Étienne's status; the militia appeared to be carrying out its mandate to a degree of efficiency rarely seen in France. In the waning hours of the war, as the Allied victory seemed imminent, Étienne's father sent him to Spain with a small collection of gold and a large assortment of false documents. While being tried *in absentia* for crimes against the state and sentenced to ten years of national disgrace, Étienne obtained a six-month student visa for Canada (that this twenty-year-old man had a high school student visa seemed not to disturb the immigration officials), and, following a ten-day voyage on a Cunard freighter, he landed in Montreal. He left immediately for Quebec City, where his uncle assured him he would find men not unsympathetic to the Cause. What that cause was, Étienne wasn't sure. But he hoped most emphatically that it had something to do with allowing him to get on with his life.

.   .   .

So you can see that Étienne's world was full of statues, which is perhaps why he found himself thinking of Medusa. A painting at the provincial gallery set this train of thought in motion, an avant-garde artist's depiction of the gorgon myth, an ugly head — nostrils splayed, asymmetrical eyes, wrinkled and hirsute skin, full, chapped lips, her hair a nest of serpents — set upon the beautiful body of young woman. She was surrounded by onlookers who, captured by either her hideousness or her beauty, had turned into marble statues in the Classic, Grecian style. Étienne had stood transfixed, considering the detail of each snake, and smiled when he recognized that Medusa, at least for a moment, had turned him to stone as well. He thought of Thérèse, for numerous reasons (most of them quite obvious), and returned to that image over and over again whenever she entered his mind. In fact, he began to think of her as Medusa, mentally transplanting her head onto the body the artist had rendered, and in his internal conversation he referred to Thérèse directly as Medusa. He even began to call the planned seduction the Medusa Project: his own little joke.

There were improprieties. In fact, Madrn's next article would expose a lot of them. Laporte's unseemly connections, for one. He had strong ties to organized crime in Montreal, and there were some, including prominent FLQ supporters, who believed that the Laporte kidnapping was actually the work of professional hit men. Perhaps they were even working with the tacit approval of Bourassa and the police. How else could you explain the fact that the kidnappers had managed to walk away — in broad daylight — with the deputy premier of the province, snatch him right from under the noses of the police and army? Even given the legendary ineptitude of Quebec's police force, this was a little too hard to believe. In allowing Laporte to be kidnapped, Bourassa had rid himself of a man who was at once a dangerous political rival and a potential embarrassment to his government.

"We should talk, comrade. I mean it. I have a lot of information. It could be useful."

The driver did not respond. None of the men did. There were at least two kidnappers, Madrn believed, probably four. That's the way the FLQ operated: safety in numbers. They were just young guys really, punks, mostly politically unsophisticated, in the game for the thrill of it, the danger, the righteousness, the brotherhood. They bombed and kidnapped like other young men gang-banged.

"For instance, do you know about Operation Essay? Hmm? This is no accidental occurrence, my friends, this 'crisis.' The government — Trudeau — has been planning this for months. A secret plan with the army and the cops. You guys think you're in the driver's seat, my friends. You're not. You're playing into their hands, I can tell you that right now . . ."

He hadn't seen their faces, hadn't seen anything of them, in fact. When he felt the pistol on his neck, he'd gone without question. He raised his hands and said, "Just tell me what to do, boys." At first, he thought — he hoped — that they would simply ask him to interview them, to get their side of the story out, and that they were merely going to extraordinary lengths to protect their identities and locations. But when they pushed him towards the box and directed him to get into it — well, that's when he knew he was in trouble.

Madrn pressed his lips to the holes and sucked in some fresh air. The van smelled new, a rental, no doubt. The air inside the box

— a storage trunk or maybe a packing crate — was mouldy, with a more pleasant undertone of wood. Cedar, he thought. Yes, cedar.

"I also have a line on some guns, my friends. Kalashnikovs. Almost new. I can get them for you for a song . . ."

Not long after his visit to the gallery, Étienne received a package from Madrn. It arrived by regular post; Anna brought the unsealed envelope to him in his study. Inside was a draft manuscript for an article the journalist was writing for a leading English-language Quebec daily, an article that more or less accurately detailed, among other things, Étienne's flight from Europe and his rise within the rightist circles of New France. A typed note invited the doctor to correct any errors and craft, if he so desired, his own rebuttal. It ended with a short, hand-written addendum, underlined for emphasis. *"We should talk!"* Étienne read the article once, then, after cancelling a ten o'clock appointment, read it again. His first impulse was to write a stinging letter to the editor, defending himself and demanding, in advance of publication, an unequivocal retraction. His second impulse was to call a lawyer friend with intimate knowledge of Étienne's circumstances. His third impulse was to call a cabinet minister or two and ask them to apply the kind of pressure that could get a story like this killed. In the end, he read the article again; there was something about Madrn's prose that appealed to him. Emotionless, motionless, almost hypnotic, not charged, as Étienne would have expected, with political rhetoric or intent. The result was that Étienne came across as a calculating fiend, coldly detached from the events of the time, seeking only to protect and further himself. Was he really such a monster?

Étienne picked up the note and scrutinized it. The hand-written message was curious. Why should they talk? Was there something Madrn wanted to say that could not be entrusted to a note? Did he want, Étienne speculated, to offer a deal? Perhaps this was part of a primitive blackmail scheme, his present (as was always the case in blackmail) held hostage by the past? He could hear his wife puttering in the sitting room next door and wondered how the revelations would affect her. She could surprise him but didn't do it often. The story would no doubt devastate her. And now Étienne put the note down and, slumping deep into his chair, dropped his head into his hands. He thought again, almost speaking the words aloud: *Am I really this monster?*

.   .   .

Étienne had grown up in the age of statues. In Rhône there were gods and statues everywhere. But now he lived in an age of radio, of television, of journalists and Marxists. Of politics. One couldn't even trust one's mistress anymore. Étienne could no longer tell who was having whom: was Sondra his mistress, or was he hers?

And now they were having lunch again, and she was playing the role of conciliator. Étienne was upset about the package he'd received. He left the precise details of the package vague and would only say that, despite the outward appearances of civility, his was a cutthroat profession.

Sondra ran her hand through her long hair, streaked with grey. She wasn't that old, really, thirty-four or thirty-five, he guessed (he'd never asked — a gentleman didn't — although he was certain she would tell him if he did), and could easily have coloured it. Most women of her age would.

"It's like anything. There's is only so much room at the top, there is always someone circling around to take your place. Anyway, enough of this business." But this business did not leave his mind, and he came back to it several times over lunch and later, back in her apartment. They'd made love in the usual manner, after coffee and the radio news, on the bed in the spare room (neither of them felt comfortable doing it in her bed, with its ghosts and shadows). He'd only just finished when he rolled off and said, "You know, this business — it will kill her."

"Kill who?"

"Anna. It will kill her. She always likes everything to be the same. She never wants anything to change. Of course, things change all the time, everything changes around her . . ."

His voice trailed off, and Sondra pulled the yellow sheet up to her neck. Étienne stood and picked up his shorts, which he'd neatly folded over the back of the armchair at the foot of the bed. He thought of how much more comfortable chairs were these days, less decorative and more utilitarian than when he was a boy. When he'd been growing up, his mother had chairs that no one was allowed to sit in. Étienne dressed in silence. These silences were beginning to define his life.

Madrn tried a different tack.

"Look, if it's money you're after, I can provide you with what you want. I'm not a rich man by any means, but I have some . . . resources."

What these men failed to realize was that Madrn had been a hostage his entire life. Born in a country that did not exist, surrounded by invaders who looked like him, talked like him, ate like him, stank like him. And the secret was . . . the secret was that once you become a captor, you also become a hostage.

"I'm just thinking out loud, of course, but what's in my mind is some sort of negotiable commodity. I'm thinking specifically of heroin right now, but that can all be discussed. The point is, I'm willing to swing a deal. But you have to tell me what you want."

In Poland, everything had been a negotiation. He'd negotiated his way out of the army and into the polytechnic institute, he'd negotiated himself in and out of bed, he'd negotiated for an ounce of caviar and for a loaf of bread. Once he'd traded cigarettes for toilet paper, only to trade it back again for more cigarettes. The What was never significant, it was what the What did for you that mattered. A man with something to trade has status, and that alone makes him a hostage.

"Do you know how I got to this country? I invented myself. That's right, comrades. I gave myself a mother and a father, I gave myself a wife and three small children. I bought my freedom on their backs, my little invented wife and our make-believe brats. They were my collateral. My money-back guarantee."

Nothing. Silence still.

"Maybe you just want your freedom, a one-way ticket out of here? Where do you want to go? Cuba? Algeria? Hollywood? Just tell me. Getting you there — the documents, the contacts — that's the easy part. It's making up your fucking mind. That's the difficulty."

It's funny how the world works. The gods at play. Étienne had called on the alderwoman because of the Pole and his blackmail scheme. He thought that maybe, somehow (to be honest, the details were not worked out yet), Thérèse could help him. She had a lot of sway in this town and at the very least could be counted on to vouch for him. She'd suggested on the phone that he come over to her apartment to speak directly, although she prefaced that remark by explaining that her husband was out of town on business unrelated (she was emphatic on this point) to the series of articles for the cardiology clinic. Of course. The articles. He'd forgotten the Medusa Project. And now here she was, providing the perfect entrée for him. He did not let it slip.

"Well, I have some general thoughts about the articles that maybe I could discuss with you, in general terms. I'd like your feedback, and I'm sure your husband would appreciate it as well."

He arrived, like any experienced seducer, under the cover of daylight. Thérèse met him at the door. She wore a billowy brown caftan which, although it did not conceal her size, did not accentuate it either. She led Étienne to the sitting area, chatting in a very animated away about the latest news on the radio: first the British trade consul, now the Deputy Premier of Quebec — both taken hostage by masked gunmen. A French Canadian terrorist group calling itself the FLQ had claimed responsibility.

"It's impossible to believe. Something like this happening here, in our country."

Étienne, who had not heard the news before, agreed. Things like this did not happen in Canada. Then he began, in as indirect a way as possible, to talk about Madrn's article. But Thérèse would have none of it; she kept dragging the conversation back to the present.

"We were in Montreal only last month, Gerald and I. There was something . . . the atmosphere was . . . tense."

"I haven't been to Montreal in years. Decades perhaps."

Still, Thérèse played it cool. She never gave the slightest inkling that she had known Étienne before. Yet there was something intimate in her body language. The way she tilted her head when she spoke to him, the way she held his gaze for a moment before quickly diverting her eyes. She was at once inviting him and pushing him away. So Étienne decided to seize the initiative. He stood abruptly to take his leave, and when, as if on cue, Thérèse protested that they hadn't even begun to talk about the clinic articles, Étienne boldly invited her to dinner that night to finish their discussion. By now she was blushing, he was certain of that. On an impulse, he took her hand and murmured some ancient nothings that perhaps he'd offered to her before, years ago, in a Spartan bedroom at the top of a Quebec City rooming house.

"You speak French." She seemed genuinely surprised.

"I *am* French."

"How quaint." Thérèse rolled her tongue through her mouth. Étienne could see the saliva sticking to her palate. "I was once French too."

She smiled, and Étienne noticed for the first time how her teeth had yellowed and cracked. She squeezed his hand and whispered a place and time where they could meet for dinner. Then she stepped back from the door, raised her eyes in a manner that she must have imagined coquettish and wished him a good afternoon. At that moment he understood. She had absolutely no recollection of their shared past, that she wasn't just cleverly faking ignorance but joylessly revelling in it, and, as he glanced at her one last time before the door closed, he realized that the woman who was already old and large in his eyes had become older and larger. He noticed too that his hands were trembling again.

The box landed upside down on a layer of thin ice. Madrn immediately felt the cold, the sour air freezing the inside of his nose. Perhaps the force of the blow had knocked him out briefly (he'd fallen, God knows, twenty feet, twenty-five maybe), but in any case, he was certainly dazed. When he became aware again, he realized that the water had begun to seep in through the air holes, and the box was filling up. Being upside down meant that his head would be the first thing to go under. He kicked and kicked again, which only freed the box from the ice and plunged him deeper into the river. In his panic, Madrn made no attempt to hold his breath. The cold water flooded his nose and his lungs, and he was certainly dead before the boxed settled on the bottom of the St. Lawrence. It was still night. The driver looked down from the bridge, flicked the dying bud of a cigarette onto the ice below. She noticed her hand; it had already stopped trembling. Anna hesitated, then wondered what she was still doing there. Étienne would be waiting for her, wondering where she was. She went back to the van. She was happy. The world — her world — was no longer different. Madrn's manuscript lay on the passenger seat. She picked it up and held it for a moment. She'd thought of dumping it with the journalist, but that could have been risky. Instead, she would stop at her mother's on the way home, burn it in her fireplace. She started the ignition and pushed forward. New snow was already falling on the dirt road, covering her tracks. Although it was still dark, it would be morning soon, it would be morning and nothing would be different. Madrn was dead and she was free again.